The Promissory 2

KYIRIS ASHLEY

U.A.D PRESENTS

URBAN AINT DEAD

P.O Box 448

Maybrook, NY 12543

No part of this book may be reproduced or transmitted in any form by any means electronic or mechanical, including photocopying, recording, or by any information storage system, without written permission from the publisher.

Copyright © 2025 By Kyiris Ashley

All rights reserved. Published by URBAN AINT DEAD Publications.

Cover Design: Akirecover2cover.com

Edited By: Shawna Brim / Ladies of Lit

URBAN AINT DEAD and coinciding logo(s) are registered properties.

No patent liability is assumed with respect to the use of information contained herein. Although every precaution has been taken in the preparation of this book, the publisher and the author assume no responsibility for errors or omissions. Neither is any liability assumed for damages resulting from the use of the information contained herein. This is a work of fiction. Names, characters, places, and incidents are either the product of the author's imagination or are used fictitiously. Any resemblance to actual events, locales, or persons living or dead is entirely coincidental.

Contact Author on FB: Kyiris Ashley / IG: @kyirisashley / TikTok: @Kyiris _Ashley/ Email: KyirisAshley@gmail.com

Contact Publisher at www.urbanaintdead.com

Email: urbanaintdead@gmail.com

Print ISBN: 979-8-218-77705-0

Stay Up to Date

To stay up to date on new releases, plus get information on contests, sneak peeks and more,

Click the link below...
https://mailchi.mp/6d21003686d1/subscribe

Soundtracks

Scan the QR Code below to listen to the Soundtracks/Singles of some of your favorite U.A.D titles:

Don't have Spotify or Apple Music?
No Sweat!
Visit your choice streaming platform and search URBAN AINT DEAD.

Currently on lock serving a bid?
JPay, iHeartRadio, WHATEVER!
We got you covered.
Simply log into your facility's kiosk or tablet, go to music and search
URBAN AINT DEAD.

U.A.D PRESENTS

Like & Follow us on social media:

FB - URBAN AINT DEAD

IG: @uadpresents

Tik Tok - @uadpresents

Submission Guidelines

Submit the first three chapters of your completed manuscript to urbanaintdead@gmail.com, subject line: Your book's title. The manuscript must be in a .doc file and sent as an attachment. The document should be in Times New Roman, double-spaced, and in size 12 font. Also, provide your synopsis and full contact information. If sending multiple submissions, they must each be in a separate email. Have a story but no way to submit it electronically? You can still submit to URBAN AINT DEAD. Send in the first three chapters, written or typed, of your completed manuscript to:

URBAN AINT DEAD
P.O Box 448
Maybrook, NY 12543

DO NOT send original manuscript. Must be a duplicate.
Provide your synopsis and a cover letter containing your full contact information.
Thanks for considering URBAN AINT DEAD.

Chapter One

VITA

I stepped out the shower and oiled by my body. It was Saturday night, and I was going out to shake some ass. I'd been calling Braylen all day to see if she wanted to come with me, but my calls had gone unanswered. I knew she was lost in that fine ass, rich man that loved the shit out of her, and I wasn't mad at it. My girl deserved the world, and that nigga, Banks, was going to make sure he gave it to her.

Walking into my bedroom, I began going through my closet, looking for something to wear. As much as I wanted my girl to come out with me, I didn't mind going out alone. I laid out a blue and cream, Dior, two-piece set with matching Dior strappy heels and bag. *I will be Dior from head to toe tonight.* Walking over to my vanity, I took a seat. The bass from my Bluetooth speaker thumped softly in the background, matching the rhythm of my heartbeat, as I perched on the edge of my velvet vanity stool. I parted my honey blonde locs down the middle. I was feeling good from the two shots I'd taken before my shower and bobbed my head to the music as I worked.

I'd started my loc journey six years ago, and now, they reached my waist – thick, golden, and soft from the aloe and oil blend I massaged into them weekly. Tonight, I wanted them full and wild but polished. I misted my hair with rosewater and twisted a few pieces back from my face, securing them with small gold cuffs I kept in a jewelry tray. Then, I pulled the rest into a half-up, half-down style with a Dior scrunchie that matched my two-piece set, giving just enough structure in the front while still allowing my locs to cascade down my back.

After finishing my edges with a gentle swoop of my edge brush and some edge control, I leaned back to admire my work. My honey-blonde locs shimmered under the soft glow of my vanity lights. I stood from my vanity and slid into my blue and cream, Dior, two-piece set, the fabric hugging my hips just right. The crop jacket sat neatly on my shoulders, showing off my pierced belly button and the glint of shimmer I'd dusted across my collarbone. I felt like a whole mood, and I looked like more money than I actually had.

I looked over the perfume tray on my dresser, looking for my scent of the night. I chose Kayali's Vanilla 28. It was both sweet and sexy, making it perfect for the night. I spritzed it on my wrists, behind my knees, my neck, and in the curve of my cleavage before spraying it on my clothes. Sliding on my gold hoops, I glanced once more ins the mirror and gave myself a wink. My skin was glowing, and I was looking like *that bitch* as I stepped out tonight.

The Uber dropped me off right in front of a velvet rope in front of Club Mariposa. There was no driving tonight because I knew I would be drinking. A sharply dressed doorman gave me one long look before asking me my name. I gave it to him, and he nodded, giving me the okay. I didn't wait in no line. I didn't have to. My name was already on the list. The moment the heavy double doors opened, the bass from inside hit me square in the chest.

Club Mariposa was one of those bougie but not-too-bougie spots downtown where the lighting stayed dim, the crowd stayed grown, and the cocktails came with fat price tags. The walls were dressed in dark marble and soft cream panels with gold accents. Everyone who came here either came to flex or find someone worth flexing on. Crystals from a massive chandelier sparkled above the dance floor, casting a glow on the entire room.

I strolled in slow, not rushing, just scanning the crowd. The DJ was spinning some smooth R&B.. I moved with it, letting my hips catch the rhythm, as I headed toward the bar, knowing every set of eyes in that room was clocking me. I didn't look at anybody directly, but I felt them all watching. That was the kind of attention I pulled when I stepped out effortlessly.

I found a seat at the far end of the bar, away from the loud clusters of conversation and close to the mirrored wall that lined the bar. I wanted to watch the room and see what was going on before stepping out on the floor. The bartender came over quick. He was light skinned with sleeves of tattoos and pretty boy energy.

"What can I get you, beautiful?"

I gave him a soft smirk. "Something sweet but with a kick. Surprise me."

He nodded and walked off, and I leaned one elbow on the bar, crossing my legs and adjusting the hem of my skirt. I could smell my perfume on me, so I knew it casted a scent bubble around me. I pulled out my phone and pretended to scroll, even though I wasn't checking for anything. I was watching the club, observing everyone as they walked through the door. A few men tried to catch my eye, but I looked away, only paying attention to the ones that had enough presence to make me look up from my phone. I wasn't here just to be seen. I was hunting for the next big money nigga to front my lifestyle, and I never missed a target.

He walked in like he owned the entire establishment. He was tall with broad shoulders, impeccably tailored navy slacks, and a dove-gray shirt rolled up at the sleeves. He had salt and pepper hair cut close, skin like melted chocolate, and a five o'clock shadow that made my thighs clench under the bar without permission. His eyes were sharp, scanning the room with practiced ease, but when they landed on me, he stopped.

He made his way over to me slowly with a swagger I'd never seen before. It was almost as though I'd already called out to him.

"How are you tonight?" he greeted, his voice deep, slow, and smooth. "I'm Victor," he continued.

His cologne hit me a second later, something woody and expensive – oud and amber with a hint of citrus. It curled around my senses like a whisper. My lips curved before I could stop them.

"I'm Vita," I replied, letting my voice drop just enough to sound sexy.

"Vita," he repeated like he was tasting the syllables. "That means life, doesn't it?"

I tilted my head slightly, pretending to be amused. "That's what my mama always said."

He chuckled and leaned against the bar beside me, close enough for the heat of him to press against my bare thighs. "I'm not here to waste your time," he said, eyes steady. "May I buy you another drink?"

I glanced at my glass then back at him.

"You can," I said, sliding my empty glass toward the bartender. "But only if you plan on sitting down while I drink it."

Victor pulled out the stool beside me without hesitation. He wasn't just attractive; he was commanding, the type of man who knew who he was and what he wanted. There was a stillness to him that made everyone else around us feel loud. Something told me I hadn't even scratched the surface of who Victor really was, and that intrigued me. Victor smiled, and it was the kind I knew had broken hearts in at least three time zones. He extended his hand, palm warm and steady.

"It's nice to meet you."

His voice was deep and smooth. I took his hand, letting my fingers rest a beat longer than they needed to. He smiled, already knowing what I was on. He rubbed my thigh, letting me know he was on the same thing. The bartender brought me my drink along with a glass of brown liquor on the rocks for Victor, already knowing his order.

"You been here before?" I asked curiously.

"Yeah, a time or two."

I nodded. We sipped on our drinks and talked, getting to know one another a little better.

"So, what do you do, Victor, besides sneak up on women and flatter them in upscale lounges?"

He laughed, eyes crinkling at the edges. "Let's just say I know how to move money fast and quietly."

"Oh, that shit sounds dangerous and illegal."

"Dangerous, yes. Illegal, nah." He winked.

I crossed one leg over the other and leaned closer, suddenly intrigued. Victor didn't just look powerful; he really was. I felt the tingle between my legs just from the way Victor spoke.

"And what do you do for work, Vita?"

"I make people regret underestimating me."

Victor's eyebrows lifted just slightly. "I like that. You seem like the type of woman I like spending time with. You want to get outta here and go somewhere quiet?"

"That depends. Where do you have in mind?"

"We downtown, so we can go anywhere. How 'bout I get us a suite?"

I smiled, already knowing what Victor wanted to get into, and I was down for the ride. I finished my drink before standing from the bar. He led us out the club, and we made our way to his car.

The suite Victor reserved was pure luxury. The moment we stepped off the private elevator and into the penthouse floor of The Marquis, a five-star hotel nestled in the heart of downtown, I knew I wasn't dealing with your average man. The suite had its own black glass double doors, and when he opened them, I stepped into something that looked like it belonged in a billionaire's home magazine spread.

The lighting was soft and sensual with recessed golden hues glowing from behind crown molding along the tray ceilings. Floor-to-ceiling windows lined the entire far wall, showing off a stunning night view of the city lights twinkling like stars below us. The skyline was wrapped in deep hues of navy and silver, casting an intimate glow across the glossy hardwood floors.

A plush cream sectional was sprawled across the sunken living room, accented with deep navy and gold throw pillows. A glass coffee table sat in the center with an untouched bottle of Dom Pérignon chilling in a sleek gold ice bucket next to two tall crystal flutes. A modern electric fireplace flickered quietly beneath a mounted flat-screen, casting a warm orange glow over the marble feature wall behind it.

To the right, an open-concept bedroom peeked from behind a partition wall of smoked glass panels. The king-sized bed was massive with a low navy velvet frame, buttery-soft white linens, and a mountain of pillows stacked neatly at the headboard. Gold fixtures accented the nightstands, while tiny vases of fresh orchids stood tall next to dimly lit lamps.

Victor slipped out of his jacket and placed it over one of the tall leather chairs by the marble-topped bar. "Make yourself comfortable," he said in that calm, rich voice that made my stomach flutter.

I turned in a slow circle, my heels clicking against the floor. The suite was quiet, exclusive, and private, just like him. I could tell this night was about to unfold into something unforgettable, and I couldn't wait to see what was going to happen. I stood in the center of a space that screamed quiet money, and dollar signs flashed in my head.

"You want a drink?" he asked, already making his way to the bar.

I nodded, but it wasn't the liquor I was thirsty for. His movements were smooth and practiced, the way he reached for the crystal decanter, how he poured just enough into the glass. He handed me a glass and brushed my fingers as I took it. His eyes were on me the whole time, steady and unreadable, like he was mentally unwrapping me layer by layer.

I took a slow sip. The drink burned down my throat, but it wasn't what made my chest warm.

"You always this quiet?" he asked, coming to stand in front of me.

I tilted my head and smirked. "You always this forward?"

He chuckled and damn if that didn't light a fuse in me. Tension buzzed in the space between us like electricity. I took a step forward, testing him. His eyes dipped low, dragging across my body like a slow touch. He licked his lips slowly as I looked up at him.

"I've been waiting to get you alone all night, Vita."

When he spoke my name, I felt it between my legs.

He stepped closer, closing the small space between us. My breath caught as he reached up, his fingers ghosting over one of my locs. "This color's fire on you," he murmured, his thumb brushing over my baby hairs. "You fine as hell, Vita."

His hand slid to the back of my neck, gripping gently, as he pulled me into a kiss. It was slow at first. However, that didn't last. The second my tongue met his, everything ignited. His other hand gripped my waist, pulling me in until there wasn't an inch of space between us. I could feel him, thick and hard, pressed against me. I couldn't help the little sound that slipped from my throat.

"You sure you want this?" he asked, his voice rough, his forehead pressed to mine.

"I want it bad," I whispered.

He turned me in his arms and guided me backward toward the bed. With every step, his lips trailed along my jaw and down my neck, until I was melting under his touch. He sat me on the edge of the bed then knelt in front of me like I was some kind of altar.

"Victor," I uttered, my voice shaky.

"Let me taste what's mine tonight."

He started slow, his fingers trailing down the length of my legs, as he pushed my skirt up, kissing every inch of skin he revealed. His tongue moved in lazy, wet circles on the inside of my thighs, teasing me, causing me to whimper.

His mouth found that aching place between my legs, and I swore my soul almost left my body. Victor had the kind of patience most men lacked. He licked me like he had all night, like there was nowhere else he'd rather be. His beard scratched gently against my thighs, as his tongue worked deep, slow circles, drawing out a low moan from deep in my chest.

I arched up off the bed, grabbing at the sheets, unable to hold still.

"Victor, shit. Damn, it feels good."

He chuckled low against me, the vibration of his voice pushing me closer to the edge. "You taste like sugar, Vita."

He wrapped his arms under my thighs, locking me in place, as he devoured me – fast, slow, then fast again, switching it up every time I thought I could keep up. My body trembled, breath caught in my throat, as the orgasm rolled through me like lightning. I cried out, clenching, trying to breathe through the explosion of pleasure. Before I could fully recover, he rose up and pulled me into his lap, his lips claiming mine, letting me taste myself on his tongue. I ground down onto the thick bulge in his pants, both of us panting, needing more.

"Turn around for me," he said, voice dark and commanding.

I obeyed without a word, crawling onto all fours, as he slid his slacks down and pressed against me from behind. The feel of him teasing my entrance made me gasp, my hands clutching the sheets again.

"You ready, baby?"

"Yes," I moaned. "Please don't stop."

He slid in slow, stretching me inch by inch, until he filled me completely. I cried out, gripping the pillows, as he began to move, deep and steady. Each stroke hit the perfect spot, dragging sounds out of me I didn't even know I could make. Victor gripped my hips, pulling me back onto him, faster now. His hand slid up my spine until he had a fistful of my locs, tugging just enough to make my head tilt back.

"Look at you," he growled, "taking this dick."

His words made my walls flutter around him. I met every thrust, desperate, greedy, and wild with need. We switched positions – me on top, riding him slow, while his hands explored my body like he was memorizing every curve. Then, he flipped me again, legs over his shoulders, pushing even deeper. His control, his rhythm, the way he watched my face the entire time all unraveled me.

By the time we both finished, sweat clung to our skin, and the room smelled of sex. I collapsed into his chest, trembling, sore, but completely satisfied.

Victor kissed the top of my head and whispered, "You're trouble."

I smiled sleepily, eyes closing. "You gon' love trouble."

Chapter Two

BRAYLEN

I couldn't sleep. The silence in our bedroom wrapped around me like a second skin. As much as I'd tried, I hadn't been able to settle myself since my doctor's appointment. Banks lay quiet beside me – not sleeping, just breathing slow and heavy like he was giving me space to think. Maybe too much space. I rolled over and looked at him. The room was dark, lit only by the soft amber glow from the small lamp on the nightstand.

Banks laid there like he didn't have a care in the world, as if he was completely unfazed by the fact I was carrying another man's child. My entire world was crashing down around me, and he was laying there like it was just another night. I felt his arm move around me slowly, his fingertips brushing the bare skin at my waist. I closed my eyes, savoring his touch. I knew having this baby would cause our dynamics to shift, but I prayed it wouldn't break us.

I never imagined something so beautiful could hurt so bad. It had been a week since the appointment. Since the ultrasound tech looked at me with that bright smile, congratulating me, while my entire world crumbled beneath the sound of a heartbeat of a baby that didn't belong to Banks. It was a sound that should've made me feel nothing but joy, but all it did was bury guilt into my chest like a dagger.

Three months. Not days or weeks but months. A child had been growing inside of me without me knowing. Three months of me carrying a baby that didn't belong to the man I now loved. The man that held me close to him at night and had completely changed my life around. Instead, this child belonged to Kyrie. My soon to be ex-husband. The same nine fingered bitch ass nigga that gambled me away like a pawn.

I was terrified of what would happen when I finally told Kyrie I was pregnant. Banks didn't press the issue. He told me not to worry about it one time when we left the appointment and hadn't said anything since. I didn't understand how he expected me not to worry; I couldn't help it. That was all I had been doing for an entire week. I wanted to be excited about becoming a mother, but how could I be? The father of my child was a no-good ass nigga that didn't give a fuck about anyone but himself. Just when I thought I would be free of Kyrie forever, here I was, being pulled right back to him.

"You still awake?" he murmured.

I nodded against the pillow. "Can't sleep."

"Me either." His voice was deep and rough. "I can feel your energy, and you worrying too much, baby. We gon' be good."

"How can I not worry? What if this changes everything? What if…" I trailed off, not wanting to say what I was thinking out loud. Saying it out loud made it too real too soon. "I know this baby I'm carrying isn't yours, but I still want you to want me. Is that selfish?" I turned to face him, wanting to look into his eyes when he answered.

His jaw clenched, and his hand came up to cup my cheek. "I do want you, Braylen. Nothing about that will ever change. It's me and you. Me loving you means loving everything that comes with you. If that means standing by your side through this pregnancy, then that's what it is."

He kissed me but not with the usual heat, not with that fire that always left me breathless. This time, it was slow and deep, as if he was reminding me that no matter what Kyrie had done, I was his now. I kissed him back, matching the rhythm of his kiss. Banks didn't rush. His hands trailed over my sides, slipping beneath my silk camisole. His mouth moved from mine to my neck, kissing it softly before sucking it gently.

I breathed his name, my voice shaking.

"Let me take care of you," he whispered against my skin.

Banks peeled the camisole up and over my head, tossing it aside, his eyes never leaving mine. There was something raw in his gaze, something I hadn't seen before. It wasn't lust. It was more like his eyes telling me that he loved me. He kissed my collarbone, lowering his mouth down to my breasts, before stopping at my nipples. I hissed, taking in the air between my teeth, as he sucked gently. He sucked them both, making sure they both received equal attention.

He kissed lower, taking his time. He slowly kissed a soft trail from my breasts down my stomach. Banks didn't stop there. He used his tongue to form a trail from my belly button to my clit. When his mouth hovered just above it, he paused. His hands rested on both my hips, grounding him.

"You don't owe me anything," I whispered. "You don't have to stay. You don't have to be a part of none of this bullshit."

"I know that," he said, eyes still fixed on my stomach. "But I want to. I want you. And a nigga like me gon' always get what he wants."

My eyes closed as he kissed me again, this time on my lower set of lips. I moaned softly as his tongue made slow circles around my love button. This wasn't just desire; this was confirmation. His mouth was like a promise that would never be broken. My back arched, allowing his mouth to take away any ounce of anything that wasn't pleasure.

He climbed back on top of me, kissing me so passionately that I trembled beneath him. I couldn't explain the way his kiss settled in my chest. It was as though I was finally coming up for air after drowning in silence for days. My hands found his face, fingers brushing his jawline, as I pulled him closer. I wanted more of him – not just his body but his peace, his strength, and his presence.

Banks had a way of making me feel like I was the only woman in the world, even when I felt the world was shattering around me. He kissed me like I wasn't broken, like I wasn't carrying a part of my past inside of me. I let my legs wrap around him, the heat between us rising, as his lips moved over mine with more urgency. My hands slid down his chest, feeling his muscles tighten beneath my touch. Every inch of him was solid and warm. His skin smelled like coconut and shea butter. I felt his breath hitch when I traced his tattoos with my fingertips.

"It's us against everything and everybody." His eyes locked with mine. "We gon' be good. All three of us. That's my word."

When our lips touched again, I felt every word he'd said. When he positioned himself back between my legs, I opened wide for him. His mouth touched me, gently at first. My hips arched as a moan slipped from my lips, my fingers curling into the sheets beneath me. Banks was patient yet attentive. His tongue traced slow circles until my body trembled beneath him, my thighs tightening around his shoulders.

When I came, his name was the only thing on my lips. Not Banks but A'zir. That was the first time I'd said his name. Up until now, he'd been nothing but Banks to me. However, when I said his name, his eyes locked with mine.

"I like the way my name sounds coming from your lips. I want to hear it while I'm inside of you."

I nodded, letting him know that I wanted the same. He moved up, sucking my nipple gently. My breath hitched. No matter how many times he'd touched me before, this time felt different. It wasn't about lust or escape; this was more than that. This was him reassuring me that I truly had nothing to worry about. He inserted himself inside of me, and his thickness filled me.

"A'zir," I moaned.

We moved together in a rhythm that felt ancient, like our bodies had been waiting for this moment long before we ever met. His mouth moved from my neck, shoulders, and lips then back again. His hands were on my waist, then gripping my thighs, pulling me closer with every thrust.

"I ain't never letting you go," he whispered, lips pressed against my skin.

I blinked back tears, wrapping my arms around him, as I met his rhythm, hips rising to meet each stroke. He groaned my name, and it shot straight through me, making my entire body clench around him. Our bodies tangled together with our moans as the soundtrack. When we came, it was together. His mouth crushed mine to muffle his groan, as my body convulsed beneath him.

He collapsed beside me, pulling me into his chest without a word. His heart was still racing and so was mine.

"I'm scared," I admitted softly, my voice muffled against his skin.

"Of what?"

"That I'm going to lose this, lose us. Kyrie is not just going to sit around and let you raise his child. This is all he needs right here to think he can get me back."

He exhaled slowly, one hand stroking my back. "You're not going to lose me, Bray. And that nigga can try whatever he wants. There's no pussy in me. Just as quick as he can run up, he can get dropped right back down."

"But the baby. He's going to want to be in his child's life."

"I don't care that the baby isn't mine biologically." He paused. "I care about you, so I care about that baby too. We will raise this baby together with love. Trust me, Bray. I got y'all."

I lifted my head to look at him. His eyes were serious, staying locked on mine. "Are you sure?"

"I've never been more sure of anything in my life."

A tear slipped down my cheek, and he caught it with his thumb. "Then I'm yours," I whispered. "If you still want me."

He smiled, brushing my hair back from my face. "You've been mine."

We stayed like that for what felt like forever, our skin still slick with sweat, wrapped in each other's arms like nothing else mattered but us. He didn't let me go, and I didn't want him to. He kissed me again, this time softer but still intense. "It's me and you, baby. And I mean that shit. You don't never have to worry about anything because I'm gon' take care of it. All you need to be thinking about is how you want to decorate the nursery."

I didn't respond, just looked at him and smiled. At that moment, any doubt I had was gone, and I knew both me and my child would be safe with A'zir. It took a different kind of man to take on the role of father to a child that didn't belong to him. A'zir was that man, and for that, I admired him. There I was, laying in the arms of a man that loved me and wanted to be with me no matter what. A man that wanted to build a family and a life with me no matter how it came. This was a type of love that I had never experienced, and I prayed it would last forever.

We lay there in silence, but it wasn't awkward or empty. It was full of love and unspoken trust that everything would work out. My fingers traced slow lines across A'zir's chest, memorizing the feel of his skin, the way his breathing gradually returned to normal. His arms stayed wrapped around me like he never wanted to let go, like I was something precious to him. I closed my eyes and took a deep breath as I took it all in. For the first time in my life, I was safe with a man.

I tilted my head, resting my chin lightly against his chest, so I could look at him. "How did I get so lucky?"

He smiled lazily. "Shit, I'm the lucky one."

His fingers brushed the small of my back, and I let my eyes close again, sighing softly. I didn't want to move. I wanted to lay in his arms forever. I couldn't wait to experience the life we were going to build with each other.

"Can I ask you a real question?" I murmured.

"Always."

I hesitated. "What are we going to do about Kyrie? Should I tell him that I'm having his baby, or do I just not say anything? I don't want to lie to my child, but is not ever knowing Kyrie what's best for him or her?"

"That's something you will have to decide for yourself. You can tell him or not tell him for all I give a fuck. It doesn't change the truth. And the truth is that he won't have no parts in raising that child. Our child. He or she will know me as daddy, just like any other children we have after this. Ain't shit he gon' be able to do about it either way. So, it really don't matter what you tell him. As far as I'm concerned, there's no need for you to say a fuckin' thing to him ever."

His hand stilled for a second, but then, he sat up, pulling me with him, so I was straddling his lap. His eyes locked onto mine.

"That nigga lost his chance the second he sold you for a punk ass hundred grand. He don't deserve to even get spoke on anymore. That nigga is your past. The future is much brighter with me, baby."

I smiled at him before lowering myself to meet his lips. A'zir kissed me softly, our tongues dancing with one another's. He held me tight in his arms, and I was finally able to close my eyes.

Chapter Three

KYRIE

The sun poured through the cracks in the blinds, waking me from my sleep. I blinked against the light, my mouth dry and my head throbbing with everything I didn't get to say to Braylen before she left me, everything I should've said. Her side of the bed was cold and had been for far too long. It had been too long since I held her and felt her body pressed against mine. I reached across the mattress like I was going to find her there anyway, like she'd somehow crept back in during the night. My fingers curled into nothing but sheets.

I sat up slow, elbows on my knees, hands rubbing my face. Every morning hit the same lately, like loss and regret had a timeshare on my chest. Some mornings, it felt like I was breathing through water, like the weight of losing Braylen was too heavy. I swung my legs over the edge of the bed, bones stiff like I was pushing sixty instead of barely pushing thirty. My phone buzzed on the nightstand. I didn't check it. I knew it wasn't her. Braylen wasn't calling. She'd made that real clear. Still, I prayed every night she'd change her mind.

I got up, tossed on a black tee, and slid into some joggers. My slides slapped the hardwood as I walked through the townhome. It still smelled like her, like the jasmine lotion she used. That scent had dug into the walls, same way she'd dug into me. I handled my morning business – checked the safe, counted the stacks, called Vic to see what moves we were setting for the day to make sure everything went smooth. I wasn't trying to be sloppy about shit, not anymore. I'd been sloppy with Braylen and ended up losing her. I wasn't making that mistake again.

I poured a glass of cold water and opened the patio doors. The mid-morning breeze felt good on my skin. I stood there a minute, phone in my hand, debating whether I should even call. My lawyer had already sent the papers once. I'd sent them back unsigned. I wasn't giving up on us. Not yet. I tapped the screen and found the contact that read *Isaiah Turner Attorney*. He picked up after the second ring.

"Morning, Kyrie," he said, all smooth and polite like this was some regular-ass business deal and not my whole heart on the line.

"You got a minute?" I asked.

"For you? Always."

I leaned against the door frame, staring up into the sky. "You said if both parties want the divorce, it's pretty much done, right?"

"That's correct. Michigan doesn't require a reason beyond 'irreconcilable differences'. You can contest it, but it won't stop the process indefinitely. It'll just drag it out."

"I ain't tryna drag it out just to be spiteful," I said, jaw tight. "I just... I need more time. She's not thinking straight."

There was a pause on his end. "Kyrie, you sure she's not thinking straight? Or is she just thinking without you?"

That one hit harder than I expected.

I clenched my jaw. "She's my wife. We been through worse."

"She filed the motion, Kyrie. That tells the court she's serious."

"She's just mad and hurt. She ain't seeing things clearly." I stepped back inside, pacing. "I put her in a messed-up position. I can admit that. But I never though the shit would end in divorce. I just need to talk to her. Get her to see things my way."

Isaiah let out a quiet sigh. "What do you want me to do?"

"I need you to slow this down. Stall it, block it, whatever you gotta do. Give me two more weeks."

He hesitated. "That won't stop her from moving on emotionally."

"She already moved on," I said under my breath, more to myself than him. "I just want the chance to show her who I am now. What I'm doing to fix this."

"Alright," he said. "I can file a motion to extend the response window. That'll buy us time. But Kyrie, eventually the court's going to move forward with or without you."

"I'm not worried about the court," I snapped. "I'm worried about her."

Isaiah paused again. "You're walking a fine line, man. Don't end up holding onto a marriage that already died."

"It ain't dead. It's bruised, yeah. But it ain't gone."

I ended the call before he could say more. I didn't need anyone else talking like it was over. I already had to live with the fact that she was sleeping in another man's bed, a man that I had sent her to. *God, what the hell did I do?* I thought as I ran my hand down my face.

I took a seat on the edge of the couch. This place felt so damn empty without her laugh bouncing off the walls, without her humming while she cooked, or arguing with me about little shit like toothpaste caps and the TV being too loud. Back then, I used to tune her out. Now, I'd give anything just to hear her voice in this place again. Braylen had been telling me for years to stop gambling, but I never listened. I thought I had it all under control. Now, I'd gambled my wife right into the arms of another man.

I needed to talk to her, to show her how I'd changed in the time she'd been away. I needed to show her that I no longer moved the way I used to. I moved with Vic and his crew, and everything we did was calculated and well planned out. Counting cards was a foolproof way to ensure I won every time I took a seat at the table.

Vic had taken me under his wing and taught me the hustle inside and out. I made sure to stack every penny I made, saving for the beautiful life I would give Braylen when she came back to me. I had given her promises at first and had broken all of them. Now, I had to show her proof. She had no idea the plans I had for us, and I knew once she saw the new life I could provide, my wife would be right back in my arms.

I stood up and walked over to the drawer where I kept her bracelet, the one I'd bought her after our first anniversary. It was real gold and the most expensive thing I'd brought her since we'd gotten married. She used to wear it every day until I lost a gambling bet and had to pawn it for money. I got it back for her in a couple weeks, just like I said, but she never wore it again.

I picked it up and ran my thumb over the clasp.

"I'm gon' bring you home," I whispered. "Even if you hate me right now."

I held the bracelet in my hand for a long time before setting it back in the drawer. My chest felt tight, like if I took another breath the ache would pour out. I didn't want to go there. I told myself I was done torturing myself like this. But I was weak for her, even now. I opened the hidden folder in my phone, the one marked *Just Bray*. It was locked with my fingerprint like it was national security.

Inside were dozens of clips, videos, and screenshots that I didn't want to delete – memories I kept like souvenirs of a love I couldn't let go of. There was one I played more than the rest.

The screen lit up with her face. She was laying on our bed, her hair wild around her shoulders, lips parted in that lazy smile she gave me when she wanted to get freaky. She had on my old T-shirt, stretched over her thighs, one hand rubbing her nipples through the shirt, the other sliding slow between her legs.

"Say my name, baby," I'd told her from behind the camera.

"Kyrie," she breathed, biting her lip. "I want you so bad right now."

I sat back against the couch cushions, one hand gripping the phone, the other slipping into the waistband of my joggers. I knew I shouldn't, knowing it would only make things worse – wanting her this bad, knowing I couldn't have her right now. However, I didn't care. I missed her in every gotdamn way a man could miss a woman.

My hand wrapped around myself as the sound of her moans filled the room, soft and sweet. I closed my eyes and imagined her right there, legs spread on the couch, back arched, whispering my name the way only she could. I stroked slow, deliberate, letting the memory swallow me whole. She was everything. The curve of her hips. The way she gasped my name like it tasted good. The little laugh she gave when I made her beg. I gritted my teeth, jaw flexing. "Braylen," I moaned.

I'd give anything to have her under me again. To feel her nails in my back, her breath in my ear. It wasn't just the sex; it was deeper than that. I missed being the one she trusted. The one she came to for comfort, for pleasure, for everything. I came hard, my entire body jerking, vision going hazy around the edges. However, instead of relief, I just felt emptier.

I walked upstairs to the hall closet, grabbed a towel, and wiped off, jaw still clenched, chest heaving. The truth was that no orgasm could bring her back. No video, no memory, no replay of the past could fix what I'd broken now. I knew the longer she stayed away, the harder it would be to get her back.

I sat on my bed in the quiet, the only sound in the room my own breathing. I stared at the dark screen of my phone like it held answers, as if maybe she was watching me suffer the way I watched her memory break me apart. I should've stopped there. Should've just swallowed the ache and moved on with my day. But pain made a man reckless. And I was hurting in ways I couldn't patch up with sex or money.

So, I opened my messages. Her name was still saved in my phone, still *My Love* with a red heart, still pinned to the top like she hadn't already unpinned me from her life. I tapped the thread and typed something simple.

Me: Can we talk? Please.

I stared at the message for a second, thumb hovering over the send button. Then, I hit send. I watched the screen like I was watching a bomb count down. Waited for the little bubbles. Waited for anything. But something was off. The message didn't go through. No "delivered". No read receipt. No response. I frowned and sent another one.

Me: Bray, just hear me out. I'm just asking for one convo.

Then, the system response hit. **"Message not delivered. This number is no longer in service."**

I froze as I read it again. I sat back slowly, the weight of that little sentence crushing the air out of my chest. She changed her number. Changed it and didn't tell me. Didn't care if I had it or not. Didn't care if I could reach her. That realization cracked something deep in me. Something I'd been trying to keep whole with denial and daydreams. She wasn't just mad. She was done.

Done with the apologies, the promises, and the tears. Done waiting on me to be the man she needed before Banks ever came into the picture. She'd cut the line. Severed the last thread I had to her voice. That silence was louder than any curse she could've ever thrown at me. I dropped the phone on the nightstand, chest hollow. The smart thing would've been to let it go. But I'd never been smart when it came to Braylen. And I damn sure wasn't going to start now. If I couldn't call her, then I would have to find her. She was going to talk to me one way or another.

Chapter Four

BANKS

I woke up early that next morning and just laid there for a moment, flat on my back. One hand was behind my head, the other resting on the curve of Braylen's thigh under the sheets. She was still asleep, breathing soft and steady, legs tangled in mine. I turned my head slightly and watched her as the morning light hit her face. Her skin was golden under the natural light, and she'd never looked more beautiful. One arm was curled under her head, lips slightly parted, hair wild across my pillow.

I slid out of bed quietly, not wanting to wake her. She stirred once, reaching for me in her sleep like her body already knew I was leaving it. I padded through the room barefoot, leaving her in the warmth of Egyptian cotton and memory foam. The sun had just come up, and I had rose with it. Discipline was what kept me sharp. It was also what separated me from most men my age.

I made my way downstairs and hit the gym room. I started with pushups, shirtless and focused, with my palms flat against the cold, rubber floor. I didn't stop until my arms burned and sweat rolled down my back in streams. Next was the weights. I didn't work out to music. I didn't need any distractions, just me in control, because in this life, control was the only currency that mattered.

Braylen had started cracking that, and I was surprised that I was allowing her. I tried not to think about her when I worked out, but my mind drifted anyway to the way she moaned my name last night. It was the first time she'd moaned my government name, and it sounded like heaven on earth. Braylen clung to me like our souls recognized each other's. Even after everything that happened to get her here. The way we fell in love might not have been ideal, but it was our story, and I wouldn't change one thing about it. She was mine, and I was hers.

After forty-five minutes, I grabbed a towel, wiped the sweat from my face, and headed down the hall to the indoor pool. The lights inside were dim, sunlight filtering through the ceiling-length windows above, casting gold hues across the calm blue surface. This pool was my sanctuary. The water was always warm, the air thick with silence and steam. I dropped the towel, stepped into the shallow end, and dove under without hesitation.

I pushed through the water in long strokes, each lap burning the last of the tension from my muscles. I ducked my head underneath the water. When I came up for air, I closed my eyes and leaned against the edge of the pool, arms stretched out wide. My heartbeat slowed as the steam rose around me.

By the time I stepped out the pool, my body felt relaxed and ready for the day. I dried off slow, wrapped the towel around my waist, and headed upstairs. On the way, I stopped by the intercom on the hallway wall and pressed the kitchen line.

"Start breakfast," I said into the mic, voice low but clear. "Something light."

"No problem, coming right up," my chef replied.

Back in the master suite, the room was still darkened by thick blackout drapes. Braylen hadn't moved. She was curled up on her side with the covers tucked up to her shoulders, one bare leg slipping out the side. I stood there for a second, just looking at her. She looked so peaceful sleeping like that, and I didn't want to wake her.

I turned quietly, grabbed fresh clothes from my drawer – a pair of gray sweatpants and a fitted tee – then hit the shower. The water was hot, pounding down on my shoulders like fists. I let it burn some of the tension out of my neck as I stood still beneath the stream, palms flat against the tile. After drying off and getting dressed, I stepped out of the bathroom. I glanced over at the bed once more to see Braylen still sleeping. I smiled before walking out the room, softly closing the door behind me.

I moved down the hallway and walked down the stairs to the main floor. The smell of rosemary potatoes, smoked turkey bacon, and fresh-baked croissants hit me halfway down the steps. My chef was plating up in the kitchen. There were two covered trays, one with a fruit medley and green juice just the way Braylen liked it. I nodded my approval as I walked through.

"Take hers up. Set it on the warmer," I told my chef. "Don't wake her."

"No problem."

I took my own tray and headed toward my office, allowing the door to click behind me. Here, the mood shifted. The dark tone of the room matched my profession. Matte black monitors glowed softly across the desk, waiting for me. I sat down, fork in hand, and ate while skimming through the encrypted email feed. Most of the messages were routine, coded logistics, payments clearing, and location verifications. But one caught my eye.

Subject: ORDER REQUEST – PRIORITY

From: Raven

Time: 4:43 AM

I clicked it open, reading the message.

Client requesting two units. Male. Clean pull. No visible marks. Prefer Detroit or Chicago-based. Budget open. Delivery within seven days. Payment ready. Need confirmation before noon.

I leaned back in the chair, chewing slowly. Placing my plate down on my desk, I sent a reply.

Noted. I'll confirm by ten.

I encrypted the message and hit send. Then, I leaned back in the chair, sipping my bottled water, staring at the screen. Braylen didn't know this version of me. However, I knew that if we were building a life together, then eventually, she would. And I knew that when she did, she would either stay or want to be as far away from me as possible.

I stayed in my office for another hour, finishing my meal, as I moved through the rest of the system. The desk in front of me was cold and clean. There was no paper trail, just encrypted files and quiet money. I approved three transfers, flagged one suspicious request from overseas, and re-routed a package I didn't like the timing on.

Normally, I would stay in my office for hours, working. The money always motivated me to do the most. However, with Braylen being in my bed, all I wanted to do was be next to her. It was fucking with me because I never did this soft shit. But Braylen had me acting different.

I confirmed the request before I powered off my monitors and closed my laptop. I moved through the office, past the shelves lined with black, leather binders that looked like legal ledgers but hid all my sins. The hallway outside was quiet. I walked up the steps to the landing just in time to hear her voice.

"Good morning, Marcus. Breakfast was delicious as usual," she said softly.

She was standing at the kitchen island, her back to me. Braylen's voice was low, still thick with sleep. I leaned against the archway, watching her with a smile on my face. She had one of my hoodies on, sleeves too long, hem hitting just below her ass. Her legs were bare, and her hair was pulled back in a loose, messy bun. Her face was fresh with no makeup, and to me, she'd never looked more beautiful.

"You sleep good?" I asked, voice low but sharp enough to let her know I'd been watching.

She turned her head slightly, eyes scanning over me once before she nodded.

"Yeah," she said. "Best sleep I've had all week. I didn't realize I was out that long."

"You needed it." I paused. "You didn't toss once. You stayed in one spot the entire night. That's rare for you." I laughed.

"You call that sleep-tracking or surveillance?" She smiled.

I smirked just a little. "Both. You know I don't miss much."

She turned around and started walking out the kitchen.

"Where you going?" I asked, eyeing the way her hips swayed as she walked.

"I was just about to head back upstairs."

"Nah," I said, pushing off the wall. "Go get dressed."

She turned, brows slightly raised. "Get dressed for what?"

"You'll see." I paused, voice even. "Don't keep me waiting, Bray."

She didn't argue or ask any more questions. She just nodded once, slow, and headed back up the stairs. My eyes followed every step. She came back downstairs about thirty minutes later, still not dressed but now in a robe. He hair was no longer in the bun but now hanging down her shoulders.

"A'zir, I need to know how I should dress for the day since I don't know where we going."

My name on her tongue damn near had me mesmerized. I stood there for a second, just taking it all in. "You can wear anything you want. It's nice outside. It's supposed to be eighty-four so just dress for the weather."

Today was going to be all about her. She'd just began finding her footing in this new life of ours. And just when she thought she had it, she was thrown a curve ball. I saw it in her eyes every time she looked at me since her doctor's appointment. The quiet fight to stay present, to not let the weight of her past with that sorry bastard, Kyrie, drag her under – the beautiful chaos that was now our life. I wanted her to know that I was going to be there every step of the way. However, I couldn't just tell her. I would have to show her. So, today, that was exactly what I was going to do.

When she came back downstairs dressed in a soft pink, two-piece, linen set that showed off her waist and hugged her hips, her glossed lips perfectly glistening, I was already waiting by the front door.

"Come on, baby. We outside today."

She blinked at me, confused. "Outside where?"

I grinned and leaned in to kiss her forehead. "Everywhere."

Our first stop was a private spa tucked in the hills of Bloomfield, surrounded by trees and beautiful rose bushes. The place didn't even have a damn sign, just a discreet gate and a long driveway. I had the entire place booked out – just me, her, and a team of Black women ready to treat her like royalty.

We were greeted with infused water, cold towels, and custom plush robes. I sat back and sipped ginger tea, while she got a ninety-minute body polish and massage with eucalyptus oil. Her sighs of relief through the cracked treatment room door were the sexiest sounds I'd heard all week.

Next came the hydrotherapy, a warm, bubbling mineral tub in the center of a glass room surrounded by greenery. She floated on her back, her eyes closed, lips slightly parted, like peace had finally caught up to her. I joined her, pulling her into my lap under the water, hands on her thighs, just holding her, while she rested her head against my shoulder.

"You good?" I murmured.

She nodded without opening her eyes. "I'm better than good. This is the most relaxed I've been this entire week."

I smiled. "Good. That's all I wanted."

I stayed in the tub, while Braylen went to get a facial. I was happy that she was enjoying her treatment, and I knew this was only the start of our day together. I needed for Braylen to know that she was special to me, and to do that, I would have to show her. So, today, that was exactly what I was going to do.

We left the spa and got into the Rolls. Zeek kept quiet as I pulled out my phone and queued a playlist of old school R&B, mostly from the 90s. It was the kind of music that hit different when you were in love or falling back into it. She leaned against the window, singing under her breath to Silk, while I kept my hand on her thigh.

We didn't say much, nor did we have to. We just drove around, listening to music and enjoying one another. An hour later, we pulled up to the heliport, and her brows shot up.

"A'zir, what is this?"

I smirked and helped her out the car. "You said you needed to get out your own head. So, I'm getting you above it."

She smiled before wrapping her arms around me. "I never would have expected this. Thank you."

"You don't have to thank me, baby. I got you forever." I wrapped my arm around her shoulder, and we walked toward the helicopter.

The ride was smooth and quiet except for the hum of the blades. We flew over Detroit, and the big city looked small from our view at the top. She held my hand the entire ride, squeezing tighter when the skyline came into view.

"This is beautiful," she whispered.

"You are," I replied.

We landed about thirty minutes later and made our way back to the car. Zeek took us to a high-rise building with a private rooftop. I'd called ahead and had everything set up just for us. A black tablecloth, gold charger plates, candles, and fresh white roses lined the table. We walked over to the table hand in hand. I pulled out her chair, and she took her seat before I took mine.

The chef served lobster risotto, grilled lamb lollipops, and berry sorbet with prosecco foam. We sat across from each other under the open sky, our knees touching under the table. She laughed more than I'd heard all week, telling me about her childhood dreams.

"I want to paint again," she spoke softly. "That night we painted together was the first time I'd painted in years. When I was a kid, that was all I ever wanted to do."

"You will," I promised. "And I'll buy every damn piece. I'll do whatever to make you happy, Bray, and I just want you to know that."

She smiled before nodding her head. She didn't push. She knew if I said I had her, then that was exactly what it was. We sat there for a few moments more, conversing under candlelight. When we were done, we made our way back to the Rolls Royce where Zeek was waiting. I didn't take Braylen back to the house, not tonight. I had a suite booked downtown overlooking the river with floor-to-ceiling windows and a private balcony. As nice as our house was, I knew Braylen needed a getaway, and that was exactly what she was going to get. The room smelled like vanilla and sandalwood. A bath was already drawn when we walked in. Rose petals, candles, the whole nine.

She stood in the doorway, staring at it all, then turned to me. "Why are you doing this?"

I stepped behind her, wrapping my arms around her waist, pulling her back into me. "Because I want you to know what it feels like to be cherished, not just tolerated. You deserve more than survival, Bray."

She turned in my arms and kissed me before I could say another word. The kiss was soft and long. I didn't want to pull away, and when she did, I was still lost in her. We undressed before I stepped inside the tub first. Braylen followed after, laying back on my chest, as I wrapped my arms around her. I held her tightly, as I softly kissed the nape of her neck.

"Today was wonderful, A'zir," she whispered softly.

"I'm glad you enjoyed it, but we just getting started. This is the first of many days like this, Braylen, because you deserve it. I want your pregnancy to be as stress free as possible. And I'm gon' make sure of that."

I lathered a towel with vanilla scented body wash before I began washing her body. I started at her neck. With slow strokes of the cloth, I moved over her collarbones and down her arms. I massaged the pads of her fingers then her wrists. I worked my way to her breasts, brushing against her nipples, as they peaked through the foam. Her breath caught, but she didn't stop me. I moved down her belly and around her hips. I washed every part of her like she was something priceless and fragile. Because the fact was that she was.

When the water started cooling, we stepped out the tub. I wrapped her in a plush towel and carried her to the bed. I laid her down and kissed the inside of her thigh gently.

"I been waiting all day for this," I murmured, eyes locked on hers, as I kissed higher. "Let me taste you, Braylen."

I pushed her legs apart wider, resting between her thighs. She was already warm, soft, and ready for me, but I wasn't rushing this. Tonight, I was going to take my time. My tongue found her clit slowly, and I moved in gentle circles, teasing her with the flat of my tongue until she arched up and gasped.

"A'zir..." she whispered. "Just like that."

I groaned against her, loving the way she said my name. I slid two fingers into her as I sucked her clit, curling them just right, while her hips rocked against my face. Her taste was everything, sweet and addicting. I licked like I couldn't get enough because I couldn't. She moaned, high and breathless, her thighs tightening around my head. She trembled as she came for me. Even then, I didn't stop. Not until she begged me to.

"Relax, Bray," I murmured, kissing her inner knee. "Let me take care of you."

I moved up from between her thighs until her lips met mine. I kissed her like I was writing an apology with my mouth. Slow and deep. She moaned softly against my lips.

"I want to taste you again," I whispered.

"A'zir," she moaned, breathless.

"Let me." Before she could answer, I crawled back down between her legs. I buried my face between her thighs and tasted her like I needed to memorize every part of her. She was dripping wet, and that only made me hungrier. My tongue moved in deep strokes, slow circles, then back again, teasing her clit, pulling soft moans from her mouth like a song only I could hear. Her fingers threaded through my locs, tugging gently, hips rising with every flick and suck.

"Damn, A'zir..." she breathed, arching. "Don't stop. Please don't stop."

I didn't. I stayed there just as she asked, eating her until her thighs trembled and her eyes fluttered shut, until she called out my name again and again, her whole body unraveling under my tongue. She came like a storm, shaky and breathless. Soft cries and gasps came from her lips, while her nails scratched my shoulders. I didn't move until she was done – until she was fully spent.

Then, I crawled up beside her, wrapped her in my arms, and kissed her forehead.

"You good?" I asked against her skin.

She nodded, still catching her breath. "Yeah... better than good."

I pulled the blankets over us both and held her there, not saying a word. I didn't need to. Us being together, holding each other like this, was enough.

Chapter Five

VITA

It had been two weeks since Victor walked into my life. Two weeks of expensive dinners, late-night drives in his matte black Maybach, and two weeks of getting whatever it was I wanted. I wasn't used to feeling soft like this. This was my first time fucking with anyone his age. It just felt different all together. Although I hadn't let my guard all the way down, he was making me feel like I would be able to eventually.

I was in my robe, fresh out the shower and lounging on the couch. I was scrolling on my phone when it rang. It was Victor, and I smiled before I answered.

"Hey, you," I answered, my voice still a little raspy.

"Open your door," he spoke, voice smooth as jazz on a late night.

I blinked. "Wait, what?"

"Go to your door and open it."

Before I could say another word, he hung up. My stomach flipped with excitement, not knowing what to expect. I pulled my robe tighter and padded barefoot across the apartment to the front door. When I opened it, my breath caught. There, sitting pretty on the welcome mat, was a massive bouquet of deep red roses in a black marble vase. Right next to it was a Chanel shopping bag with a white envelope on top. I glanced around, half-expecting him to pop out from somewhere, but the hallway was empty. It was just me and these beautiful ass gifts that I wasn't expecting.

I brought them inside and set the roses on the counter. They smelled just as beautiful as they looked. The Chanel bag was heavy, but I opened the envelope first.

Be dressed by 7. I want to show you off. —V.

That alone made my thighs press together. Inside the bag was a dress that looked like it cost more than my rent. It was midnight black and sleeveless with a plunging neckline and a slit that ran up the thigh. Underneath it, nestled in tissue paper, was a red-bottom heel so high and sleek that it screamed bad bitch. I held the dress up to my body and looked into my full-length mirror in my living room. *Alright, Mr. Mysterious. Let's see what tonight is about.*

By the time six-thirty rolled around, I had transformed. The dress fit like it was sewn onto my body, hugging every curve like a second skin. I'd oiled my skin down until it gleamed like bronze under my bathroom light, slipped into the heels, and let my locs fall down my back. My makeup was sultry – smokey eyes, a glossy nude lip, and a hint of gold shimmer on my cheeks. I looked like a walking bag of money.

At exactly seven o'clock, there was a knock at my door. Not a second early. Not a second late. I took a deep breath, adjusted my dress, and opened the door. Victor stood there, tall and handsome, dressed in a black Tom Ford suit that looked tailor-made. He was clean. Grown man clean. His crisp white shirt opened at the collar just enough to show off the tattoo that peeked from his chest. His pants fit him to perfection, and on his wrist was a Rolex that glinted beneath the light.

He smelled like Creed Aventus. He looked like a man that commanded his respect, and that was something I liked about him. He smiled when he looked at me before leaning in to kiss my cheek gently.

"Damn, baby," he spoke low, licking his bottom lip. "You trying to make me cancel dinner and take you straight to the floor right here and now?"

I laughed softly, a blush creeping up my neck. "Is that an option?"

"You look like trouble. Beautiful fucking trouble. Are you ready for the night of your life?"

I nodded, and we both walked out the door. He didn't let go of my waist the entire walk to the car. When we got closer, I saw the driver standing outside the door waiting for our arrival. When we approached, he opened the door, and we slide into the soft leather seats. Once inside the back of the Maybach, Victor reached for my hand and kissed my wrist gently then laid it on his thigh.

"In whatever room we walk in, just know you're going to be the baddest in it."

I smirked. "Thank you but I already know that."

He chuckled, low and deep. "Facts."

I didn't ask where we were going. I didn't have to. With Victor, I had learned to sit back and let him drive, both literally and figuratively. He looked over at me once more, eyes hot, then said, "Tonight, Vita, I'm showing you what my world feels like."

My breath caught. I knew that tonight would be unforgettable, and I was ready for whatever Victor had planned.

The first stop was a rooftop restaurant I'd only ever seen on Instagram. It was the kind of place with a waiting list months long, where the menu didn't have prices, and the food came out looking like art. But Victor? He walked in like he owned the damn place, hand at the small of my back, speaking low to the hostess who immediately nodded and led us to a private terrace that overlooked the city.

The table was set for two. Candles flickered in the warm summer breeze. Soft jazz floated through the air, and the sun was just beginning to set, bathing the whole city in gold.

Every course that came out was better than the last. Wagyu beef that melted on the tongue. Hand-rolled pasta with truffle cream. The red wine was so smooth that I drank my first glass down in one gulp.

Victor was quiet, but his eyes stayed on me. It was as if he was admiring my every move – possessive but in a way that made me feel protected, not owned. After dinner, the driver was waiting again. This time, we pulled up to an art gallery that had closed early in preparation for our arrival. Victor had arranged a private viewing – just me, him, and walls filled with soft-lit paintings and sculptures. He walked me through the exhibits slowly, pointing out pieces he liked, asking for my thoughts on them. The intimacy of it all, the way he paid attention to every little reaction I had, was more seductive than any bedroom act could be.

By the time the night ended and we were driven back, my heels were dangling from my fingers. I was still tipsy from both the wine and Victor's gaze. I slid back into my shoes before we stepped out of the car into the cool night air. Victor's hand was firm on my lower back, guiding me through the glass doors of his building. The elevator hummed quietly as it climbed, and I could feel his eyes on me.

When the doors slid open, the apartment was darker than I expected, bathed only in the soft glow of the city lights through the floor-to-ceiling windows. Victor closed the door behind us and didn't say a word. He just took me by the hand and led me toward the center of the room where a massive black leather couch waited alongside a low table.

I was still catching my breath from the beautiful night Victor had shown me. My heels clicked softly on the marble floor as I followed him. Without warning, he reached for the straps of my dress and slid them down my arms. The silk slipped from my skin with ease, leaving me in nothing but a black lace thong. He watched me, his eyes never leaving mine, as his fingers traced my collarbone.

"You didn't think the night was over, did you?"

I swallowed hard, heart pounding in my throat. Victor stepped closer, his breath warm against my ear.

"You're mine tonight. Every inch of you. And you'll beg me to show you just how far that goes."

His words were a command, a threat, and a seduction all at once. I was trembling beneath him, but it wasn't from fear. It was from need. As much as Victor wanted to own me, I wanted him to. I watched as he walked over to the glass bar in the corner of the room. He poured brown liquor into two glasses and handed one to me. We drank them down before setting the glasses down on the table. Victor didn't speak. He didn't have to because his eyes said it all.

Grabbing my hand, he guided me down the hallway and into his bedroom. In the middle of the room was a huge bed with black silk sheets. However, I felt the cold marble flooring against my knees as I dropped to them. I slowly unzipped his pants and pulled out a dick that was already rock hard. I took him into my mouth, listening to him hiss, as my tongue circled the tip.

Victor licked his lips before speaking in a low but steady tone. "You're mine. And tonight, I'm going to show you why."

He pulled himself from my mouth before helping me to my feet. He laid me on the bed gently. I didn't hesitate when he took the two silk ribbons from the nightstand and wrapped them around my wrists, tying them tight enough to both thrill and scare me.

He kissed my neck then whispered, "Let's begin."

The ribbon tightened around my wrists, cold silk biting gently into my skin. My breath hitched. However, it wasn't from pain but from the delicious tension curling through my body.

Victor's hands slid down my arms, tracing over every inch of me, as if memorizing the map of my body.

"Look at you," he said, voice low and rough. "So eager to be claimed. You want me to be the one to claim you, don't you?"

I swallowed hard, eyes locked on his. The way he moved with slow precision made me dizzy. Made me want to beg for him. To surrender to him. This was something I'd never felt before.

"Yes," I moaned, breathless.

His mouth found my neck, teeth grazing lightly before pressing kisses on my skin. My hands twitched against the silk, but I couldn't pull free nor did I want to.

"Good girl," he murmured.

He slid down my thong before spreading my legs across the black silk sheets like I was his canvas. He positioned himself between my legs. His breath was hot as he lowered his mouth to my skin, licking a slow trail from my hip bone up to my belly. My body shuddered at the contact, the thrill of his dominance wrapping around me like a drug. Victor's tongue flicked over my sensitive skin, teasing, tasting, driving me crazy. His hands gripped my thighs firmly, pressing me open for him.

"Tell me you're mine," he demanded.

"I'm yours," I whispered, voice trembling.

He smiled against my skin, teeth nipping gently before he plunged his tongue inside me, swirling and sucking with relentless hunger. I moaned, hips rising, as my fingers clutched the sheets. Victor didn't rush; he took his time tasting me. He came up several moments later, his mouth glistening with my juices. He stripped off his shirt slowly, muscles rippling under the low light.

"Say it again," he ordered.

"I'm yours," I breathed.

"No limits, just let me do what I do."

It wasn't a question. It was more like an order. He was telling me that he was going to do whatever he wanted to my body. For some reason, I wasn't scared. I trusted Victor and was going to allow him to do whatever he wanted.

"I'm yours," I repeated, heat flooding me, letting him know that he could take me however he saw fit.

He entered me slowly, taking his time, making sure I felt every inch. His pace was merciless, deep and deliberate. My hips bucked, syncing with his thrusts. Our bodies moved together like a perfect storm.

"You belong to me now, Vita. Every part of you."

I nodded, chest heaving, letting him know that I would be his.

Victor's hands were everywhere, gripping and claiming every inch of my body. He placed his finger under my chin, guiding my eyes to his. I looked at him, eyes filled with desire. He bit down on my shoulder, not hard enough to draw blood but enough to remind me he was in control. His pace was relentless, deepening and hitting spots I didn't even know I had. Every thrust was a command, and every growl was a warning. I was drowning in pleasure, and Victor knew it.

"Say it again," he demanded.

"I'm yours," I gasped, breath hitching.

"Good girl. And don't you ever forget that."

His hands trailed down my body, fingers digging into my skin, as he shifted me, flipping me over onto my stomach. He licked a trail up my spine, and I moaned softly. His nails racked over my ass cheeks before he grabbed them. He slid back inside me, my pussy curving to his dick like it was made for it.

Hours could have passed or minutes. I wasn't sure. Time lost meaning as he stroked deeper. Victor didn't let up. Every movement was filled with brutal pleasure. The way he held my hips in place. The low growl of the whispers of my name. It all sent shock waves through my body. The bed creaked beneath us as we moved together in a rhythm we made. The passion was pure, and I knew we both felt it. We climaxed at the same time with our names on each other's tongue.

That next morning, I woke up to breakfast in bed. Victor had ordered it while I was still sleeping and placed the food on a tray next to a glass of apple juice. I couldn't help but smile as he placed the tray into my lap.

"Thank you."

"You're welcome. After last night, I thought you deserved breakfast in bed."

We ate together before showering. He dropped me off at my house, and the first thing I did was call Braylen.

"Bitch, I found me a man. A fine ass, grown ass, rich man," I screamed into the phone the moment she answered.

"Aw, shit, best friend. Tell me all about it."

I could hear Braylen smiling through the phone. Hell, I was smiling too and had been since the first night I met Victor. I started telling Braylen all about him, trying not to miss any details. I spoke about how we met and the date he'd taken me on the night before.

"I met him a couple weeks ago at a club downtown. That was that night I was trying to get you to go out with me, but yo' ass wouldn't even answer the phone."

"Girl, I been going through a lot these past couple weeks. But it's all good now."

"Going through some shit? I know Banks' fine ass ain't no fuck nigga, is he? Because I will fuck his ass up for you, Bray. What the fuck that nigga do?"

"Nah, he has been wonderful. It's some other shit that was on my mind."

The one person I knew better than I knew myself was my best friend. So, I could hear in her voice that something was off. Not giving it a second thought, I told Braylen to get dressed and meet me at the Blind Owl for brunch. She agreed, and the call ended.

I arrived at the restaurant first, grabbing us a table and ordering our lemon drops, as I waited on Braylen to arrive. She walked in about five minutes later, and I waved her over as I sipped from my glass.

"I ordered us our first round of lemon drops already," I informed the moment she took her seat.

"I can't even drink it, sis." She pushed the drink over toward me.

"You can't drink it? Why not?"

Braylen took a deep breath before answering. "Bitch, I'm pregnant."

I smiled wide as I stood up and ran around the table, hugging her tightly. "Oh, my God, Bray. I'm about to be a god mama. I knew you was gonna let that fine ass nigga knock yo' ass up. I'm so happy for you, sis. You deserve all the good things that's coming."

Braylen's smile slightly faded as I spoke. I looked in her eyes and immediately knew that something was wrong, seeing the tears that were starting to form. I grabbed her hand and wrapped one of my arms around her shoulder.

"Bray, what's wrong?"

"I went to the doctor a couple of weeks ago. When I got my ultrasound, the tech told me that I was three months along. That means it's not Banks' baby, Vita. It's Kyrie's."

My mouth fell open with her words. The tears that had formed in her eyes were now falling down her cheeks. I knew how much Braylen wanted to get away from Kyrie, and I wanted her to be rid of that nigga too. However, I knew this baby would bring her right back to him.

"What did Banks say?"

"He told me not to worry about it. Told me we would raise the baby together and that Kyrie wouldn't be a part of the baby's life. But how could I do that? How could I lie to my child?"

I took my seat again, my hand still on Braylen's. "You wouldn't be lying to your child; you would be saving that child. Kyrie sold you to a man he thought was going to kill him. What the hell do you think he would do to that baby? If Banks wants to step up and be a father to that child, then I say let him."

Braylen dropped her head as tears fell from her eyes. I didn't understand why she felt anything. She had a chance to have a great life, a life free from all the fucked-up shit Kyrie had ever put her through. My girl deserved that, and I wanted her to have it.

Chapter Six

KYRIE

I stood in front of my closet, trying to decide what to wear for the night. Over these past few weeks, I'd completely changed my wardrobe, stocking my closet with several designer items. Gone was the broke ass nigga I used to be. The Kyrie I was now was a man that I knew Braylen would be proud to be with. I just needed for her to see it for herself. Until that day came, I was going to continue to stack my money.

I unhooked my gold-plated watch from its velvet box and slid it over my wrist. It wasn't real gold, not yet anyway, but it *looked* like it was. And that was half the battle. It was all about illusion when we went out to the casino. Look like you had way more money than you actually did. As long as you looked the part, you could make the money.

I pulled a black turtleneck over my head and smoothed it down over my chest. Over it, I threw on a double-breasted charcoal blazer with a subtle herringbone pattern. I adjusted the lapels before grabbing my pants. They were slim, black, dress pants, Italian-cut and ankle-length with a slight break at the shoe. I slid into a fresh pair of black leather loafers that were polished to perfection.

My braids were freshly done, and my line up was clean. I sprayed my cologne before looking at myself in the mirror once more, making sure everything was perfect. Although my finger wasn't completely healed,

I'd been able to remove the huge bandage and replace it with a smaller band-aid.

My phone buzzed, and I knew it was Vic letting me know that he was outside. Walking over to my closet, I took the five thousand I was going to play tonight out of one of the shoe boxes I kept it in. I grabbed my wallet and walked out the house. The black SUV idled at the curb, waiting for me to hop inside. The windows were tinted darker than legal, but I could still make out the silhouettes inside. I adjusted my blazer one last time, rolled my shoulders back, and climbed in.

Vic sat up front, laidback in the passenger seat like a don. His black suit jacket was open just enough to show a gunmetal chain sitting thick against his chest. Tasha drove, her long braids pulled into a tight ponytail, lashes thick enough to cast shadows across her cheeks. Simone sat in the back corner seat, arms crossed, black lipstick flawlessly painted on her lips. She eyed me like she was still deciding whether I was built for this life.

"You look decent tonight," Simone said without looking directly at me.

"Appreciate it," I replied, keeping my tone neutral.

Vic turned halfway in his seat, sunglasses on even though the sun had long dipped behind the skyline. "You ready?"

I nodded. "You already know I am. Let's get this money."

He grinned, but it didn't touch his eyes. "Good."

Tasha pulled off, and we cut through Detroit's back streets and merged onto the highway, heading south toward Columbus. The drive was just over three hours, long enough for nerves to creep in if I let them. But I didn't. I kept my mind sharp and eyes focused on the prize. Tasha played a curated playlist of trap music with a heavy bass. Nobody talked much. Vic scrolled through his phone, occasionally making a call in that low voice of his, talking about numbers and percentages. Simone dozed off for a bit, her head leaned against the window.

I rehearsed the system in my head like I hadn't done it a dozen times already. Card counting wasn't magic like most people thought. It was math and memory. If you could count fast and remember numbers, then you could count cards. The foundation was the hi-lo count. Every card that left the shoe either helped me or hurt me.

By the time we pulled into the casino parking garage, everyone was ready for the night. Vic turned in his seat before speaking.

"Aight, this is it. Kyrie, you're takin' the anchor seat at the blackjack table. Simone's on your left, Tasha's floatin'. Don't look for us. Don't speak unless it's in the script. Let the dealer push the rhythm and you ride it."

I nodded once, my palms dry but breath steady. I was born for this shit, and I knew it. The thrill of taking something that once fucked up my life and using it to better my life, this right here was the real flex.

The moment we stepped onto the casino floor, it was like entering a different world – bright lights, the metallic clatter of slots, and the many voices of people both winning and losing money. Most of them didn't even know the game they were playing was rigged from the jump.

I moved through the crowd with my head held high. I sat at table seven, just close enough to the dealer's eye line to seem interested but not enough to be memorable. Simone took the seat beside me, ordering a vodka and cranberry, laughing too loudly at nothing at all. Tasha circled like a hawk in heels, occasionally brushing by the table to drop a cough, a laugh, or a tap on her lip, all pre-set signals, letting us know what to do next.

I didn't start playing right away. That was the first mistake most amateurs made. I watched, observing the dealer's style, speed, and shuffle. I watched for imperfections in the deck and consistency in how often they changed cards. It was a male dealer, maybe mid-forties, Asian, with sharp eyes but an unfocused posture. I waited until the shift break ended. That was when fresh shoes got loaded. I knew from Vic's recon that they changed decks every ninety minutes.

When I finally bought in, I did it with a crisp five thousand, handed in hundreds. It was nothing that screamed suspicion but enough to mark me as a serious player. I let the dealer think he had a shark at his table.

Card counting seemed to come easy to me. Every card that left the shoe adjusted the count in my head. Low cards, two through six, gave the house the upper hand. High cards, ten through Ace, favored me. I tracked them like it was my own heartbeat. Plus one, zero, minus one, plus two, plus three, then back to zero. Bet small, bet small again, then the count jumped to plus four. That was when you doubled the bet. Maybe even tripled it.

Simone gave a soft laugh, brushing my arm. That was the signal. Plus six count. It was time. I upped the bet from two hundred to eight hundred. The pit boss was still across the room. Dealer didn't blink as he flipped my cards. An ace and a ten.

"Blackjack," the dealer called out.

I smiled faintly, taking the chips without a word. On the next hand, the count stayed positive. This time, I bet twelve hundred. Tasha walked by behind me, dragging a finger across her chest, a reminder to back off if the boss started circling. I backed off the next hand, let the count drop, then surged again once it hit plus five. Over the next forty minutes, my stack grew. I was up seventeen thousand before the dealer changed again. I knew this was going to be a great night.

The adrenaline was still riding high when we stepped out of the casino. Vic clapped me on the back like he was proud of me. His gold rings flashed under the lot lights as we made our way back to the SUV.

"You a fuckin' problem, Kyrie," he spoke, grin wide as hell. "That little brain of yours was made for this shit."

Tasha and Simone were laughing, both of them holding onto Vic's arms like they'd just come from a damn movie premiere.

Simone popped the SUV trunk and tossed a backpack inside then turned to me. "When you first came around, I ain't think you was gon' be good at this shit. But I stand corrected."

"I just watch everything," I said simply, slipping into the backseat and feeling that high I got every time I left a casino richer than I walked in.

Vic slid into the passenger seat and turned to look at all of us. "Y'all good? 'Cause I'm thinkin' we don't stop here. There's a place about forty-five minutes south. Smaller but the pit bosses are green. We can eat down there. What y'all think?"

I nodded without hesitation. "Let's get it."

He smiled as we all agreed. The drive to the next casino was quiet, felt heavier. Nobody was talking much anymore, and that was probably because we were all focused. Simone drove this time, listening to old school R&B, as she kept her eyes on the road. Tasha leaned her head against the window and pulled out a vape pen. She took several puffs before closing her eyes for the rest of the ride.

Vic stayed on his phone for most of the ride, texting back-and-forth with someone. I just sat there, letting the first win settle into my bones, while my mind shifted gears. This wasn't about luck. This was about intention and control. About winning at life when I'd been losing for years.

When we pulled up, the second casino wasn't nearly as flashy as the first. It was a lot smaller, and the air smelled like cigarettes. However, all we needed was tables and real chips, and they had those. We entered in pairs – me and Simone first then Vic and Tasha two minutes behind us.

The goal was the same – slide in, don't look too sharp, blend in with everyone else. I went into the pit with more confidence. I chose a table with a tired-looking dealer and a full circle of small-time players. A guy in a denim vest. A woman with a thick Southern drawl and a Mountain Dew beside her chips. I bought in for just under five hundred, didn't want to look flashy. Simone sat behind me, legs crossed, playing bored but ready. I started slow again, letting the shoe cycle through a few hands, while I counted in my head.

We were about halfway through the shoe when I saw the pattern forming. I leaned forward and raised my bet to a hundred and fifty dollars. Then three hundred next. By the next hand, I had a blackjack, and the lady next to me sucked her teeth.

"Damn," she muttered. "I been trying to get blackjack for hours."

That was when the heat started creeping. I could feel one of the floor staff watching, but I kept my eyes lazy, mouth shut, and body language cool. I didn't draw attention to myself, just kept playing.

Vic slid past the edge of the table, sipping from a glass like he'd just wandered in from the bar. "Y'all good?" he asked casually.

"Winning," I replied, voice dry.

"You don't say."

Another hand and the count was climbing. I knew the aces were hot, knew the tens were buried in the middle. I dropped five hundred and then split the tens when the dealer laid them on the table. People around the table gasped like I didn't know what I was doing. Dealer raised a brow, but I kept my face straight. I kept my face cold. And just like that, blackjack twice.

The dealer coughed like he'd swallowed bad air. "Damn."

Vic walked past again, whispering near my shoulder. "You up enough?"

I nodded. "Let me run three more hands," I whispered back.

Vic nodded and walked off. I played my three more hands and won all three. When the floor manager started walking over, I stood and stretched like I was just getting tired.

"Y'all, good luck," I spoke to the table, and they laughed like I was just some dumb kid who got lucky. They had no idea I'd just walked out with several grand in profit and a pit boss on my heels.

We all made our way back to the SUV and headed back to Detroit. We went back to the spot where Tasha and Simone's cars were already waiting. We split our money four ways. Each one of us were going home with a little over thirty thousand. By the time Vic took me home, I was more than tired. I peeled out of my clothes the moment I stepped into my room. I didn't even bother with a shower. My bed was calling me, and as soon as I laid down, I went to sleep.

I woke up hours later with a tightness in my chest that wouldn't let me breathe right. At first, I thought it was just exhaustion from the night before – two casinos, over fourteen hours, and a bag filled with money in my closet. I lay still for a second, listening to the silence of the house. That was when I knew exactly what it was. It was Braylen. I missed her, needed her. Now.

The weight of her absence hit me like a ton of bricks all at once. She'd been gone for months, but today, it felt like she'd just left. I rolled over, dragging my hand across the side of the bed she used to lay in. I was hoping that maybe, somehow, I'd catch a trace of her warmth. But it was empty, just like it had been. It had been too long since I saw her, since I felt her, or even heard her voice. I missed her deep in my bones. It was like a part of me was gone, and I didn't know if it was ever coming back. It had been far too long since I saw her, held her, smelled the scent of her perfume. I missed her in a way that was bone-deep, like missing a piece of myself I wasn't sure I'd ever get back.

I sat up, rubbing the heel of my palm over my eyes. My body ached from the hustle, but my mind was sharp with thoughts of her. It was not just how she looked but how she felt. How she used to sit cross-legged on the couch, eating cereal and watching TV. Or the high-pitched laugh she had when something was truly funny. I hadn't heard that laugh in months. I missed her so much and knew that I needed to see her.

I got up and headed to the bathroom, dragging my feet like I was mourning something. In a way, I guess I was. I was mourning the loss of a good wife that I'd taken for granted. I turned the water on hot and stepped into the shower, letting the water hit me hard. As I stood there, I let my head fall forward under the pressure of the water. I thought about that last day she was here – the way she walked out of the house without looking back. She deserved better, and I knew that now. I should've never let things get as far as they did. I should've protected her. And now, I knew that it was the old me that she needed protection from.

I stayed in the shower longer than I should have, like I was trying to rinse off all my regret. But the thing about guilt was it didn't wash off. When I got out, I dried off slow, standing at the sink for a long time, just staring at myself in the mirror. The man looking back was different, better. However, I still had the same love for her. I was still the man who'd do anything to get her back. And that wouldn't change – not til I had her.

I walked into the bedroom and opened the closet, pulling on a fresh black tee and jeans. There was no need to dress up for what I had planned today. I wasn't hitting any casinos. I was staying right here in the city because the next move I made was gonna be for her. I sat down on the edge of the bed and picked up my phone. My thumb hovered over her name. I didn't press it though. There was no need since she'd already changed her number. Instead, I opened my notes app and started typing out a list of everything I still needed to do. The amount of money I still needed to stack and calls I still needed to make to my lawyer to see how long we could stall the divorce. I needed Braylen to see who I was now because I knew once she did, she would come back to me.

Once I was done, I sat there, just looking off into space. I wished like hell that I could talk to her. Tell her how much I needed her. Standing up, I walked down to the kitchen and grabbed the bottle of tequila from the counter. I took a shot, hoping it would take the edge off. When it didn't, I took another one.

"I need to fucking talk to you, Braylen. I need you to hear me, to see me." I spoke out loud as I downed my third shot.

Fuck it. If I couldn't talk to her over the phone, I would just have to go to Banks' house. I put on my shoes and grabbed my keys and wallet from the table and walked out the door. The fear that I once had for Banks was gone and replaced with determination. It was like something inside of me cracked open. She hadn't been here in weeks, but today, it was as if my soul was starving for her, like I couldn't go another hour without catching at least a glimpse of her. I didn't know if I was in love or had a death wish, but I got into my car anyway and headed to Banks' house.

I parked a few houses down and couldn't see anything past the long ass driveway. The house was so far back from the road that it made it impossible for me to see from where I was. I sat there for a good twenty minutes with the windows cracked. My knee was bouncing, fingers twitching like they had a mind of their own. The waiting was making it worse. Not knowing if she was in there or not. Not knowing if she was happy and smiling or sad because she missed me.

About five minutes later, a black Escalade eased out of the driveway, tinted windows so dark I couldn't see a thing. I knew it was Banks' SUV, the same SUV that he had put me in the day I did the unthinkable and traded my wife.

That was when something in me snapped. I didn't even think twice. I jumped out the car and sprinted across the grass. The moment my feet hit the gravel of his driveway, my heart started pounding like I was dodging bullets again. The driveway was long, but I moved fast, keeping low behind the trees and hedges where I could. I didn't know what I expected to see. Maybe I could catch her in the window or walking outside. Anything was better than not seeing her at all.

As I crept up the side of the house, my breath caught in my throat. The place was huge and modern with tall windows and the blinds drawn. My stomach twisted. Did he have her locked in there? Did she even go outside anymore? What the fuck was he in there doing to her? I moved around the side, past the garage, staying low in the bushes. I saw the backyard, wide open with a high privacy fence and some fancy-ass patio furniture. There was no sign of her yet.

I was just about to turn around when a curtain shifted upstairs. I froze, hoping that I wasn't spotted. My eyes locked on the window, praying that it was her. Then, I saw the shadow. It was her. I couldn't help but smile. She looked beautiful standing in front of the window, wearing a butter yellow dress. Just the sight of her was enough to light me up and break me down at the same time. I swallowed hard, wanting to call out to her, but I couldn't. My feet were planted in the dirt, but my soul was running toward her full speed. She was right there and yet so far away.

I knew then that I couldn't take it anymore. I couldn't live a life without her in it. I wouldn't. I was going to do whatever it took to get her back in my arms again. She was mine. We had taken vows in front of God to be together forever, and that was exactly what we were going to do. Fuck everything that happened. I was going to take my wife back, and nothing or no one was going to stop me.

I stood there for several more moments until Braylen was no long in the window. When she disappeared, so did I, making my way back to my car. I sat there for several more moments, thinking about how beautiful she was. She had this glow about her that I'd never seen, and I couldn't help but get jealous. She should be glowing because of me, not because she was with another man. I started my car and smiled, knowing my wife would soon be back with me.

Chapter Seven

BANKS

The morning sun peeked through the half open curtains. I rolled over in bed and watched as Braylen slept peacefully. Her skin looked soft in the morning light, the sun casting a golden glow across her face. I slid out of bed, careful not to wake her. Marcus was already in the kitchen when I got downstairs.

"Morning," he greeted without looking up, already dicing shallots like his hands were on autopilot. "What are the two of you in the mood for this morning?"

"Morning. Make something light. Scrambled eggs, smoked salmon, and toast. Oh, and some fresh fruit."

"No problem."

I nodded once and turned toward the patio windows. I watched the breeze roll across the grass as I thought about what I was going to do today. I knew I was going to have a long day, and I was ready for it. Braylen came down about twenty minutes later. She had on a black, two-piece, Victoria's Secret pajama set with her hair pulled into a messy bun. She smiled as she joined me at the table.

"You let me sleep too long," she said, voice still soft with sleep.

"You and the baby needed y'all rest." I motioned to the seat across from me. "Come eat."

She sat, pulling her legs up into the chair, looking at the plate in front of her. She reached for a strawberry and popped it into her mouth. We ate in a comfortable silence for a while, trading slow glances. When I was done eating, I pushed my plate back and leaned forward.

"I've got a few errands to run," I told her. "I'll be gone for at least a few hours. You gone be good?"

Braylen nodded, tapping the sides of her mouth with her napkin. "Yeah, I'm good."

"Cool. I'll try not to be gone too long."

She rolled her eyes. "I'm a big girl, A'zir. You do know that, right?"

My jaw relaxed when she used my real name. I nodded my head and stood to my feet, walking up the stairs to get dressed. I walked into my closet and looked at the many rows of crisp lines, black suits, imported fabrics, and hand-stitched Italian leather. There were several shelves that each housed dozens of bottles of cologne. For the errands I had to run, I didn't need a full suit, but I never stepped out sloppy.

I chose a pair of black slacks with a slight taper at the ankle and a fitted short-sleeved charcoal gray button-up. I sprayed on Maison Francis' Grand Soir all over me. It was expensive as hell but worth every penny. I placed a vintage Rolex around my wrist and a gold Cuban link chain around my neck. My locs were freshly re-twisted yesterday, pulled back into a half-knot at the crown with the rest falling clean down my back.

When I came back downstairs, Braylen was still at the table, sipping from a glass of apple juice.

"You sure you'll be good?" I asked again.

She glanced at me, licking jam off her thumb, and smirked. "Go handle your business, A'zir. I'll be here waiting for you when you get back."

I walked up behind her, bent down, and kissed her shoulder, inhaling her scent. I rubbed her stomach softly and whispered to her, letting her know I'd be home in a few hours. I pulled my phone from my pocket and placed a call to Zeek, telling him to pull the SUV around. I had a few stops in mind, the first being a private art supply boutique in Midtown. I had plans on making Braylen's day, and she didn't even know it.

She'd told me that she wanted to start painting again, and that was all I needed to hear. Art lived in her, and I knew it. As much as she tried to put it off like it was just a hobby, I knew it was her passion. I wanted Braylen to have everything her heart desired. So, if panting was what she wanted to do, I was going to make sure she had everything she needed to do it.

We arrived at Pigment & Press about twenty minutes later, a discreet storefront behind a frosted glass gallery. There was no logo on the front of the small brick building, just a small 'open' sign that rested in the window. I walked through the door, and the smell of fresh paint hit my nose immediately.

The owner, a short French woman named Claudine, greeted me with a polite nod the moment I walked inside.

"Good morning, welcome to Pigment & Press. Please let me know if you need help with anything."

"I'm building something," I told her. "A basement studio and I need it to be top quality. It's for someone very important."

Claudine smiled and gestured for me to follow her. She walked me through the store, showing me everything I would need to create the space I wanted for Braylen. I took my time as I walked around the store, taking everything in. I planned on spending a lot of money in this store, so I walked back to the front and grabbed a shopping cart.

The first thing I placed inside the cart was an easel. It was hand-crafted in solid beechwood that had been imported from Italy. It was adjustable and sturdy enough to hold extra-large canvases. The wood was polished and soft to the touch. Next, I walked over to the canvases. I wanted Braylen to be able to paint as much as she wanted to. So, extra canvases were a must. I picked up three dozen canvases, all in various sizes. I hoped I'd gotten enough, but I knew we could always buy more.

I slowly walked through the store, looking around, until I got to the paint. I knew I couldn't half step on the paint. It was the main thing she needed. I brought her the entire Winsor & Newton Artists' oil color line. The pigments were so rich in color that I knew they wouldn't fade over time. I also added a full acrylic paint set as well. I then grabbed several sets of brushes, some with natural and others with synthetic bris-tles, not knowing which she preferred. I made sure that all the brushes came with handcrafted handles. I knew that real artists cared about the brushes they used to paint with, so I wanted to make sure that Braylen had the best.

I grabbed two wooden palettes, one with an open-hand grip and one for table mixing. Claudine also included a glass palette with edge guards and a cleaning blade free of charge. I grabbed a nice set of palette knives, a charcoal and graphite set, and a high-weight sketchbook. I also grabbed a few watercolor pads and canvas paper. I knew she'd need storage drawers and lighting, and this was a one stop shop because it had all of that and more. I picked out a matte black modular drawer along with a matching rolling cart and custom daylight-balanced LED studio lighting with adjustable warmth. I wanted her eyes to see every color exactly as it was meant to be seen.

Next, I grabbed Braylen several linen aprons and gloves along with anything else I thought she might need or like from the store. By the time Claudine finished tallying the order, the total had climbed high. I didn't so much as blink as I pulled out my credit card.

Claudine gave me a small smile. "Whoever this is must be very special."

"She is." I smiled.

After I paid for all the items, I rolled the two full baskets out to the SUV where Zeek was waiting. He helped me pile everything into the trunk, and then we got inside. We sat there for a moment, while Zeek waited for me to tell him our next stop. To me, it wasn't enough to give Braylen just some paint and canvases. I wanted her to have a sanctuary, a place where her spirit could stretch without fear or pressure, a space that felt like it belonged to her and no one else. It had to be beautiful and a place she would be proud to be in.

"Head over to Maison Élan," I spoke, still looking out the window. "The one in West Bloomfield. Call ahead. Tell them I need the show-room cleared. I'll be there in twenty."

Maison Élan wasn't just a furniture store. It was an entire experience. Everything inside was custom-designed, one-of-one, and imported from different places. Once you bought something from that store, you knew no one else would ever have it. Those were the exact vibes that I wanted Braylen to have inside her art room. When I walked in, the manager, Vera, met me at the door.

"Mr. McFarland, it's nice to see you again. We've prepared a private walkthrough per your request. We are ready whenever you are."

"I need everything delivered to my home within the next two hours," I spoke, letting her know there was no room for negotiation.

She hesitated as if she was thinking about it. I just stared at her, ready to walk out the door if she said she couldn't make it happen. She nodded, letting me know that it could be done, before motioning for me to follow her. We walked the floor together, and I pointed out the things to her that I wanted to purchase.

I chose a deep sage green, oversized, velvet armchair with gold legs, something she could curl up in and draw in her sketchpad, and two worktables, one oak and the other one glass. I also picked out several matte black floating shelves with hidden hardware. I added a scented diffuser along with different oils of all different scents, an area rug, and a mini refrigerator that I was going to fill with bottled water and all her favorite juices. I added a few personal touches such as a gold, full-length mirror and gold handcrafted sculptures of women's hands holding a brush. I knew that once everything was put together, the space would be beautiful, and I hoped she would love it.

"Pack it up," I told Vera. "I'll pay whatever you need. But it all needs to be at my house within two hours. Delivered, carried in, and set up according to the floor plan I'll send."

"Yes, Mr. McFarland, everything will be delivered and set up in the time frame that you requested."

I handed her my credit card, paying for the items, before walking out of the store. I got into the car, eager to see the smile I knew I was about to put on Braylen's face. She had no idea what I would be building right beneath her feet. By the time we made it back to my house, it was a little after four. I was glad that Braylen was nowhere in sight when I walked in. Zeek and I quickly took the items inside. The moment we were done bringing in the last item, the delivery truck pulled up.

Two hours later, the studio was done, and everything was in place. I placed the diffuser on one of the floating shelves, turning it on before placing Lost Cherry oil inside. I stood there a second longer, looking at the space I'd created for her. It was beautiful, if I did say so myself. I didn't want to rush the reveal, so instead of going to find Braylen right then, I walked up to my bedroom and peeled off my sweat soaked shirt. I threw my dirty clothes into the hamper before heading straight for the shower. I let the hot water run until steam kissed the mirrors and my muscles stopped twitching from lifting and moving.

When I stepped out, I tied the towel low on my waist, wiped my face, and walked into my bedroom. I pulled out a simple white tee and a pair of gray sweatpants before putting them on. Once I was dressed and had sprayed myself with cologne, I walked through the house in search of Braylen. Finally, after about ten minutes of looking around, I finally found her. She was curled up in a lounge chair by the far side of the indoor pool, legs folded under her, with a book open in her lap. Her curls were half up, soft tendrils falling around her face. She wore a light-yellow dress, that looked comfortable on her skin, with no makeup and bare feet. She looked so peaceful.

I didn't say anything at first, just stood there and watched her for a moment. The way her brow furrowed when she read something intense. The way her lips moved like she was mouthing the words silently. I stepped forward, letting the sound of my feet echo just enough so I wouldn't startle her.

She glanced up and smiled when she saw me. "Hey."

"You having fun reading your book?" I asked.

She nodded. "Yeah. This one is pretty good. I'm glad I decided to read today."

I walked over, leaned down, and kissed her forehead before leaning down even more and kissing her stomach. "You hungry?"

"Starving," she said. "Can the chef make that lemon butter salmon again? With the asparagus and wild rice? And maybe those little rolls he does with the garlic butter and sea salt?"

"Say less." I walked to the intercom panel mounted beside the pool entrance and pressed the button.

I called out to him, and he replied swiftly. I ordered the meal that Braylen had requested, and he told me he would have two plates ready in thirty minutes. I clicked off and turned back to her.

"Anything else you want?"

She stretched and smiled. "Umm, maybe something sweet."

I raised an eyebrow. "You want chocolate or something else?"

She tilted her head, smirking. "Surprise me."

I nodded my head and smiled, already planning what would come after dinner. And if she liked what I had waiting downstairs, tonight would be more than just dessert. While the chef worked his magic upstairs, I was ready to show Braylen her surprise. I couldn't wait any longer. I'd spent all day building that room, handpicking everything down to the rug on the floor, and I was ready to show her what I'd done for her.

"Come with me," I ordered, nodding toward the hallway.

Braylen looked up from the pool chair, her eyes curious. "Where we going?"

"You'll see."

She didn't ask any other questions, just slid on her slippers and followed behind me. I led her past the kitchen, down the hallway, and to the door that opened to the basement stairs. I unlocked it and pushed the door open slowly, turning on the dimmed LED lights as we descended.

"Is this a surprise?" she asked softly, fingers trailing the railing as we walked down.

I didn't answer, just continued to walk her down the steps. When we finally made it down the stairs, I walked her to one of the closed doors and stood in front of it. Slowly, I placed my hand on the doorknob and turned it, opening the door, so she could see what was inside. She froze, and just like that, I saw her heart bloom through her eyes. The room wasn't loud or flashy but warm and inviting. A space made just for her.

The walls, which had already been painted a soft cream, had one sage green accent wall that was added. It was the same shade of the velvet chair I'd bought, which was nestled in the corner of the room. The light wood floor had been polished until it glowed with a woven ivory and sage rug that had been placed across the floor. The glass art table rested against one wall with her brushes already lined up in ceramic cups. Canvases of all sizes were stacked neatly beside it. Across from that sat the oak art table which housed her palette knives, water jars, and the sketchpad I'd purchased for her.

To the left, a set of floating matte black shelves displayed jars of paint arranged by color. There were so many that I didn't even know all of those colors existed. The stocked mini fridge sat in the far corner of the room, and the full-length mirror hung on the wall next to the chair.

Braylen finally stepped forward into the room, her hands covering her mouth.

"Oh, my God."

She walked to one of the tables, fingertips trailing the glass, then to the floating shelves. Her hand touched the soft bristles of one of the brushes. The back of her fingers grazed the edge of the velvet chair. She turned slowly to face me, her chest rising with emotion.

"A'zir," she spoke, voice barely above a whisper, "you did all this for me?"

I nodded once, watching her take it all in. "All of this is yours, baby. Every inch of it. However you want to use it. However you want to paint. This is your space."

Braylen stepped toward me slowly, her eyes full of tears. She wrapped her arms around me and held me tightly.

"Do you have any idea what this means to me?"

"I do. That's why I did it."

Her hands found my chest, and she looked up at me like she was seeing me all over again. "No one has ever done anything like this for me. Not even close."

I leaned down, pressing my forehead to hers. "I want you to get back to the woman you want to be. So, whatever I can do to help with that, I'm going to do it."

She kissed me hard, her body soft and trembling against mine. I felt her gratitude in the way she gripped my shirt. Felt her awe in the way she lingered, like the moment had taken hold of her and wouldn't let go. Once she had went over everything in the room, we walked up the stairs hand in hand and went into the kitchen for dinner.

Braylen sat across from me, still glowing from the surprise but quieter now. I could tell she was still taking everything in. She dipped a roll in the lemon butter sauce then looked up at me with that calm, curious stare.

"A'zir," she said softly, "can I ask you something?"

I leaned back and wiped my mouth with a cloth napkin. "Always. Ask me anything you want."

She hesitated then set her fork down before looking up at me. "What were you like as a kid? I mean, what was your childhood like? Your parents?"

That was a question I wasn't expecting. Most women didn't ask. Maybe it was because they didn't care. They were either scared of what made me or too obsessed with what I'd become. But Braylen wasn't most women. I took a sip of water before answering.

"My parents ain't together," I said plainly. "Ain't been for a long time. But they always kept a solid relationship for me."

She watched me closely, nodding. "You close with them?"

"I am. In our own way. My pops is real disciplined and about his money. Taught me structure, how to move with purpose. Moms is softer but strong as hell."

Braylen smiled gently, brushing a loose curl behind her ear. "Do you think they'd want to meet me?"

I paused and looked at her in the eyes. I had never introduced a woman to my parents before. This was going to be something different for me. It let me know that Braylen wasn't trying to play house. She wanted to meet my parents, which meant she was planning to be here for the long haul.

"You wanna meet them?" I asked.

She nodded. "Yeah. I do."

I leaned forward, my fingers brushing the top of her hand where it rested on the table. "Alright then. I'll set it up. We'll do something small like go out to dinner or something."

"You think they'll like me?" she asked with a soft smile.

"They'll love you," I uttered without blinking. "Just like I do."

That made her go still for a second. Her eyes were on me, lips parted like the words melted somewhere in her chest. Her eyes stayed locked on mine for several seconds like she was trying to detect a lie. Finally, she spoke.

"I love you too, A'zir."

We were still sitting at the kitchen table long after the food was gone. Her plate was pushed off to the side with only her fork and napkin left on it. Her legs were pulled up into the chair, and her arms were crossed on the table. She looked at me as if she was trying to read me, but I didn't feel judged, just seen. After several moments of her watching me, I spoke.

"You got something else you wanna say?"

Braylen blinked like I'd pulled the thought right out her head. Her voice came low. "What do you do for a living, A'zir? Really?" she said it softly, but the weight of it filled the room.

I leaned back in my chair and rubbed my jaw once. I'd known this was coming. Truth was, I'd been waiting for it. She had every right to know, and I wasn't going to lie about it.

"I traffic people. People call me when they want to pay top dollar for someone specific. Most people think I sell drugs, but that's never been my style. I like the dark side, so that's what I do. I built an entire empire from it. For some people, I might very well be a monster, but to me, I'm just a man that does what he has to do to get the things I want in life."

She didn't move. She didn't even flinch or gasp. She just looked at me.

"Does that scare you?" I asked.

Braylen paused then shook her head slowly. "No. Not in the way you think."

I leaned forward, elbows on the table. "How then?"

"I already knew you weren't just some regular businessman. I could feel it in the way you move. The way people listen when you speak. You're calm but dangerous. That didn't scare me though. The part that scares me is how easy it is to feel safe with you anyway."

That hit something in my chest.

She looked down then back up. "What made you get into it? Like how does that even start?"

"All my life, I been good at reading people. Not just reading but studying. I was seventeen when I realized most people weren't loyal to who fed them. They were loyal to who made them feel useful. That was my in. I started small, running people across borders for someone else. Then, I figured out I could do it better. I knew where to find the desperate, how to spot someone willing to disappear. Girls who wanted out. Men who owed debts they couldn't pay. I found ways to give them purpose or profit off the ones who didn't care anymore." I paused, looking her dead in the eyes. "It wasn't about greed. It was about control. About being the user and not the one who got used."

I stopped for a moment, allowing her to take it all in. She didn't blink, didn't say a word, just looked me in my eyes. So, I continued to speak.

"I built a network with my three best friends that we run like a company. We have employees and all. Everything we do is quiet and only accessed on the dark web. You never saw my name in the news and you never will. What I do is so discreet that the people that buy from me don't even know who I am. Although my morals are on the fence, I do have rules. No kids – ever. Other than that, nobody else is off limits."

I looked down for a second. When I looked back up, she was still watching me.

"You think I'm a monster yet?" I asked.

Braylen leaned forward, her voice calm, steady. "No."

"Why not?"

"Because monsters lie. You didn't. I could never judge you, A'zir. You're ready to take care of a baby that you know is not yours. A monster wouldn't do that. I'm actually glad you told me."

"I owed you that. If we building a life together, then you deserve to know everything."

Braylen didn't say a word, just stood to her feet and walked around the table and over to me. She sat on my lap, wrapping her arms around me, as she kissed my forehead. That one simple kiss was the most intimate kiss I'd ever experienced.

Chapter Eight

BRAYLEN

I couldn't stop smiling. Every time I blinked, I saw it again – my studio. The way the soft sage chair cradled me was like it had been made only for me. The way the paint was organized by hue, it was like he knew I needed order even in chaos. The way the shelves weren't just functional but beautiful, it was all so thoughtful, and I wanted him to know that I appreciated it all. A'zir didn't just give me a space. He gave me proof. Proof that he watched me. That he heard me even in silence. He'd taken the parts of me that others tried to destroy and started putting them back together again, even when I couldn't do it for myself. That did something to my soul.

This man had come in and changed my life completely. There was nothing about him that I didn't love. I didn't care what he did for a living. I cared about the man inside. The man with a heart so big he would take me out of survival mode and bring out the soft woman that I never knew I could be. The man who wanted to build me up into the best version of myself. The man who would take on the responsibility of a child he knew wasn't his when he had none of his own. That was the man I saw. And no matter what else he did, that was the man I would always see him as.

I was all smiles when we left the kitchen and headed upstairs. He walked a few steps ahead of me, slow and calm like always, one hand dragging lazily along the railing. His locs fell around his shoulders. He smelled like amber, leather, and something sweet underneath it. I smiled as I inhaled his scent. I watched the way his back flexed through the fitted tee he'd thrown on. The way his sweats hung just low enough to make my stomach tighten. The way he walked – controlled, quiet, like a man who didn't need to say much to be heard. And he didn't. I heard him loud and clear before he even opened his mouth to speak.

I followed him past one of the guest rooms and into the master suite. He didn't notice the way I closed the door behind us or the slow way I locked it. He sat down on the edge of the bed and pulled off his watch, glancing at me briefly before tossing it onto the nightstand.

"You tired?" he asked.

"No," I said softly, walking toward him. "You?"

He looked up at me, one brow lifted. "Nah."

I stepped between his knees, placing my hands on his shoulders. "Then good," I whispered, running my fingers down his chest, "because I got plans."

He leaned back slightly, eyes dark with amusement. "And what kind of plans are we talkin'?"

"The kind where I show you how much I appreciate what you did for me today."

I slid my fingers up the back of his neck, curling them into his locs, gently tugging until he was looking up at me. His eyes didn't waver.

"You really surprised me, A'zir. No one's ever did anything like that for me before."

I bent down and kissed the side of his neck slowly, trailing my lips from the line of his jaw to his collarbone. My lips pressed against the hollow of his throat, and he exhaled. I continued kissing his neck gently, as he wrapped his hands around my waist. I ran my hands down his chest and settled on his crotch. I could feel his hardness through his pants.

"You don't gotta do nothin' for me," he murmured.

I pulled back just enough to look into his eyes. "I know. That's why I want to."

His jaw flexed. I took a step back and slowly lifted my cotton dress over my head, letting it fall to the floor behind me. I wasn't wearing any underwear underneath. His gaze dropped slow as if he was memorizing everything he already owned. I pulled him to his feet, and I watched as he slowly took off his shirt. His pants soon followed. He pulled me close to him, kissing me passionately.

I led him back to the bed, fully prepared to take my time with him. I wanted to kiss every inch of his skin, trace my name into the heat of his body with my mouth, show him just how good I could make him feel. He sat down on the edge of the bed first, letting me stand between his knees again. I watched the way his eyes roamed over me like he couldn't decide what to touch first. He grabbed my hips and placed soft kisses right at my bikini line.

I placed my hand under his chin, lifting it, as I bent down to meet his lips. My tongue slid along his bottom lip, and he gripped the back of my thigh like he couldn't hold back much longer. His kiss deepened, as his mouth moved over mine. I felt it in my toes, that heat curling through me, slow and deliberate. I thought I was in control. I thought I was going to take my time, straddle him until he moaned my name. However, he had other plans.

Without warning, A'zir stood and gripped the back of my thighs, lifting me effortlessly and laying me down on the bed like I weighed nothing. His eyes flickered over my body, as I sprawled back on the cool sheets, my breath quickening, as he slid his hands down my legs and pushed them apart slowly.

"A'zir," I whispered, already aching. "Let me..."

"No," he growled softly, positioning himself between my legs. "Let me."

His hands gripped my thighs, as he lowered his mouth between them, spreading me open like a gift he'd been waiting to unwrap. The first flick of his tongue made my back arch off the bed. He licked me slow, like he'd been waiting on this all night. He didn't rush to make me cum. I could tell he wanted the pleasure to build. His tongue circled my love button, causing my breath to hitch.

I moaned before I could stop myself. One hand was gripping the sheets, the other tangled in his locs as his mouth worked in slow, deliberate motions. His tongue moved in tight circles then long strokes up, down, then back again. When his lips sealed around me and he sucked just a little, his name rolled off my tongue. He added more pressure when I whimpered. His fingers gripped my hips tighter, holding me in place when I started to squirm.

"A'zir..."

His name spilled out of me in a shaky gasp. Waves crashed through me hard, pulsing in time with every moan I couldn't hold back. He didn't stop until I was panting, writhing, whispering curses under my breath, and still trying to pull him closer. When he finally pulled back, he kissed the inside of my thigh, slow and soft, like he hadn't just made my soul leave my body. I looked down at him, still breathless, my skin flushed and my heart racing.

He climbed up over me, eyes dark and steady. He kissed me, his eyes never leaving mine. I slid my hands up his chest and pushed gently until he lay back on the bed. His brows lifted a little, but he didn't stop me, just smirked like he was curious to see what I'd do next. I swung one leg over him and straddled his chest slowly, teasing him with the roll of my hips. His hands gripped my thighs like he already knew where I was headed.

Without breaking eye contact, I rose up on my knees and shifted forward, lowering myself onto his face. His hands slid down to the curve of my hips and held me there. The first stroke of his tongue made me hiss, the position making everything sharper, deeper. I gripped the headboard, my body rocking against his mouth. A'zir held me still as he licked me with intention over and over again. Every flick of his tongue made my thighs tremble. Every slow circle pulled me closer to the edge.

I gasped his name again, but this time, I didn't stop moving. I grinded down on him, my hips moving in slow circles. I turned, twisting my body around, lowering myself and coming eye to eye with his manhood. He was already hard, thick, and waiting, his breath uneven, as I slid my hand around him. I licked my lips then lowered my mouth to him, slow and warm, taking him in inch by inch, as he continued licking me beneath the weight of my body.

We moved together, his tongue matching the way my lips moved over him. The deeper I took him, the better he licked and the wetter I got. I was so close I could feel it building in my body. His mouth was relentless, his tongue working in a steady rhythm. A'zir gripped my hips and lifted me gently, setting me beside him on the bed like I weighed nothing. My breath caught, lips parted in protest as he sat up, his chest rising hard beneath a thin sheen of sweat.

"Why'd you stop?" I breathed.

He leaned down, kissed the inside of my knee, then stood. "Because we not done," he said, voice low, controlled. Then, he walked over to his closet.

I sat up, still catching my breath, watching as he bent down and pulled out a familiar black leather bag. He turned and held it up slightly, eyes locked on mine.

"You sure you want all of me tonight?" he asked. "You're pregnant. I'll go easier if you want me to."

I smirked, heat pooling low in my belly all over again. "Don't," I said softly. "Don't hold back."

He nodded once, showing me that he wasn't going to hold back. He unzipped the bag slowly, never taking his eyes off me. I shifted on the bed, watching his hands, as he removed a bottle of lube and placed it on the nightstand. When A'zir reached into the bag and pulled out the sleek, black vibrator, my breath caught.

"Turn around," he ordered.

I obeyed, turning around and placing my back to him. My knees sank into the mattress, as I placed my palms flat in front of me. I felt the shift in the air behind me before I felt his touch. His hands slid over the back of my thighs, spreading me just a little wider. Then, I felt his tongue. He licked me slow at first, the sensation making my breath hitch and my eyes flutter shut.

Every stroke of his tongue sent tremors through my body, the position making it more intense. His hands gripped my hips like he needed them to stay grounded while he lost himself in me. I whimpered his name, my fingers digging into the sheets. He groaned against me, the vibration of it making my hips roll back into his mouth. He licked deeper, using his tongue to explore every fold. Each stroke of his tongue hit differently. His lips sealed around my love button, while his tongue flicked in a rhythm that made me shiver.

Then, I felt the cool press of the vibrator against my inner thigh, making me hiss. He moved it around my clit, as his tongue stayed buried inside my wetness. Then, he stopped, and I felt him line himself up. His hand gripped my waist, the other still holding the vibrator, as he pressed it between my ass cheeks. He entered me slowly, his manhood filling me to capacity. I gasped, arching forward instinctively, every inch hitting exactly where I needed it.

"A'zir," I whispered, my voice already unraveling.

"You feel that shit, baby?" he growled behind me, his strokes slow and heavy. "You feel how deep I'm in you right now?"

I nodded, mouth open, unable to speak, as pleasure flooded through me in waves. He moved his hips with precision, rolling into me like he was molding us together. He rocked into me again, deeper this time, the toy still gliding between my cheeks, adding just enough sensation to make my body go tight. I whimpered, my fingers clutching the sheets tighter.

I was already trembling under him, his body moving into mine with a rhythm that was all power and precision, like he knew exactly how to pull me apart. Each slow, deep thrust stole my breath and left me grasping for something to hold onto. Then, I felt the vibrator move again. This time, I felt the coldness of the lube, as it ran down my crack. He pressed the tip of the vibrator to my asshole before easing it in.

"A'zir," I whispered.

He leaned forward, his chest pressing into my back, lips brushing my ear. "Relax," he spoke low. "Trust me."

The toy slid inside, as he matched his stroke with the rhythm. His hand was steady as he held onto my hip. The double pressure made my entire body lock, my breath catch, and my toes curl hard against the bed. He growled softly behind me, like the way my body clenched around him drove him somewhere darker. I'd never felt like this before, and I begged him not to stop.

"Fuck, A'zir, please don't stop!"

My words broke into a moan, as a new wave of heat spiraled through me, my body shivering uncontrollably, caught in a rhythm that blurred pain and pleasure in the most wicked and addicting way.

"You're takin' it like you were made for this," he murmured against my skin, his voice low and dark.

And maybe I was. Every thrust, every press of that toy, every breath that passed between us felt like a ritual. Like he was teaching me something I didn't know I could feel. I couldn't stop the sounds falling from my mouth. Couldn't stop the way I bucked back into him, and I didn't want to. My body wasn't mine anymore. It was his. Every inch, every nerve ending, every desperate moan that spilled out of me belonged to A'zir now.

"Yeah, this pussy mine. You feel how you wrapped around this dick? This pussy was made for me."

I nodded helplessly, mouth open, breath caught in my throat. My stomach clenched, my thighs trembling, as I tried to breathe through it, but it was too much. He didn't stop. The deeper he moved, the more I came undone. My body locked up, the wave rising so high it felt like it might break me when it crashed.

"Don't run from it," he said, his voice right in my ear now. "Fall."

I shattered around him, crying out, as the orgasm ripped through me like lightning. My legs gave out, my fingers clawed at the sheets, and still he kept moving, drawing it out until I was writhing under him, completely lost in the pleasure he'd poured into me. He pulled the toy out slowly, but he wasn't finished.

A'zir gripped my hips harder and drove into me faster now, chasing his own release. I could barely hold myself up, my body still convulsing around him, oversensitive but I wanted him to have all of me. I pushed back against him, moaning through the overstimulation, and that was when he cursed low, his rhythm stuttering. He grunted my name, rough and raw. Slamming into me one final time as he came, his fingers dug into my skin like he couldn't bear to let go.

His body dropped over mine, chest heaving, sweat slicked against my back. We stayed like that for a long moment, both of us trembling, breathing each other in. Neither of us spoke because there was no need. What we'd just done said it all.

Chapter Nine

VITA

I was curled up in bed with the AC humming low and the TV light flickering across my bare legs. A half-eaten bowl of kettle corn lay beside me. My bonnet rested on my head and hadn't been removed all day. I was in relaxation mode and planned to be for the rest of the night. *Gone Girl* played on the screen. I'd seen it before, twice, but I loved the movie. I was mouthing the line, "I'm not a quitter. I'm that cunt you married," when my phone lit up with Victor's name. A little flutter ran through me at just seeing his name. I wiped popcorn salt off my fingers and answered.

"Hey," I spoke, sitting up straighter without meaning to.

"You busy?"

"Just watching a movie. Why, what's up?"

There was a pause on the other end then a low chuckle. "You feel like stepping out with me tonight? Taking a walk in my streets?"

My brows pulled together. "What does that mean?"

"It means you might see something different tonight. But only if you're ready."

My stomach flipped. "I'm always ready," I said, voice calmer than I actually felt.

"Cool. Get dressed. I'll be there in thirty."

Victor hung up before I could say another word. I stared at the phone for a second then back to the TV. Amy Dunne was mid-monologue, faking her murder like it was a craft project. Something told me that tonight, I'd find out exactly what kind of man I'd let into my life. I stood to my feet and walked over to my closet.

I grabbed a black, body-hugging, slip dress that stopped mid-thigh. The fabric had a soft sheen under the light, thin straps crossing low at the back – simple yet still seductive. Underneath, I planned on wearing a black lace thong and nothing else. I rushed into the bathroom and freshened up a bit before going back into my room and getting dressed.

My locs had been freshly retwisted just two days ago, so I styled them into a high ponytail, laying my baby hairs perfectly. My makeup was minimal – lashes, liner, blush, and gloss. For my scent, I layered Ariana Grande's Cloud and Sol de Janeiro's Brazilian Crush 40 body mist. I grabbed a tiny black clutch and slid into a pair of black strappy heels. I looked at myself once more in the mirror, loving what I saw.

Victor pulled up exactly thirty minutes later. He was driving himself this time in a black-on-black BMW M8. The windows were tinted so dark that no one would be able to see inside. I smiled as I slid into the passenger's seat. He wore a pair of black slacks, a black button-up shirt, and a gold chain that winked just above his collar. His cologne hit my nose the moment I got into the car, and I knew it was something expensive.

We didn't say much on the ride. His hand rested low on my thigh, thumb stroking small circles into my skin like it was second nature. I didn't mind the silence as I sat back and enjoyed the ride. We passed blocks of boarded-up buildings with graffiti painting the broken bricks. When Victor turned down an unmarked road, my eyebrow raised, but I still didn't say a word. We pulled up to what looked like an old, abandoned warehouse with rusted doors and cracked windows. A chain-link fence surrounded the lot. One faint light glowed above a steel side door like it was daring someone to come inside.

I looked at him, eyes narrowing. "What is this?"

Victor killed the engine and leaned back in his seat, completely unbothered. "Just waiting on a few members of my crew."

Crew? What the hell is this, and what type of crew is he waiting on? I thought. I looked back at the warehouse then at the empty lot. There were no cars or people anywhere around, and it didn't look like it had been in a while. No cars. No people.

"Your crew meets in abandoned buildings?" I asked.

He turned toward me, slow and calm, one brow raised. "Sometimes the safest places are the ones no one pays attention to."

I didn't respond nor did I ask any more questions. It wasn't because I didn't have any but because I wanted to see how this would play out myself. So, I leaned back in the leather seat and crossed my legs, keeping my voice even. "You know I look too good to be sitting in front of some old warehouse, right?"

That made him smirk. "You look good no matter where you go."

He leaned in and kissed my neck, slow and deep like he wasn't even thinking about where we were. Then, he pulled back just slightly and whispered, "Tonight's about showing you what my world looks like."

Goosebumps swept down my arms. Before I could say a word, headlights cut through the dark as a black Jeep turned into the lot. The car parked beside us, and when the door opened, a woman stepped out looking like she meant business. She wore a long, emerald green dress with gold jewelry around her neck, wrist, and on her ears. Her jet black braids were neatly placed in a low bun, and her makeup was flawless.

Victor got out the car before walking around to the passenger's side to open my door. I stepped out the car, and Victor grabbed my hand.

"Vita, this is Tasha. She's one fourth of my crew. Tasha, this is my lady, Vita."

I smiled when Victor referred to me as his lady. We hadn't spoken about titles, but when he gave me one, I wasn't complaining.

"What up doe?" She extended her hand, her voice low but her eyes warm.

"Hey," I replied, just as calm.

"Tasha's been with me for a few years. She's cool as hell, and I hope the two of you will be just as cool as we are." Victor smiled, looking over at me. "There's usually one more young lady with us. Her name is Simone. She couldn't join us tonight due to a family emergency, but you will soon meet her too."

I nodded, not saying anything. I was still trying to figure shit out. I didn't want to jump to any conclusions, but if this nigga thought he was going to pimp me out, then he would have another thing coming. If I was going to sell a bit, I would be the only one making money. Not being able to hold my tongue anymore, I finally opened my mouth to speak.

"What exactly do you do in there?" I asked, eyes locked on the steel door.

"In there?" He pointed at the warehouse. "We do a lot in there – train, have meetings, count money." He stepped closer to me, placing his hands into mine, as he looked me in the eyes. "I feel like I can trust you, Vita."

I nodded my head yes, not knowing if his words were a question or a statement.

"Tonight, I'm going to show you exactly how I make my money. I have some really late nights when I'm working. And if we building something together, then I want to show you exactly what I'll be doing on those late nights."

"Oh, we building something?"

"Are we not? Am I wrong about your place in my life?"

I stepped closer, closing the space between us, before kissing his lips softly. "You're not wrong."

Victor smiled, kissing me again, once on my lips and the other on my forehead. I didn't know why, but something about him made me trust him completely. It was as though I knew he wouldn't allow any harm to come to me without him even having to say it. The fact that he wanted to show me this side of him, whatever side it was, only made me want to trust him more. I didn't know if it was blind curiosity or the way that his eyes felt like they were looking through my soul. However, whatever it was, I knew I was down for this ride.

Victor glanced at his watch then looked toward the street. "We're just waiting on one more. He'll be pulling up any minute. Once he gets here, we can leave."

I nodded my head okay. Just a few moments later, a familiar car pulled into the parking lot. My eyes widened as I watched the car park. The driver's side door opened, and Kyrie stepped out. He was wearing a navy blue suit that looked expensive – more expensive than anything I'd ever seen him in before. His black loafers were polished, and his braids were freshly done. My stomach turned just from looking at him. I'd hated Kyrie for years due to the way he treated Braylen. If there was ever a man I would go three rounds with in a boxing ring, it would be him. And please believe I would beat him the way his mama should have done when he was little.

Kyrie looked at me as if he was shocked to see me. I was sure he was because the feeling was mutual. He didn't speak to me, and I figured he wanted to pretend he didn't know me. Which was cool with me because he was someone I wanted to forget I even knew. Braylen had moved on to bigger and better things, and I loved that for her.

Victor didn't say much either, just looked toward me and said under his breath, "That's Kyrie."

I kept my expression flat, but inside? I was fuming. *Out of all people that could have pulled up, why him? How the hell does he know Victor, and what kind of business do they do?* I couldn't wait to find out what was going on so that I could call Braylen and tell her. Victor told us that it was time for us to go, and we all got into Tasha's Jeep. I sat in the back, sliding in beside Victor, while Kyrie sat in the front seat next to Tasha. I wondered if she was his new girlfriend or just his business partner like Victor said. If there was one thing that I knew about Kyrie, it was that he was no businessman. So, I hoped Victor knew exactly what he was getting himself into.

Tasha started the engine, and the low rumble of bass kicked in almost immediately, old-school Three 6 Mafia. Victor's arm stretched along the back of my seat, his fingers lightly touching my shoulder. I didn't speak the entire ride, and it wasn't because I had nothing to say but because I was busy thinking about how I couldn't wait to tell Braylen. Victor said I was stepping into his world tonight, and I had no idea Kyrie would be a part of it. I glanced at Kyrie, turning up my nose.

Victor leaned in, clearly noticing the look on my face. "If you have any questions, I'll answer them later."

I nodded, not wanting to press the issue. I knew I would have a lot of questions, and I planned to ask them the moment we got back to Victor's car. About fifteen minutes later, we pulled up at Greektown Casino. I should have known that if Kyrie was involved, then a casino would be too. Victor reached into his pocket and pulled out a wad of hundreds. He handed them to me and told me to play the tables with him. I smirked, not knowing why he needed a crew to go to the casino and gamble.

"I don't know how to play the table. I might lose all your money. What table?"

"It's Blackjack, and if you lose, it's all good. This is just fun for you. It's only work for us." He pointed between him, Kyrie, and Tasha.

"Work?" I questioned.

He looked at me once more, letting me know that he would answer questions later. I nodded and took the money, placing it into my purse, before we all got out the car. Kyrie and Tasha walked in first. Victor told me to wait a moment. I didn't ask why, just waited. A few moments later, we walked into the casino. Victor placed his hand on the small of my back again, guiding me through rows of slot machines and toward a Blackjack table. His touch was both firm and reassuring amongst all the chaos around me. Tasha walked off with Kyrie and headed to a table near the far end of the floor, not even glancing back at us.

Victor and I sat side by side, and within the first five minutes, it became clear that I wasn't built for this. I kept second-guessing myself. Hit when I should've stayed. Stayed when I should've hit. Meanwhile, Victor was calm, cool, and calculated, stacking chips with a casual rhythm like he could do this in his sleep. The man next to him lost three hands in a row and walked off, cussing under his breath.

Victor leaned over to me, voice smooth and smug. "I can teach you the game if you want," he spoke, his hand slipping to my thigh beneath the table.

"I doubt I'll have to learn the game. I don't even gamble. I'm just here with you."

He smirked. "That's what they all say."

I laughed a little, even though my stack of chips had been reduced to crumbs. An hour passed, maybe more. The room blurred a little from the free drinks I was receiving while playing the table. I touched Victor's arm gently, leaning in, telling him that I was going to the bathroom. I stood to my feet, adjusting my dress, before grabbing my purse.

"You want me to walk with you?"

I shook my head. "I can handle a hallway."

He grinned and went back to stacking his wins. The women's restroom was tucked down a carpeted corridor near the poker room. I washed my hands, reapplied my lip gloss, and stared at myself in the mirror for a second too long. Gambling wasn't my scene. I had watched it tear my best friend down firsthand. I could only hope that Victor wasn't anything like Kyrie because if he was, this would end here. I walked out the bathroom and was stopped in my tracks when I saw Kyrie standing there.

"Vita, I need to talk to you. I need to get in touch with Braylen, and I guess she changed her number," he spoke, walking up on me.

I stared at him, knowing that he couldn't be serious. This nigga had to be insane. *Why would he think that Braylen would ever want to speak with him again?* Kyrie had never been shit, and Braylen had always been too good for him. I was glad that she finally moved on, and I damn sure wasn't going to allow Kyrie to pull her back into his bullshit.

"If Braylen wanted you to have her number, then you would have it. It's clear that she is finally over yo' bitch ass and is moving on like she should."

"I just want to make sure she's good. Braylen is still my wife, Vita."

"Yo' wife? Nigga, my friend stopped being your wife the moment you sold her to pay yo' bullshit ass debt. And look at yo' ass, ain't learned shit. You still got yo' ass in the casino gambling all yo' money away. You just so fucking trash, Kyrie."

"Have you talked to her?" Kyrie asked.

"I talk to her all the time. Now get the fuck out my way so that I can get back to my business."

His face hardened with anger, but he didn't say anything. I silently dared he would push the issue because I was ready for his ass right then and there. He had the nerve to be coming to me, talking about Braylen was his wife. He was clearly delusional and would have to come to reality quickly before I knocked him into it.

I turned to leave but not before I added, "Stay away from her, Kyrie. Whatever game you think you're playing, she ain't a piece on your board anymore."

I walked away, heading back to Victor, who was still sitting at the table, stacking his chips. He looked up at me, smiling, as I took my seat. He asked me if I was good, and I nodded yes before getting back into the game.

We played for a couple more hours before Victor decided it was time for us to go. We stood up, and I walked with Victor to go cash out his winnings. I'd lost all the money Victor had given me, so I didn't have anything to cash out. However, when the teller handed Victor twenty-five thousand dollars, my eyes widened. I had no idea he'd won that much and for it to be all in one night intrigued me. We walked back to Tasha's Jeep, arm in arm, without saying a word. Kyrie slid into the front passenger seat, while Tasha adjusted her mirrors and pulled onto the highway.

A few miles into the drive, Victor leaned forward between the seats. "What y'all make?" he asked.

Tasha didn't hesitate. "Fifteen and some change."

"I made nineteen," Kyrie replied.

Fifteen and nineteen thousand? They really won that much? I thought, not wanting to let them know that I was really into their conversation. *This is why Kyrie gambles so much if he winning like this every night.*

"This wasn't out best night. Something light but it's cool. Tomorrow will be better," Victor assured.

The fact that Victor said that twenty-five thousand was a light night for him made my pussy wet. Victor leaned back and placed his hand on my thigh. I leaned in closer to him, melting into both him and the leather seat for the rest of the ride. Once we got back to the warehouse, we all went inside. The inside was nothing like I expected it to look. It was nice and had everything one would need in a secret hideout. Victor told me to take a seat on one of the couches, while the three of them sat around the table. He began running the bills through a money counter before dividing the money up into four stacks.

"Tash, can you take Simone her cut?" Victor asked, pushing two stacks of cash over to her.

"Yeah, I'll take it over to her in the morning."

Victor nodded his head, and we all walked out the warehouse and to our cars.

We hadn't even pulled out the lot good enough before I started with the questions. I turned in my seat, so I could look at him while he answered. "I need to ask... Why do you need a *crew* just to go to a casino?"

Victor smiled, turning to look at me quickly, before placing his eyes back on the road. "We don't just go to the casino; we work the casino."

I crossed my arms, never taking my eyes off him. "What does that even mean?"

"We count cards. We don't gamble; we calculate."

"Is that even legal?"

He grinned. "It's not illegal. It's just frowned on."

"And you make thousands doing this?"

"Sometimes tens of thousands," he confirmed. "Depends on the night."

My mind was spinning. Victor was making gambling a business, and it seemed to be actually working. I saw it for myself.

"And Kyrie? What is he doing with you? Do you trust him?" I asked.

"He's been working with me for the past few months. I met him one day at the casino, and I could tell he was trying to make some money, so I put him on. He can really work the numbers and been making a lot of money. He never gave me a reason not to trust him. You talking like you know him."

"I do. He's my best friend's ex-husband. Well, soon to be ex. They're getting a divorce now."

"Why didn't you tell me you knew him?"

"I would much rather forget I ever did. That nigga ain't nobody for anyone to know."

"Shit, that nigga been making good money since he been working with me. I don't know. I think yo' friend might want to think again on the ex part."

"Hell nah, it's fuck that nigga for life. If he making money with you, that's cool, but I don't want to be around him."

"You don't ever have to. We still good, right?"

"We better than good," I replied.

The rest of the car ride was quiet. We drove back to Victor's place. He parked the car, and we went inside. I followed him without a word as he took my hand and led us to his bedroom. He pulled me closer to him, closing the distance between us. He kissed me like he'd been waiting to do so all night. His hands moved down to my backside, gripping it firmly, as his kiss deepened. I moaned against his mouth, my hands flying to his chest, grabbing hold of his shirt like I needed something to anchor me. The heat off him poured into me in waves, and my knees went soft just from the way his tongue moved against mine. He pulled back from me just enough to speak.

"Take off that damn dress."

I stepped back, peeled it up and over my head, then stood in front of him in nothing but my black lace thong. I smiled at him before licking my lips as his eyes roamed my body.

"Turn around," he ordered.

I did as I was told, turning around, giving him a full view of my ass cheeks. He came up behind me, lips brushing the back of my neck, hands skating down my hips. He kissed my neck softly as he pressed himself into my backside. I could feel his hardness through his slacks.

"You looked so damn good tonight. I been ready to see you with that dress off the moment I saw you with it on."

Goosebumps scattered across my skin as his fingers trailed to my breasts, cupping them, as his fingers rubbed slow circles on my nipples. My entire body tingled as a soft moan escaped my lips. He turned me back around, kissing me, as I unzipped his slacks. I unbuttoned his shirt, peeling it off of him, revealing his toned body. Victor picked me up into his arms and wrapped my legs around him as he carried me to the bed. He laid me across the black silk sheets, rubbing his hands over my skin, as he looked down at me. I spread my legs for him, and Victor leaned down and kissed me again.

I was already moist between my legs, waiting for Victor to enter me. When he finally lined up and slid in, I gasped. I wrapped my arms around him as I pulled him in deeper. My eyes rolled in the back of my head, and I bit down on his shoulder, trying to control the loud moan that threatened to escape. He leaned up, still looking down at me, as he pumped. He opened his mouth, allowing his spit to trickle from his lips. I moaned as I opened my mouth and caught it.

"Yeah, that's right, baby. Take all of me," Victor moaned.

And I did, just as he told me to. I wrapped my legs around him as he went deeper inside of me. His mouth landed on my collarbone, licking and kissing, as he kept his pace. His tongue swirled around my nipple, lips sucking hungrily, as if I was his last meal. He looked me into my eyes before sitting up and flipping me over. His hand slapped my ass cheek firmly, and I yelped, welcoming the painful pleasure. He slapped it again, loving the way my ass jiggled.

I watched as he grabbed the baby oil from the nightstand. He poured it on my ass and between my ass cheeks. He rubbed his hardness over my asshole several times before easing it in. I was so tight that it burned at first.

"Relax, baby," he whispered into my ear.

I did, and this time, he was able to get all the way in. The first few pumps hurt, but I took them. But then it started to feel good to both myself and Victor. He grabbed my hips, pumping in and out of me, now in a steady pace. The deeper he went, the louder I moaned. When he came, it was inside of me. Warm liquid spilled over into me, filling my asshole with his seed. He collapsed beside me as I laid there, breathing hard.

"I want you to stay the night with me," he spoke. It was more of a request than a question.

Still, I said yes, walking into Victor's en-suite bathroom to take a shower. Victor joined me moments later. It was like he couldn't get enough of me because he couldn't keep his hands off my body. We had sex in the shower then once more once Victor carried me back to the bed. By the end of the night, we were both spent when we cuddled up in each other's arms and went to sleep.

Chapter Ten

BRAYLEN

I woke up tangled inside the soft sheets. The air in the room still held the faintest scent of A'zir's cologne. I could tell he wasn't in the bed anymore; his body would have been wrapped in mine if he were. He was probably off handling something before the day fully started. He always woke up bright and early. I pushed the covers off slowly and sat up, pausing to breathe. My body felt heavier than usual. It wasn't just a tired feeling; this was something different. It was as if my entire body was shifting.

I made my way to the bathroom, walking barefoot on the cool floor, rubbing my hand over my stomach like I had the past few mornings without even thinking. When I flicked on the bathroom light and stepped in front of the mirror, I froze. My heart skipped as I looked at my baby bump. It was as if it had formed overnight. My hands went to it immediately, fingers splayed across the smooth skin stretched tighter than it had been just yesterday. It wasn't huge, but it was visible.

I turned to the side and lifted the hem of my T-shirt higher. The curve of my stomach was small but undeniable now. And I couldn't help it – my eyes watered. *This is happening. I am becoming a mother, and no matter if I am ready or not, the baby will be here soon.* My hands moved in slow circles over the bump, and for a second, I imagined what it would feel like when I felt a kick for the first time. When I'd see my stomach rise and fall from movement inside me. When we'd bring this life into the world.

I whispered, "Hey, little one."

I stood in front of that mirror for a long time, one hand braced on the sink, the other resting on the curve that hadn't been there the day before. It felt like my body had decided to catch up all at once, like the life inside of me was tired of hiding and had chosen this morning, of all mornings, to make itself known. I wasn't ready, but I wasn't scared either, not the way I expected to be.

"Oh, my God, I'm really pregnant," I spoke out loud to myself.

Saying it didn't make it feel any more real but seeing it did. The way my stomach poked out let me know that there was truly life growing inside me. The moment washed over me in waves. It wasn't joy or fear but something in between that I couldn't put my finger on. When I first found out I was pregnant, I was terrified. I didn't know what I was going to do. However, Banks had changed all that. He'd promised me that he was going to be there and raise the baby as his, and I knew he meant it.

With A'zir, I never had to second guess what he said. If he told me he was going to do something, then it was always going to get done. Being pregnant by Kyrie wasn't in my plans, but it happened. Now, A'zir was going to be here to make sure everything went right. And despite everything, all the mess and pain from my past, it had all led me right to A'zir. So, I wouldn't change one thing. What me and A'zir had might not have started out perfect, but it was ours, and we were perfect for each other. This was something that I wanted to protect, something that I needed to protect.

Even though Kyrie was the biological father, he wouldn't have any parts of my child's life. At first, that was something that I was battling myself about. However, there was no way I was going to allow a man like Kyrie around my child. He never had to know, and I was fine with that. It wasn't out of revenge or hate, not because he'd sold me like property, but because I couldn't trust him. Not with my child.

I gripped the edge of the counter and stared hard at my reflection. What I saw was the old Braylen leaving and a brand new woman blooming, a woman becoming someone new. Kyrie had fumbled me, and I'd allowed him to. However, I'd be damned if I allowed him to fumble my baby.

This baby was growing inside of me. Being nourished by my strength. Held together by my healing. Becoming whole inside a body that had already survived too much to offer more pieces to someone who had no clue how to care for them. Kyrie had made his choice, and now, I was making mine.

This baby would know A'zir as its father. The man who stayed up with me when I couldn't sleep. The man who made me feel safe even when I didn't ask him to. The man who saw the cracks in me and never once tried to patch them with lies. I knew my child would never have to wonder if A'zir loved him or her because A'zir would show it every day. This child, our child, would never know neglect. Would never see me begging a man to stay or love me. Would never hear raised voices or feel the sting of being an afterthought. This child would never hear me pleading for his father not to gamble our rent or grocery money away because A'zir would never do any of that. With him, I didn't have to wonder because I already knew.

I pulled myself away from my thoughts, took off my t-shirt, turned on the shower, and stepped inside. The hot water rolled down my back, tracing every curve, soothing every thought that had been moving too fast. I let the silence hold me for a while before I began washing my body.

When I finally stepped out and wrapped myself in a towel, I felt lighter, not just physically but emotionally, like something had shifted in me and was ready to move forward. I noticed my phone screen light up. Looking at it, I saw I had a missed call from Vita. I stared at the screen for a second then let it go dark again. I'd call her back in a few – after I dressed.

Today wasn't a glam day, not with the way my body felt, not with the weight I was carrying. I reached for a pair of light-wash, baggy jeans, soft, worn denim that hung low and loose on my hips. I folded the waistband once for a better fit and paired it with an oversized white T-shirt. I cuffed the sleeves then looked at myself in the mirror. *Cute and comfortable,* I thought. Around my neck, I placed a gold Cuban link chain that A'zir had purchased for me a few weeks back. I slid a pair of small gold hoops into my ears and a stack of thin gold bangles around one wrist.

I reached for my hair oil and brush. I oiled my hair before brushing it into a low bun. I applied edge control to my edges and swooped them to perfection. For my fragrance, I layered Masion Margiela's Bubble Bath with Kayali's Vanilla 28. The blend was both sweet and comforting.

Picking up my phone, I went to Vita's contact, calling her back. I took a seat in one of the accent chairs by the window and pressed the phone to my ear. Vita answered on the first ring.

"'Bout time you called me back," she said, half-playful, half pressed.

I smiled faintly. "I was in the shower."

"Well, bitch, I got some tea that you gotta sip," she spoke into the phone.

My stomach knotted. "Okay, Vi, tell me what's up."

"I saw Kyrie last night."

"Saw him where?" I rolled my eyes, not giving a damn about Kyrie.

"So, you remember the older cat I been talking to, right? Well, last night, he took me out. We pulled up at some abandoned warehouse off Junction. Shit was crazy. Anyway, when I asked him what we were doing there, he told me we were waiting on his crew. Well, guess who was a part of his crew? That's right, Kyrie's fingerless ass."

"His crew?" I was so confused.

"Yes, girl, Victor has a crew. It's him, Kyrie, and two other females. Girl, they going to casinos, countin' cards, and hittin' they ass for big money. Victor asked him what he made that night, and that nigga said nineteen racks. He came a long way from the bum ass nigga he used to be. He even looks better. Still ain't made enough money to get all ten fingers, but it's a start. He asked me about you. I told him you moved on to bigger and better things and not thinking about him."

I swallowed hard. My hand slid back to rest on the slight swell of my belly. I didn't give two fucks about Kyrie's ass. Not anymore. There was a time where I would go to war for him; now, I wouldn't spit on him if his ass was on fire. I wasn't shocked to hear that Kyrie was still doing the same shit. That was all he knew.

"So, he's still the same old gambling ass nigga. You should have told him to sign them fucking papers and stop trying to hold off on our damn divorce."

"Nah, he ain't gamblin' no more. That nigga counting cards. It's a foolproof way for him to win every time. Victor got an entire system, and that shit seemed like it was working. But hold up. What you mean? That nigga still trying to hold off on the divorce? I thought that shit was going to be clean and easy."

"It was supposed to be easy, but Kyrie keep acting like he don't want to let go when he was the one that ended our marriage in the first place. He keeps having his lawyer do stupid shit, so legally, we not divorced yet."

"Man, that shit is crazy, Bray. I'm really sorry you going through this shit, especially while you're pregnant. Speaking of that, did you figure out what you're going to do?"

"Yeah, I'm going to let Banks raise the baby. I can't trust Kyrie's ass, and that's even more clear now. He still the same person. I don't care how much money he making now. He still doing the same shit that has always ruined his life. I can't have my baby around a person like that."

"I completely understand. You know I'm always team Braylen, no matter what."

"Thanks, girl. Now, about your new man, Victor, right? You say he's counting cards? Look, Vi, just be careful, okay? I been down the road with a gambling addict. Trust me when I say that's not a road that you want to travel."

"I hear you, Bray, but Victor is different. He's not an addict; he's a boss. A real one. I saw it firsthand. Plus, his dick game is strong as hell. I didn't know the old heads had it like that."

"Bitch, shut up! That old nigga got it like that? My mama always told me that old men will give you worms."

Vita burst out into laughter. "Bitch, what? I ain't never heard of no shit like that."

"Well, that's what my mama said, so I never fucked with older men."

"Bitch, that shit is not true." Vita continued laughing.

I sat in the chair for a while, talking and laughing with Vita. When we ended the call, I stood to my feet, grabbed a pair of red and white Jordans from my closet, along with my red Telfar bag, and pressed the intercom.

"Zeek?" I called out.

His voice crackled through the speaker. "Yes, I'm here, Braylen."

"Can you pull the car around for me?"

"Yeah, I got you, Braylen. Just give me five minutes.

I walked back into the closet, grabbing a pair of oversized sunglasses for my face. I looked at myself once more in the mirror, loving my cute and comfortable look. I shot a text to A'zir, letting him know that I was going shopping and would be back later. When I walked down the stairs, Zeek was already waiting by the open front door. I wasn't sure if I was having a girl or a boy, but today, I would be doing some shopping.

Chapter Eleven

KYRIE

The door slammed behind me harder than I meant it to. The sound echoed through the apartment – empty, dim, and cold. My footsteps followed it, slower now, heavier, but every one of them pulsed with something I couldn't name. I tossed my keys on the counter then just stood there in the dark, staring at the wall like it had answers. *Vita of all people?* I thought. I hadn't seen her since Braylen left me. She hated me, always in Bray's ear, telling her to leave me. I should have known she wouldn't tell me shit about Braylen.

I knew she was going to tell Braylen that she saw me, if she hadn't already. I wondered what Braylen would say when Vita told her about all the money I was making now. I hoped she would want to at least talk to me. I paced the kitchen, every nerve in my body buzzing. I made myself a bowl of cereal and sat down at the table to eat it. I prayed that whatever Vita said would cause Braylen to reach out. I needed her, and I knew if she would just listen to me, then she would see things my way. I ran my hands down my face, tugging at my cornrows, breathing hard through my nose.

This was crazy. Life without Braylen was something that I never prepared for. I never thought that she would have left me. I thought that no matter what, Braylen would always be there. However, I'd pushed too far, overstepped too much, and now she was in the arms of another.

It hurt twice as much to know that I had put her into the arms of that man. It was never supposed to be this way. She was only supposed to be there for a week then come back to me. Now here I was, looking stupid in the middle of a divorce while trying to hold on to a woman that was pretending not to want me.

Braylen and I had taken vows before God to always be with each other until the day we died. From what I could see, we were both still living and breathing, so I didn't understand why she thought we weren't going to be together. I might not be able to buy her the things Banks could buy her now. However, give me a couple more months working with Vic and the crew, and I would be able to buy her anything she wanted.

Once I was done eating, I washed my bowl and took a shower, trying to wind down. It was five in the morning, and I'd been up all night. I wasn't sure if it was the high that I was feeling from winning at the casino, but I wasn't tired. In fact, I was wide awake. I knew there was no point in me even trying to sleep.

I sat on the couch, turned on the TV, and flipped through Netflix, but nothing looked good enough to keep my attention. All I wanted was Braylen; all I needed was her. I walked up to my room, grabbing a bag of weed from my nightstand drawer along with a pack of leafs. I rolled a blunt, lighting it and taking a deep pull. I wanted her back; I needed her back. It was clear to me that Braylen wasn't just going to come back to me on her own. I would have to do something to make her come back or force her back.

So, I made a decision right there in my living room. If she wasn't going to call me, if she was going to hide away in that big ass house with a nigga who wore cashmere and played protector, then I was going to tear the whole thing down around them. Brick by muthafucking brick.

And I wasn't gonna stop until she saw me again. Until she felt me. It was nothing to me anymore, just a drop in the pot. Vic had been feeding us all week, casino to casino, city to city. And I hadn't even been spending. I was stacking and waiting. I shoved several stacks of hundreds into a slim black envelope and wrote her name on it in Sharpie – not her first name, just *Mrs. Banks*. Not thinking twice, I grabbed my keys and got into the car, making my way to Banks' house.

It was still early, and I didn't think anyone was up inside the house.

It didn't matter because the house couldn't be seen from the street, so that meant they couldn't see me. Or maybe they had cameras facing the street and were looking at me right now. Maybe I didn't give a fuck either way. I slid the envelope inside the mailbox and walked off and got back into my car, pulling off down the street like I was never there.

I knew this was only the beginning. I'd been silent long enough. If Braylen thought I was just going to bow out gracefully and allow her to be happy with someone else, she was crazy. She was my wife. I owned her, and I wasn't going to stop until I had her back.

On the ride home, I called Jason. I knew he had a cousin that could help me with my next step. He called me within ten minutes, telling me to meet him at a Coney on Six Mile. I didn't hesitate; I hit a U-turn in the middle of the street and made my way to the restaurant.

When I arrived, he was already seated at the table, sipping Coke through a straw. I walked over, taking my seat across from him.

"Jason told me you needed some shit done," he spoke.

"Yeah, I heard you the nigga to go to when you need some quality footage of places."

"I've been known to make some good money selling photos of celebrities and their homes to all kinds of media outlets and blogs. So, it's safe to say that if you want footage, then I'm your guy. All I need is the address and five thousand, and I can get you photos and video footage. For an extra two thousand, I can get you audio too."

I nodded my head, pulling a white envelope from my pants pocket and handing it to him. "That's ten. Get me everything you can get."

He handed me a pen, and I wrote down the address on the envelope along with an email address where he could send everything to. When I finished, I stood without a word and left the restaurant. I felt better knowing that I would finally have eyes on Braylen. I walked back into my townhome smiling. Suddenly, I was tired. I walked into my room, removed my clothes, and got into bed, finally able to sleep.

I woke up around six that evening. I hadn't gotten more than five hours of sleep, but I felt rejuvenated, as if I'd just gotten a full night's rest. Walking into my kitchen, I made myself a sandwich before walking into the living room and turning on the TV. I turned on ESPN before I began eating. I was only a few bites into my sandwich when my phone chimed. When I looked at it, I noticed it was an email from a sender I didn't recognize. I clicked the link to find it was a live video feed of Banks' house. The feed showed every angle of the home so that I wouldn't miss a thing. I synced my phone to the TV, playing the feed on the big screen, as I continued to eat my sandwich.

Everything was quiet with the exception of a few cars passing by on the street. I sat and watched like it was a good ass Netflix original, waiting to see her face on the screen. I finished my sandwich, never taking my eyes from the screen. An hour went by, then two and three, yet I was still sitting there, watching the live feed, switching the angles, waiting on Braylen – waiting on any movement at all. Finally, after four and a half hours of watching, a black SUV pulled up to the front gate. I watched as the gate opened, and the SUV drove down the long driveway.

"Please be you, baby. I need to see you. Let me just see your face," I spoke out loud.

I watched, eyes glued on the screen, as the driver's door opened. A man in a black suit stepped out. I didn't know his name, but I recognized him as Banks' driver. He walked around and opened the back passenger door and reached his arm in. I smiled when I saw Braylen appear into view. She looked so beautiful, almost glowing. She stood there, saying a few words to the driver. She was wearing a pair of oversized jeans and a t-shirt, but she was still the most beautiful woman in the world.

I needed my baby back; she had to come back, and I was going to do anything to make that happen. I watched her walk up the steps and into the front door. I continued watching, praying she would walk back outside. I watched as the driver opened the trunk. He removed several shopping bags and took them inside the house.

"You wanna go shoppin', baby? That shit ain't nothing to me now. You can go shopping every day when you get back home," I spoke out loud.

Outside, the sun set, causing the sky to go dark. Inside my town-home however, my eyes were still glued to the screen. I watched as another car pulled up, and I saw Banks get out. My jaws clenched as anger set in. There he was, the man that stole my woman – the man I used to fear but hated now. I knew he was in the way. If he wasn't around, then Braylen would be here.

He was brainwashing her, making her think that I didn't love her just because I gave her to him for a week. He knew why I did that shit, but there he was, walking around with his chin up like he was some good guy. The old me was scared, but this me just wanted my wife back – even if I had to kill Banks to do it.

I continued watching the feed, praying Braylen would walk outside again. I just wanted to see her once more before I went to sleep. But she didn't. Instead, she stayed inside, probably wrapped in the arms of the man that had taken her from me. By two in the morning, I finally went up to my room and went to sleep.

Chapter Twelve

BANKS

It was four in the morning when I rolled over to a text. Braylen was sleeping beside me with her leg twisted in mine. I reached for my phone on the nightstand and saw I had a text. Opening my messages, I read it.

DeShawn: Check your email. Priority.

I was already sliding out of bed by the time I typed back. Braylen barely stirred, her breaths slow and even, one arm stretched across the pillows where I'd been. I pressed a soft kiss to her forehead then pulled on my sweats and padded out of the bedroom without a sound.

By the time I reached the office and flicked on the recessed lights, I was fully awake.

It was not because I wanted to be but because DeShawn never sent messages at this hour unless something serious was in motion. I powered up the monitor, logged into the private server, and found the flagged email sitting right at the top.

Subject: NYC Select Private Client Request

The sender was encrypted, as I knew it would be. I opened the email and began reading.

Mr. Banks,

We're prepared to finalize the Manhattan delivery within the next twenty-four hours. Client would prefer you and DeShawn make the selec-

I leaned back in my chair and dragged a hand down my jaw. This was typical rich bastard shit. They send me an email at this hour and tell me I have twenty-four hours to deliver just because they want to play. Then, they didn't want to just take what I had on hand. They wanted me to go to New York and hunt for their fantasy. The number, the five million, called out to me. I was never one to turn down any money, and I wasn't about to start now.

Scrolling through my contacts, I called my pilot and told him to gas up the private jet because I was on my way. After that, I sent a test to Deshawn, telling him to meet me at the airport in forty-five minutes. He agreed, and I left my office, locking the door behind me. I walked into my bedroom, moving quietly because Braylen was still sleeping. I took a quick shower and put on a black fitted tee, a pair of black slacks, and a pair of black leather loafers. I oiled my locs before placing them back into a low ponytail. I grabbed my black leather bag from the closet – not the one that I used when I had fun with Braylen in the bedroom but the one I still had packed from my last business trip. I kissed Braylen softly on her forehead once more before walking out the room.

I didn't call Zeek; there was no need to wake him. Instead, I got into my Tesla SUV and made my way to the airport. DeShawn and I arrived at the same time, both exiting our SUVs, black leather bags in hand. We entered the private jet, letting the pilot know where we were headed.

By nine that morning, we were touching down. I slid my Cartier shades on as we descended the stairs. DeShawn followed, dressed in all black as well. We knew we had business to take care of, and we were going to get it done so that I could go back home to my woman. We'd done this too many times to flinch. As soon as we stepped onto the runway, the concierge handed over our keys and a clipboard. It was a matte black Escalade, similar to the one I had at home. I nodded once, taking the keys, before we both got inside.

DeShawn checked the email once more, checking the list of the clients' demands. "Couple, mid-twenties, urban background." He spoke out loud.

I nodded my head, already having the demands memorized. We hit Harlem first. There was no better place to find real urban love. DeShawn parked a few blocks up from Lenox, and we walked – slow, heads down but eyes up.

"You got a spot in mind?" he asked, low.

"There's a juice bar over here that turns into a hookah spot by night. Young crowd, chill vibe. Let's start there."

We didn't speak much after that. There was no need to. We both had a job to do, and we both understood that. Inside, the spot was warm and loud. There were wooden accents with neon quotes on the wall. "Protect Black Love" glowed in pink behind the bar. Couples sat close on low couches, sharing smoothies and conversation. We posted up in a corner and ordered water and watched.

A girl in a red crop top with curly hair laughed hard enough to make her man grab her hand under the table. I clocked them for five minutes. She was sweet, but he was anxious. He kept checking his phone, looking around like he wasn't supposed to be there. *They ain't solid enough,* I thought. Two booths down, a dark-skinned couple in sweats were whispering. Body language seemed to be comfortable with each other. They seemed to be vibing as they smiled when they spoke to each other. The man was light skinned and skinny with a low haircut. The woman was a deep chocolate – beautiful with flawless skin and a short pixie.

I leaned toward DeShawn. "Them?"

He shook his head. "Seen him before. He a local rapper. Taking him would bring too many eyes. Muthafuckas gonna notice he gone."

"Damn, I'm glad you noticed that shit 'cause I ain't never seen that nigga before." Too many eyes on him. People would notice if he disappeared.

We remained at the juice bar for an hour, scanning the place and filtering through the couples walking in and out. None of them really fit the profile the clients were looking for. We stood up and walked out, ready to hit the streets again. We hit the lower eastside, Union Square. We walked through outdoor flea markets and sat on stoops, watching people pass by. We ducked into a few coffee shops and corner stores, even a damn laundromat on Myrtle Avenue, just to watch how folks moved.

Our clients were asking for a couple, and we were going to deliver. What they wanted to do with the couple after that was their business. By early afternoon, we hit a park in Fort Greene. The sky was heavy with clouds with not much sun peeking through, but that still hadn't stopped people from being outside. That was when I saw them. She had brown skin and honey locs piled up high, jeans ripped at the knees, and a fitted white tee. He was lanky with skin like molasses and a crooked grin. They were sitting on the edge of a fountain, splitting a bag of dried mangos and talking so close their knees were touching. I stopped and so did DeShawn.

"You see it?" I muttered under my breath.

"Yeah."

They weren't flashy nor poor, just two regular people, clearly in love. We walked past them once, just close enough to take a good look at them. They didn't even know we were watching them, not even looking up at us once.

"Let's loop around the back," I murmured.

DeShawn nodded and peeled off across the grass. I slid into a bench a few feet away and pulled out my phone, pretending to scroll. However, I was really watching them. He touched her face once, and she leaned into it. That was all I needed to see to know that they were the couple we'd been looking for. I took a photo of them to send to the client while they were in transfer.

"Let's follow them. We move the moment we get the right chance," DeShawn spoke.

I nodded my head, ready to finish this job, so I could get back to my woman. We watched as the couple stood and walked hand in hand. They walked to their car, and the man opened the door for the woman, allowing her to get in the car, before he closed the door. When they pulled out the park, so did we. I was sure not to follow too closely, not wanting to alert them.

By sundown, we'd tracked the couple back to a third-floor walk-up not far from Barclays. We parked three blocks away from the apartment, sitting and watching for any movement. I looked up at the brownstone building we'd been watching for the last two hours. The window was still open, causing the curtains to sway in the wind. I'd watched her come to the window twice with the last time being just ten minutes ago.

"You ready?" I asked DeShawn, glancing over at him.

He nodded once. "We go in clean and quiet. If we make too much noise, one of these neighbors gon' hear and call the police."

I smirked. "You sayin' that like I'm new to the game. I'm the one taught you this shit."

The air felt heavy as we approached the building. It was not from weather but from what we were about to do. This wasn't the first grab I'd been on, not by a long shot, but something about being in someone else's city always raised the stakes. We didn't know the neighbors here. We didn't know if the couple had a dog or any extra roommates. It didn't even matter if they did because the time was now.

DeShawn kept his head low with his hood up and gloves already on. The moment we walked up to the door, an older woman was walking out. I held the door for her before we walked into the building. We moved up the stairs like shadows with quiet steps. The third floor smelled like fried food and weed smoke. We walked down the narrow hallway and stopped in front of apartment 3B.

I placed my ear to the door, listening to the music that was being played inside. It took DeShawn all of six seconds to pick the lock and open the door. We walked in quietly, looking around. The woman was in the kitchen with her back turned to us. She wore a short, light pink robe, and she was barefoot, standing at the stove with her locs pulled back into a ponytail. We crept up on her slowly, but she must have sensed us behind her because she turned around quickly. Her smile faded when she saw us dressed in all black. DeShawn moved fast, grabbing her and placing one hand over her mouth before she could even scream.

"Shhh," he murmured, calming and deadly all at once. "Don't make this harder than it has to be."

She squirmed, trying to get away from DeShawn's tight grip, but to no avail. I rushed to the back of the house where I knew the man had to be. My gun was already in my hand. He was laying across the bed with his back to the door. His phone was in his hand, and he was scrolling through TikTok. He didn't move a muscle as I inched toward him, my gun leading the way.

"Baby, I thought you were making dinner," the man spoke, not so much as rolling over or removing his eyes from his phone.

I nudged his arm with my gun, and he took the Air Pods from his ears. When he looked up at me, his eyes widened as he jumped back. I placed my index finger to my lips, telling the man to stay quiet. He nodded his head, and I told him to stand to his feet. I walked him back into the living room, where DeShawn was still holding onto his woman, at gunpoint.

"Sit the fuck down," I spoke, motioning with my gun to the couch.

They sat down without words. The man wrapped his arms around the woman as if he could protect her from us. We injected them both with a tranquilizer we'd brought with us. It was a low dose, just enough to make them both groggy and compliant. They slumped into the couch, disoriented.

"They good, right? You didn't put too much in there, did you? I ain't never seen nobody pass out this fast," I spoke.

DeShawn checked their pulses. "Yeah, they still alive. At least we know they will stay quiet until we get them there. I'ma go get the car."

Deshawn returned a few minutes later, telling me he'd parked out back. We carried them both to the car, one by one, and placed them inside the trunk. They were both still out cold, and I was happy about that.

Fifteen minutes later, we were pulling into the industrial lot outside Manhattan. The spot had been arranged the minute the email hit our inbox. It was an old produce warehouse converted into a private distribution hub, perfect for people like us. Security was at the gate and didn't ask questions. They knew who we were. The gate lifted, and we drove straight to bay door three.

A tall guy in all black waited by the loading dock. He was clean shaven with a sharp jaw and glove covered hands. He nodded at us once we stepped up.

"Which van?" I asked, noticing the three that were in front of us.

He pointed. "Gray one right there. It's prepped and ready."

We popped the trunk and slid them both into the van.

"How long till they move?" DeShawn asked.

"Within the next couple hours. They'll be off grid by tomorrow afternoon."

"Good." I nodded, rubbing my gloved hands together.

We were back on the road fifteen minutes later, silence stretching between us, as the sun dipped behind Manhattan's skyline. I stared out the window, wondering how long the girl had lived there. How many memories had they built in that apartment? Who would report them missing first? And how long would it take before they realized no one was ever going to find them?

I stepped off the jet into the humid Detroit night, my body tired from the trip, but I couldn't wait to get home to Braylen. The mission was done, and the money would be in my account by tomorrow. DeShawn gave me a parting nod before sliding into his own SUV, and I drove myself back home, craving the feel of my shower and the softness of Braylen's skin. The house was dimly lit when I walked in, the air inside cool and scented faintly with vanilla and lavender. I dropped my duffel by the door and stripped my shirt off on the way to the master bathroom. I rolled my neck to shake off the tension of the day.

Hot water streamed over my skin as I stood in the glass shower, leaning forward with my palms braced on the marble tile. When I was done, I dried off and walked into the bedroom with a towel slung low around my hips.

Braylen's voice rang out from the hallway, bubbling with energy. "Baaaabe, come see what I got!"

She burst into the room before I could answer, her hands full of pastel shopping bags. Her face was lit with excitement, brown eyes wide, smile stretched so big it dimpled her cheeks. She looked like pure joy wrapped in a fitted sweatsuit. I raised my eyebrow, amused by the storm she was bringing into my moment of calm.

"Damn, slow down. What'd you do, buy the whole store?"

"Maybe!" She beamed, dropping the bags on the bed. "I couldn't help it. Everything was so cute. And I just don't know. I want the baby to have the best of everything."

I walked over and kissed her forehead then sat down as she began pulling items out of the bags with the energy of a kid unwrapping gifts on Christmas morning.

"Okay, look!" she said, holding up a tiny black leather jacket no bigger than her forearm. "Tell me this ain't some little baby Banks type shit."

I smirked. "That's hard. We already dressing 'em like a boss?"

"Period." She grinned.

She moved on to a set of soft cotton onesies in earthy tones, sage green, mustard yellow, and warm beige. Each had minimalist designs, tiny crowns, stars, and abstract rainbows. She rubbed one between her fingers. "Feel that. It's organic cotton. Only the best for our prince or princess."

Next was a white bassinet with gold trim, foldable legs, and breathable mesh siding. "I had it delivered," she explained, gesturing to where it was already set up beside the bed. "Isn't it beautiful? It rocks gently on its own. Look, touch this button."

I pressed it, and the bassinet let out a gentle hum, rocking slowly back-and-forth.

"I got a matching changing table too. Oh, and this diaper bag." She held up a sleek, black, designer bag with gold zippers. "It doesn't even look like a diaper bag, but it is. A'zir, look inside. It got bottle compartments, a wipe slot, and even a fold-out changing pad."

I leaned back against the pillows, watching her. She was glowing, not just from pregnancy but from excitement. I smiled. In a day that had been filled with violence and calculated silence, this right here? This was life.

"I see you went all out." My eyes traced every curve of her body as she twirled, showing off a baby wrap carrier in soft taupe.

"And I'm not done!" She laughed. "You ain't even seen the books I got. And the bath stuff, lavender baby lotion, tear-free shampoo, a baby tub that collapses for travel. I got lil' towels with ears on 'em, ears, A'zir, and they're so cute. You wanna see?"

I chuckled. "I'm good, Mama. You doin' your thing."

She softened then, walking over and crawling onto the bed beside me. Her voice lowered. "I just want our baby to feel loved. From day one. I didn't grow up with a lot of this stuff. But I want them to know we were ready. That he or she was wanted."

I wrapped my arm around her waist, pulled her close, and kissed her temple. "Our child gon' know. He or she already do."

She leaned back. "Do you like all the things I bought?"

"I love it. You did real good, Bray, and we just getting started." I wrapped my arms around her and pulled her in close. "I love everything you got. I love you, and I love our baby."

She turned in my arms, her eyes searching mine. "I missed you while you were gone."

"I missed you too, but I'm here now."

Her lips met mine. It started soft and sweet, but something always burned hotter between us, the kind of love that couldn't stay polite for long. I cupped the back of her neck, deepening the kiss, letting my tongue taste the corners of her mouth as I pulled her body closer to mine. The towel slipped a little lower, and I didn't stop it. She reached up and pushed it off completely.

Braylen dropped to her knees slowly, her hands tracing down my abs as she went. She looked up at me, eyes wide. "Let me show you how much I missed you."

I watched her lips part, felt the warmth of her breath, as she wrapped her hand around my shaft and let her mouth follow. The first touch made me exhale sharply through my nose, my hand going straight to her hair.

"Shit, Bray."

Her lips were soft and wet. She moved slowly at first, teasing me, letting her tongue circle the head before taking more of me in. The heat of her mouth was a drug, warm and tight, her tongue dancing along the underside, her throat opening inch by inch until I could feel the back of it. I groaned, tipping my head back, my fingers curling against her scalp.

"Damn, B, fuck. That mouth."

She hummed around me, the vibration making my knees lock. Every motion was deliberate – slow suction then a fast, eager rhythm that made me grit my teeth. She looked up while she did it, eyes glassy and greedy. She wanted every bit of me, and I gave it to her. My hips started to move with her rhythm, subtle but deep. I couldn't help it. She had me and she knew it. The grip of her lips, the way her hand stroked what she couldn't take, the way her other hand braced on my thigh, it was too much and just enough.

"You missed me this much?" I rasped, watching her swallow me deeper, eyes never leaving mine.

She nodded with her mouth full, and fuck that did something to me.

"Keep goin', baby," I whispered, voice rough. "Just like that."

She worked me with practiced, passionate finesse – mouth gliding up and down, spit glistening on her lips and dripping down her chin. She didn't care. She wanted to taste all of me. She wanted to show me that her craving hadn't dulled in my absence. That her body was still synced to mine like muscle memory. My stomach tightened, breath quickening.

"Bray, fuck, I'm close."

She sucked harder, faster, deeper, and then slowed again, teasing me right on the edge. I growled low, a warning she knew too well. My hand tightened in her hair, my hips jerking once against her lips, as my orgasm threatened to unravel. She kept me there, hovering and desperate. I came so hard, I saw stars. A guttural moan ripped from my throat as I filled her mouth, my body shaking with the force of it. She didn't flinch. She took it all, swallowing me with no hesitation, eyes fluttering closed for just a second before she let me slip from her lips.

She looked up at me, licking her bottom lip. "Welcome home, Daddy."

Chapter Thirteen

BRAYLEN

I walked down the stairs to find A'zir already waiting for me in the foyer. He wore a navy blue fitted turtleneck and a pair of charcoal slacks. His locs had been weaved into four cornrows to the back, and his gold chain glistened around his neck. He wore a pair of Cartier frames and a gold Rolex on his right wrist. I smiled when our eyes collided. It was my five-month checkup, and we both were excited.

It was mid-October, and the weather had started to break in Michigan. I wore a black, long-sleeved one-piece with a pair of black Prada boots and a black cropped jacket. I'd gotten my hair braided the day before in jet black knotless braids down to my butt. I had on gold Fendi jewelry on my wrist, neck, fingers, and ears. My scent was Le Labo's Another 13. My baby bump seemed to be getting a little bigger every morning I woke up. I rested my hand on my stomach, looking up at A'zir.

"You ready, baby?" I asked.

"Hell yeah, and I hope lil man has moved so that he can show Mommy that he really is a boy," A'zir smiled, taking my hand in his.

"How do you know that our little princess not ready to show Daddy that she's a girl?" I countered as we walked toward the door.

"Well, I guess we gon' hope that we finally find out today."

We got into A'zir's Tesla SUV. He didn't have Zeek drive us, telling me that he wanted it to be just us any time we went to my doctors' appointments. The late-morning sun spilled through the windshield, warm and golden, and I leaned back in the passenger seat, rubbing slow circles over my growing belly. I couldn't believe that I was five months already. It was going by so fast, and in only four short months, we would meet our baby. It still didn't feel real sometimes. That was until I caught the soft kicks at night or the steady reminder in the way my clothes now fit. Today was the day I'd been waiting on since my last appointment when the baby wouldn't uncross its tiny legs, so the tech could tell if I was having a boy or a girl.

A'zir's hand rested on my thigh as he drove, his thumb brushing in absentminded strokes. "You know," he said, glancing at me with a little smirk, "I setup something for us Friday."

I turned my head toward him. "Something like what?"

"Dinner with my mama and pops. You said you wanted to meet them, right? Well, it's happening Friday."

I blinked, caught off guard, and then felt my face breaking into a smile I couldn't hide. "Really?"

"Yeah, really. We are building a life together, so it's only right."

"I can't wait." I smiled, looking over at him.

His eyes flicked to my belly then back to the road. "They're excited to meet the woman carrying their grandbaby."

A little flutter shot through me, one part nerves, the other joy. Meeting his parents was a big step to me. But the way he said it was like it was the most natural thing in the world. When we arrived at the doctor's office, we were called back almost immediately. I lay there on the table, looking at the screen, waiting for the ultrasound tech to tell me what we were having. The room was dimly lit except for the soft glow from the monitor. She moved the wand slowly over my belly, her eyes narrowing in concentration before her lips curved into a smile.

"Well," the tech said warmly, "it looks like you're having a boy."

For a moment, the world felt still. My eyes went wide, my mouth opening in a soft gasp, as I turned my head toward A'zir. I could feel my heart racing, not just from the news but also the huge smile on A'zir's face.

"A boy," he repeated, his voice low and reverent, as if saying it too loud might break the magic. He reached over, taking my hand in his. I could feel the warmth of his palm, the strength of his grip. "That's my son in there," he continued.

My throat tightened with emotion. I thought I'd cry, but instead, I just smiled, a deep, radiant smile that came from deep within. "Our son," I whispered back. In my mind, I was already picturing the tiny clothes, the little socks, the soft baby skin. I imagined the way A'zir would hold him, how his deep voice would sound saying the baby's name for the first time. This man had to have been sent to me – sent to save me, to show me love like I'd never knew it. Here he was, smiling and ready to raise my son as his. At that moment, I knew just how in love I was with A'zir.

<hr>

When we got home later, my mind was buzzing with plans. I pulled out my laptop, scrolling through paint ideas, until I found the one that made my heart skip. I wanted something that would feel magical, something my son could grow up surrounded by. I pictured deep navy walls fading into soft twilight blues, dotted with hand-painted stars and constellations. A glowing moon in one corner. Tiny, whimsical hot air balloons drifting among the clouds. A shooting star stretching across the main wall above the crib. It would feel like a little universe just for him, a room where dreams would always feel possible.

I placed the order for all the paint, brushes, and stencils I'd need, already imagining the smell of fresh paint filling the air as I worked, music playing softly in the background, and my hands bringing my vision to life.

I could hear the water running before I even walked into the bathroom. The soft scent of vanilla and amber was already curling into the air, making the whole space feel like it was wrapped in a slow exhale. A'zir stood at the tub, testing the water with his fingers, his gold chain catching the light when he turned to look at me.

"Get in," he said, his voice deep but quiet, like the room belonged to us and no one else.

Steam swirled around my skin the moment I stepped in, the heat licking over my body like it was glad I'd finally arrived. I sank down until the water hugged me from every side, bubbles clinging to my arms, my knees, even my hair. A'zir crouched beside the tub, his hands warm, even through the water, as he began running the soapy cloth over me with slow, deliberate strokes that made my skin tingle.

He didn't rush. Every part of me was treated like it deserved time and attention. He moved from the curve of my shoulders to the dip of my back then over my stomach. His palms molded around my hips, sliding down my thighs under the water in a way that made my pulse thrum in my ears. I kept my eyes on him, the way his jaw flexed, the quiet concentration on his face, like this was his way of speaking without words.

When he finished, he didn't hand me a towel. Instead, he wrapped me in one himself, pulling me close for a moment before guiding me into the bedroom. The sheets were turned down, candles flickering low on the nightstands, their glow soft against the walls. I lay down, and he straddled the back of my legs, his hands finding my shoulders first. The massage was like Heaven – firm, slow pressure that worked its way down my spine, each muscle giving way under his touch. He worked over my arms, my hands, then lower, my calves, my ankles, then lower until his fingers wrapped around my feet. He kneaded them gently, his thumbs digging into the arch in a way that made my toes curl.

Then, his lips touched them. A shiver went through me before I could stop it, his mouth warm and deliberate as he kissed along the tips, sucking each one slow enough to make my breath catch. His eyes met mine when he looked up, like he wanted me to feel everything he wasn't saying. And I did.

The lights in the room were dim, the warm glow from the lamps casting a golden halo across A'zir's skin when he flipped me over on my back. He leaned down, hovering over me just above my lips.

"Come here," he whispered.

I pushed up and met his lips. He brought his hand to the back of my neck, holding me into the kiss. I moaned against his lips, wanting more.

"You know how much I've been thinking about you all day?"

I didn't answer. I just leaned into him, my forehead pressed to his. His thumb brushed along my jaw softly. His kiss deepened as his eyes locked with mine. It was slow, claiming, his lips moving against mine in a way that made me forget where one breath ended and the other began.

"Braylen," he murmured against my mouth, and the way he said my name made it sound like both a prayer and a promise.

His lips traced the curve of my cheek, the line of my jaw, the sensitive skin just below my ear. I shivered, and he felt it because his arm tightened around me, his chest rising and falling with slower, deeper breaths. His hands moved with purpose, mapping me like he already knew every detail but wanted to memorize them all over again.

The mattress dipped under our weight, the cool sheets brushing my skin. He didn't rush. Instead, he hovered above me, his eyes locked on mine, one hand cupping my face as his thumb brushed along my bottom lip. The intimacy of it made my pulse race faster than anything else. His kisses deepened, his touch growing warmer and slower, more deliberate. Each movement built on the last until it felt like the room itself was holding its breath. And when the moment finally came where the heat between us tipped over into something unstoppable, it wasn't just desire. It was the kind of connection that anchored itself in your bones, making you certain you'd never be the same again.

His body pressed into mine like a tide I couldn't stop, each movement drawing me deeper into him. My hands found his shoulders, gripping as though the ground beneath us had vanished. The heat between us pulsed, syncing with my heartbeat. A'zir's gaze never left my face, watching every change in my breath, every shiver that rolled through me. His touch mapped my skin with a kind of reverence that made my chest ache. I felt surrounded, claimed, yet cherished, like he was carving his name into my soul with every moment.

The air around us was heavy with our shared rhythm, with the soft, ragged sounds we made. My senses drowned in him – his scent, the warm slide of his skin, the low rumble of his voice when he murmured my name. The world beyond this room faded into nothing but heat, shadow, and the rush of us moving together in perfect sync.

When his arms wrapped tighter around me, pulling me flush to his chest, it was like being anchored and set free at the same time. My head fell back, my lips parting in a gasp that wasn't just about the sensation. It was about what he made me feel. We moved until time felt suspended, until thought blurred into instinct, and instinct into need. Every shift, every press, every pause between breaths became another way he told me without words that I was his, that there was no distance between us.

His movements had a rhythm that stole the breath from my lungs. Every press of him inside me was like a wave breaking over and over, one that was relentless, beautiful, and impossible to resist. My skin tingled everywhere he touched as though his hands were waking parts of me that I didn't know had been sleeping. I could feel the strength in his body, the way his muscles flexed under my fingertips, the subtle shifts in his pace that sent shivers running down my spine. Each deep pull drew a sound from me I couldn't hold back, a soft cry that seemed to spur him on.

It was more than physical. There was something electric in the air, an invisible thread tying my heartbeat to his. Every time his gaze locked with mine, I felt undone, stripped bare in a way that had nothing to do with clothes. His eyes told me I belonged here, in this moment, in this space where nothing else mattered. The heat between us was molten now, curling low in my belly, building with every breath. My nails dug into his shoulders when he shifted just right, a helpless reaction to the way pleasure surged through me like a lightning strike. He groaned my name, and it wrapped around me like silk and smoke, dark and soft and dangerous all at once.

I was floating and anchored all in the same moment. My body trembled under his, my heart racing as though it was trying to catch up to what I felt. The world outside didn't exist. There was only the scent of his skin, the sound of our breaths mingling, the hot press of his mouth against my neck as if he couldn't stand the thought of letting me go. Every second pushed me higher, pulled me deeper, until I didn't know if I wanted him to slow down or never stop. It was dizzying, consuming. It was like standing at the edge of something vast and letting myself fall without hesitation.

I could feel it coming, slow at first, a low hum deep inside me, then growing hotter, heavier, until it was all I could focus on. Every thrust, every grind of his hips, sent me closer to the edge. His pace was deliberate, like he knew exactly how to keep me there, trembling and waiting. My hands gripped at him, like he was the only thing holding me together, my body arching into his as heat pooled low in my belly. His breath was ragged against my ear, his voice a deep, rough murmur saying my name in a way that made me feel like it belonged to him alone.

"Look at me," he whispered, and I did. My eyes locked with his, chest tight with everything I couldn't put into words. The way he was looking at me was almost too much – possessive, tender, and fierce all at the same time – like he could see every part of me, even the pieces I kept hidden.

My body tightened around him as the rush came like fire. I gasped, clinging to him as waves of pleasure rolled through me, leaving me breathless and shaking. The world narrowed to the feel of him, the heat of his skin, the deep, steady way he held me while I came apart in his arms. He didn't stop moving with me, coaxing out every last shudder, until I was spent, my chest heaving, my pulse pounding in my ears. Then, he buried his face in my neck, his own release finding him with a groan so deep it vibrated through me, his arms wrapping around me like he'd never let go.

When it was over, we stayed tangled together, foreheads pressed, breathing the same air. My body still hummed, my heart still raced, but there was a different heat now – slower, sweeter, like embers that refused to die out. I didn't want to move. Didn't want to break whatever magic was wrapped around us. All I could do was hold him and hope he felt it too.

Chapter Fourteen

VITA

I was sprawled across my couch, one leg hanging off the side, half watching some random true crime show, when my phone lit up. I grinned before I even answered, seeing that it was Braylen.

"Hey, girl."

Her voice was practically buzzing through the line. "Vita, I'm having a boy!"

I sat up so fast that my blanket slid to the floor. "Shut up! Are you serious?"

She laughed, the sound bright and infectious. "Dead serious. We just left the appointment. I saw him on the ultrasound. His tiny little feet, tiny little hands, he's so perfect."

I couldn't help but smile so wide my cheeks hurt. "Oh, my God, Bray. A little boy. Do you realize how spoiled this kid is about to be? I'm talking designer sneakers before he can even walk."

She laughed again, softer this time, like she was letting herself savor the moment. I could hear how happy she was in every breath. And I loved that for her. I loved how she was still strong, still moving on. I was happy that she didn't allow this baby to bring her back to Kyrie. Braylen was my best friend, and I knew she deserved all of this and more. I leaned back into the couch, curling my legs underneath me.

"So, tell me everything. What's the plan for the nursery? Don't tell me you're gonna be one of those plain beige moms."

Braylen snorted. "Please. I already ordered the paint. I'm doing a full galaxy theme. My baby boy's room is going to be perfect."

I grinned. "You're going all out already. I love it. And you know I'm getting him the flyest baby Jordans, right?"

"I wouldn't expect anything less," she said, her tone playfully smug. Then, her voice softened. "It's weird, Vita. Seeing him on the screen today, knowing he's real. I didn't think I'd ever feel this way."

I let a beat of silence hang there because I knew what she meant without her having to explain. "You deserve every bit of this happiness, Bray. And you know I've got your back. Whatever you need, whatever he needs, I got y'all."

"I know," she said, and I could hear the smile in her voice.

We stayed on the phone a little longer, talking baby names, laughing over ridiculous options. I promised I'd come over soon to help her paint, even though I knew I'd mostly be there for snacks and moral support. My best friend was having a son. And I couldn't wait to meet him.

"I'm about to start planning your baby shower right now."

Braylen laughed. "Girl, please, a baby shower? I don't need all that. I'm just happy for a beautiful, healthy baby."

"Bitch, yes the hell you do need all that. Yes, we pray for a beautiful, healthy baby; however, you having a baby shower," I said, leaning forward on the couch. "I'm planning you the best baby shower anyone's ever seen."

Braylen laughed. "Vita..."

"Nope, don't argue with me. It's already decided. We're talking full decorations, a theme, food that'll have people talking for weeks, and games so good folks will forget to post on Instagram."

She chuckled, a warm, almost shy sound. "Alright, alright, do what you do because I know you gonna do that anyway. But nothing too over the top, okay?"

I grinned even though she couldn't see me. "Girl, my 'not over the top' is still luxury. Just let me handle it. All you have to do is show up looking like the glowing goddess you are."

Braylen sighed, but it was the kind of sigh that meant she was giving in. "Fine. But I get to approve the guest list."

"Deal," I said quickly. "And trust me, you won't regret it."

I was still smiling as Braylen and I went back-and-forth about whether she'd let me do an ice sculpture for the baby shower when my other line started buzzing. I glanced at the screen to see it was Victor.

"Hold on, girl," I said into the phone. "My man's calling. I'll call you back."

Braylen chuckled. "Alright, go tend to your man then. Call me back later."

I clicked over. "Hey, you."

Victor's deep voice rolled through the line. "Get dressed."

I raised an eyebrow even though he couldn't see me. "Good morning to you too. Why am I getting dressed?"

"Because," he said, like it was the simplest answer in the world, "I'm taking you shopping. So, get dressed and I'll be there in an hour."

My lips curled into a slow smile. "What's the occasion?"

"You," he replied without hesitation then hung up before I could push for details.

I set the phone down, heart doing that weird little skip it always did when he was in one of his decisive moods. Shopping with Victor wasn't the kind of trip where you picked up a candle and a pair of jeans. It was the kind of trip that left you with bags you couldn't carry yourself and a glow that had nothing to do with the store lighting.

I shot off the couch, the excitement buzzing in my chest. If Victor said an hour, that meant I really had forty-five minutes before he was pulling up outside. I headed straight for my bathroom, taking a quick shower, before going to my bedroom. I flung open the closet doors. I wanted something that felt effortless but still showed that I looked good. My fingers slid past a row of sweaters before landing on a sleek, cream-colored ribbed midi dress that hugged my curves without suffocating them. It was soft but had enough shape to make him look at me the way he always did.

For shoes, I went with nude block heels – comfortable enough for walking around the mall, tall enough to give me that extra sway in my hips. I padded over to my vanity, pulling my locs out of the messy bun I'd slept in. I spritzed them with rosewater, running my fingers through until each coil fell into place, then twisted a few pieces in the front into loose, face-framing spirals. The rest flowed down my back, swaying when I moved.

Once I was dressed, it was time for me to choose my fragrance. I layered Zara's Red Vanilla with Sol de Janeiro's Brazilian Crush 62. Together, they made this warm, sweet, slightly fruity scent bubble. By the time I was slipping my gold hoops in, I heard my phone chime, and I knew it was Victor telling me that he was outside. A quick swipe of gloss, one last check in the mirror, and I was out the door.

Victor was leaning against his car when I stepped out, black turtle-neck hugging his chest, sunglasses perched low on his nose. The slow grin he gave me when he saw me made my heart flutter.

"Damn," he said, his gaze running down my body and back up again. "You look good enough to skip shopping altogether."

I laughed, sliding into the passenger seat. "We can shop first then you can figure out what to do with me later."

Victor drove with one hand on the wheel, the other resting lazily on my thigh, as if he owned it and me. The city rolled past in a blur of storefronts and traffic lights, but all I could think about was the slight squeeze of his fingers and the smug smirk tugging at the corner of his lips. We pulled into the kind of high-end shopping district I usually only admired through Instagram posts – polished sidewalks, sparkling glass windows, sales associates with smiles just this side of rehearsed. The air smelled faintly of espresso from the café on the corner mixed with the faint perfume drifting from the boutique doors that stood propped open.

Victor parked in front of the first store, something European with a name I couldn't pronounce without embarrassing myself. He opened the door for me when we walked into the store. Inside, the lighting was soft but somehow made everything shimmer like it belonged in a fashion editorial. Racks of silk blouses and tailored trousers lined the walls, and shoes were displayed like art.

"Pick what you like," he spoke casually, as if he'd just told me to grab a bottle of water from the fridge.

My instinct was to gravitate toward the sale rack, but his gaze cut across the space between us. "Don't even think about it. I said what you like, not what you think I want to pay for."

So, I let myself look, really look. My fingers grazed over buttery leather jackets, cashmere sweaters that felt like clouds, and dresses that would make my most confident days feel like a runway moment.

Victor stayed close, occasionally reaching over my shoulder to pull something from the rack. "This one's you," he murmured, holding up a sleek emerald dress that dipped low in the back. I didn't argue, just added it to the growing pile in the sales associate's arms.

By the time we hit the fitting room, I was carrying enough clothing to warrant a fashion montage. Victor leaned against the wall, arms crossed, watching me emerge in outfit after outfit. He didn't comment much, just let his eyes do most of the talking.

"That one's coming home with us," he'd say in that low voice whenever I stepped out in something he particularly liked.

After clothes came shoes, rows upon rows of them, each pair more tempting than the last. I tried on a pair of strappy black heels so comfortable it felt criminal, and Victor just nodded. "We'll take them in every color."

I laughed, thinking he was joking, until the associate started pulling out the same style in nude, red, and metallic gold. Bags were next. Victor had a way of holding each one against me like he was testing how it looked in his hands before deciding if I was worthy of it, or maybe if it was worthy of me. By the time we left the third boutique, I was loaded down with sleek branded shopping bags, the kind that crinkle differently because they're made from thick, expensive paper. My arms were tired, but my heart felt light in a way I couldn't explain.

"You're spoiling me," I teased as we headed toward the next shop.

He gave me that slow, dangerous smile. "No, I'm investing. There's a difference."

We stopped for a break at a quiet rooftop café. It was beautiful with marble tables and little gold spoons for the sugar. The city stretched out below us, all glittering windows and bustling streets. Victor ordered without asking me, and somehow, he got it exactly right, iced lavender latte with an almond croissant on the side.

We sat there for a while, the afternoon sun spilling across the table, our shopping bags piled high like trophies. I caught him watching me more than once, his expression soft in a way that made me feel like the most important thing in the world. When we finally called it a day, the trunk of his car looked like we were moving into a designer showroom.

He drove one-handed again, his palm warm and steady on my thigh, and I realized this wasn't just about clothes or shoes or handbags. This was Victor marking me in his own way, making sure the world saw me the way he did, letting everyone know that I belonged to him. And I couldn't even pretend I didn't like it.

Victor's hand was at the small of my back as we got out the car and started walking up Woodward Avenue toward a boutique.

"This is the last stop," he announced as he held the door open after we were buzzed in.

Inside, the air was warm, scented faintly of vanilla and something floral I couldn't place. A thick, light-skinned woman with multiple tattoos across her arms stood . She was short and stood on her tiptoes when she hugged Victor. She had on a long blonde lace frontal that went well with her skin tone. Her presence filled the room, confident and effortless.

Victor's lips curved into that small, knowing smile.

"Vita, this is Monique," he said smoothly. "Monique, this is Vita."

She gave me a quick once over. There was nothing nasty about it, just the kind of measuring glance a woman like her could give without making you feel slighted. Then, she smiled at me genuinely.

"Well, aren't you stunning?" she said, her voice low and rich like she'd swallowed honey.

Before I could thank her, Victor leaned in slightly toward her. "Why don't you grab us some champagne?"

Her brows arched just for a second. Then, she nodded and disappeared toward the back, the faint click of her heels following her.

I turned to Victor. "Champagne? For shopping?"

He grinned. "For you, this isn't just shopping. This is me showing you the best."

We settled into the plush velvet chairs near the window, the city lights beginning to twinkle outside like scattered diamonds. Monique handed us each a flute of champagne, the bubbles tickling my nose as I took a careful sip.

"I have to say," I told her, swirling the glass in my hand, "you have some really beautiful pieces in this boutique."

She smiled, eyes glinting with something both warm and knowing. "Thank you, Vita."

Her gaze flickered to Victor, who gave a slight nod, just enough to tell her the message without saying a word.

"He's made it clear," Monique said smoothly, voice dropping to a more private tone, "that anything you want here is yours."

I felt a flush rise to my cheeks as Victor's eyes locked with mine, his usual confident smirk playing at the edges of his lips. Monique downed the rest of her champagne in one elegant tilt of her head then stood and crossed the few steps to sit beside me. Her presence was magnetic – close enough to feel the warmth of her skin – the subtle scent of her perfume mixing with the champagne haze.

"You have great taste," she said softly, leaning in just a bit. "I'll show you a few things I think you'll love."

Victor stayed back a step, watching us with that same slow, deliberate intensity. The moment stretched between us, thick with promise and something unspoken. Monique slid a little closer on the plush velvet sofa, her hand drifting to rest softly on my thigh. The touch was warm, sending a slow shiver up my spine. Her eyes held mine, dark and full of something unspoken, as she smiled and whispered, "You're absolutely beautiful, Vita."

I swallowed hard, my gaze flickering up to Victor, who sat back watching us with that knowing, pleased smile. It was like he was fully enjoying this moment as much as I was. Monique's fingers moved slowly, tracing gentle circles on the inside of my thigh, her touch feather-light but electrifying. My breath hitched when she shifted her hand slightly, fingers teasing beneath the fabric of my dress, finding the sensitive skin just beneath.

Through the thin material, her other hand found its way to the swell of my breasts. I felt her fingers press lightly against my nipples, both playful and possessive, sending a rush of heat spreading through me. It was both shocking and intoxicating, the way she dared to touch me like this, with confidence, with desire.

I leaned back slightly, heart pounding, eyes locked on Monique's, as the moment stretched between us, a delicious dance of teasing and anticipation. Victor's gaze never left us, his smile deepening with silent approval.

Monique's fingers lingered, her touch light but purposeful, as if she wanted me to feel every inch of her attention. She leaned closer, the faint scent of her perfume mingling with the warmth of the room. Her eyes sparkled with a mix of mischief and something softer, something more intimate.

My breath caught again as her hand slid just a bit higher, tracing delicate patterns along my thigh. I could feel the heat pooling inside me, the flutter of nerves and excitement that came with being wanted like this. Monique slid my panties down, placing my thighs over her shoulders as she positioned her face between them. The first lick from her tongue sent shockwaves throughout my entire body. Her hands pushed my dress over my thighs as she continued to lick. I hissed when her tongue flickered my love button.

I watched as Victor walked around the couch, bending down and pulling my dress above my head. Removing my breasts from the cups of my bra, he twirled his thumbs around my nipples. My breath hitched with the dual sensations. Victor's hands on my breasts and Monique's tongue on my pussy, licking hungrily, had me making sounds I'd never made before.

"Fuckkk," I moaned breathlessly, my hand now fisting Monique's hair.

"Don't stop. Fuck, don't stop." I looked up at Victor while I spoke; however, I was talking to Monique.

Monique's licks grew more confident, more controlled, her tongue tracing slow circles over my clit. She licked, sucked gently, then licked again, all while Victor's fingers teased my nipples. I looked down, watching her, just as she looked up.

"Does it feel good, beautiful?" she whispered against my skin.

"Too good." I licked my lips. "Make me cum." The command was so bold even I couldn't believe it came from my mouth, but I meant every word.

"Oh, I'm going to make you cum. You can be sure of that."

I felt Victor release my nipples, but at that point, I didn't care. I was too focused on Monique and the way she was making me feel that I didn't care. Every lick and suck made me shiver. The loud slurping noises her tongue made against my juices were the bassline to the soundtrack of my moans. Her lips and tongue traced delicate patterns, awakening every nerve ending I had.

I moaned as Monique moved in a slow trail from my clit to my asshole. The tip of her tongue moving in slow circles. A soft presence that sent shivers down my spine. I closed my eyes, breath hitching from the sensation. Victor was back, hands working my nipples softly, as Monique licked my ass. When I finally looked back up to Victor, his pants were off, and his manhood was standing at attention.

Slowly, I leaned up, letting my lips brush against him before opening my mouth and taking him in. A low moan escaped his lips as I sucked deep. He rubbed his thumb on my cheek softly as he looked down at me.

"That's right, baby. Suck that dick while she eats your pussy and ass. Show Daddy you like it."

And I did. I sucked Victor's dick sloppily as I grinded my hips on Monique's face. I cupped Victor's balls, allowing one of my fingers to rub slow circles on his asshole.

"Fuck! Yes. That's it, baby. Make me cum. Make me cum down that pretty little throat."

I could feel my orgasm building; I was about to cum right in Monique's mouth, and I was ready for it. When she sucked my clit once more, that was all she wrote. I came in her mouth. Victor pulled his glistening dick from my mouth. Monique kissed my pussy once more before standing to her feet.

"You taste like sugar. Next time, lick each other."

Chapter Fifteen

KYRIE

It had been a few weeks since Jason's cousin hooked me up with that live feed to Banks' house. At first, I told myself it was enough. Hell, it was more than I'd had in months. I could see her whenever I wanted. Watch her move through her day like I was right there in the room with her. But the more I watched, the worse it got. I'd sit there for hours, glued to the screen, letting everything else in my life fall away. Missed calls, skipped meals, it didn't matter. My entire world was in that little glowing square. The only time I was away from the TV was when I was with Vic and the crew, making money. Other than that, I was in the house, waiting for Braylen to come outside so that I could see her.

Every week, I'd put some cash in an envelope, label it 'Mrs. Banks', and slide it into their mailbox. I wanted to take care of her, even if she didn't want me anymore. But even with the feed, even with the envelopes, it wasn't enough. It was never enough. Watching her only when she went outside was like starving while staring at a table full of food I couldn't touch. My chest ached with it. My skin itched with it - the need to see her all the time, to hear her voice, to see her face up close.

It was eating me alive, the way I wanted her – not just her body but her, all of her. The way she'd look at me when she was mad, like she was trying to burn a hole straight through my skull. The way she'd touch me without thinking, like I was hers without question. The way she said my name unlike any other. But now, I was just a shadow, a ghost in her life, watching from the outside, feeding my hunger with stolen moments and blurry glimpses. And the more I watched, the more I realized I wasn't gonna survive like this for long.

I sat, hunched over on the couch, the glow from my laptop painting the living room in cold light. Braylen was on the screen, walking out the front door, smiling as she walked to the black SUV that was waiting for her. She wasn't even doing anything special, just existing, and I couldn't look away. My eyes followed every tilt of her head, every movement of her fingers. Weeks of this, hours every day, and still it wasn't enough.

The feed was a blessing and a curse. Yeah, it let me see her, but only when she left the house. And it ate at me, day by day, like rust chewing through metal. The hunger for her was constant. It crawled under my skin, gnawed at my ribs.

My phone rang, jolting me out of my trance. I snatched it up without looking, my eyes still locked on the screen.

"Mr. Parker," the voice on the other end started. It was Isaiah, my attorney. "Just calling to let you know the divorce had been finalized."

I froze. "What?"

"It's official. Papers are stamped, and Braylen has signed them. You're a free man."

Free man. The words hit like a slap. My stomach clenched, heat rushing up my chest. "No, no, no. You told me I had more time. You said we could stall this. What happened to that?"

There was a pause, then his voice came back, too damn calm. "We did stall it. We stalled it for over a month. But the court moved it forward this week. It's done."

Something in me snapped. My voice came out low and sharp, almost shaking. "You lied to me. You promised me more time. This wasn't enough."

"I told you I could try to stall it, but eventually, the courts would push it through, and that's what happened. I delayed it as much as possible."

"I don't wanna hear that shit!" I barked, my hand tightening around the phone so hard my knuckles ached. My jaw locked until it hurt, my pulse thundering in my ears. That sick, boiling feeling spread through my veins, like gasoline just waiting for a match.

The thought of Braylen being *officially* gone, on paper, made me feel hollow and on fire at the same time. It was more than anger. It was loss. It was knowing someone had ripped something out of me I wasn't ready to give up.

I wanted to throw the phone. Smash it against the wall. Drive to this lawyer's office and put my hands around his neck just to make him *understand* what he'd done. Instead, I sat there, teeth grinding, hand trembling, eyes flickering back to the laptop screen. The black SUV was gone and so was Braylen. I'd missed her.

I sat there, still seething, after hanging up on Isaiah, my eyes locked on the grainy live feed like it was the only thing keeping me from losing my mind completely. The anger burned under my skin, but the sight, the hope, that Braylen would soon come back to the house, and I could see her again, gave me hope. I'd been living off these stolen glimpses for weeks, telling myself that it was enough just to see her for a short time. Enough to just watch her walk out to check the mail or walk to and from the car. But now, I knew I needed more.

The thought started as a whisper in my head, but it grew until it was shouting, clawing at my skull. I didn't just want to watch her for short moments a day. I wanted to see her closer. See her face when she was sitting in her living room. See her laying in bed at night. Hear her voice when she thought nobody was around. Before I could overthink it, I picked up my phone and called Jason's cousin. The line rang twice before he answered, his voice lazy, like I'd woken him up.

"What up doe?"

"It's Kyrie," I announced, my tone flat but sharp enough to cut. "We need to meet. Today."

He gave a short chuckle. "What, you runnin' out of envelopes already?"

"Just meet me," I snapped. "Rouge Park, thirty minutes."

The park was mostly empty when I got there. It was still early in the day and a bit chilly outside, so that was expected. I sat on a bench under a half-dead oak, keeping my hood up over my head as if I didn't want to be seen. Jason's cousin rolled up fifteen minutes later in a black Impala. He spotted me and strolled over, wearing a smirk that I already wanted to knock off his face.

"What up doe?" he asked, hands in his pockets like we were just two friends catching up.

I got straight to it. "The cameras you set up for the live feed, they're good. But they're not good enough."

He smirked. "Not good enough? You gettin' clear visuals of her driveway, the porch, the backyard. What more do you want?"

"I don't care about her driveway," I cut in, leaning forward. "I want to see her inside the house."

He blinked, tilting his head like he was trying to figure out if I was serious. "Inside? Man, that ain't no small thing. That's a whole different kinda setup. Different risks and a different price tag."

"I didn't ask about the price," I spoke, locking eyes with him. "I asked if it could happen."

Jason's cousin rubbed at his jaw, glancing toward the basketball court like he was debating if this conversation was worth the trouble. "Anything's possible depending on how bad you want it. But you're talkin' about inside cameras. That's risky and takes planning. That's not just something I can just walk up and do."

I shifted on the bench, my knee bouncing. "Jason told me you was the plug for this type of shit, so I'm sure you can come up with a way. I don't care what it cost. I need to know if you can get it done."

He let out a low whistle, studying me. "You sound pressed, man. Like, real pressed. What you tryna see so bad? You can't sleep at night without it or something?"

My jaw tightened. "Look, you don't need to be asking no questions about why or what. Can you do the job, or am I wasting my time?"

He thought for a second then grinned slow, like he'd just pulled a card from his back pocket. "You ever heard of long-range Wi-Fi cameras? I ain't talking about them cheap Ring doorbells. I mean something military-grade, small enough to sit inside a tree knot or a birdhouse. They can link up to any device within a certain range, including whatever smart devices they got inside."

I frowned. "Inside?"

"Yeah. Everybody's house got smart TVs, smart speakers, tablets. If you plant a signal repeater somewhere close enough, I can hijack the devices that's inside the home. Use them all as cameras and link them to a feed that you will have access to."

"How close we talking?"

His eyes scanned the park, like he was measuring distances in his head. "Close enough that the signal can catch. Maybe fifty yards from the house. But it gotta be hidden somewhere it won't get moved."

My mind was already racing. "Where would I hide something like that?"

"Bird feeder. Decorative lawn lights. Even one of them fake rocks for a sprinkler system. Anything that can sit on their property line without looking suspicious. I don't need it to be inside. I just need it to be close enough to piggyback off their Wi-Fi and start pulling the video feeds from their own cameras or devices. Hell, some of these smart TVs got built-in mics and cameras that people forget are even there."

I sat back, processing it. "So. you could put me in the living room with her? The bedroom, the bathroom, anywhere in the house?"

"If she's in range of one of the devices, yeah. And it wouldn't be just seeing her. You'll hear her too."

My hands balled into fists without thinking about it. "Do it. Whatever it takes. I'll get you the money."

He raised an eyebrow. "No, you'll pay upfront, twenty-five thousand, cash. When you pay, then I'll give you the device to plant. After that, I'll set everything up, and you can start whatever freak show this is."

"Cool, meet me back here in an hour, and I'll have your money," I assured before going back to my car.

Exactly an hour later, I was back at the park with twenty-five thousand cash in an envelope just as requested. I handed him the money, and he handed me a small black device. It was no bigger than a deck of cards. He told me to hide it good, but close, and to call him when the job was done. Getting back in my car, I headed back home. I knew the device had to be close to the house in order for it to work, so I knew I would have to wait until night in order to place it. Sitting on my couch, I watched the feed that I had until night fell and I was able to go plant the device.

I threw on a black hoodie, a pair of gloves, and black jeans. I made sure to take off all jewelry, leaving everything shiny or traceable at home. I put a ski mask in my pocket, just in case. The matte black device with a magnetic back and a waterproof shell was in my hand. It wasn't just a tracker; it was a feed transmitter. Once it was live, Jason's cousin could pull video, audio, GPS everything, and I'd be able to watch it.

I waited until just after midnight. I wanted to make sure that their neighbors would be sleeping, and I wouldn't be seen. The street was quiet enough to hear my own pulse in my ears when I turned onto it. I killed my lights halfway down, coasting slow like I knew exactly where I was going. His house sat back behind a thick iron gate, floodlights on either side. That was what made it tricky. At night, you couldn't get too close without being lit up like a stage. But there were blind spots; every setup had them. I'd studied his property from the little glimpses I'd gotten from the outdoor feed. The northwest corner, just past the edge of the fence line, and a trail with no cameras or streetlights were still close enough for the device to pick up their Wi-Fi.

I parked down the street. Getting out the car, I slid my ski mask over my head. The night air was cold as I walked up toward the back of the house. I ducked low, jogging toward the trail. I looked over at the house. It was dark except for one light on upstairs. A warm yellow glow spilled out, and my chest tightened when I pictured her moving around in there. She didn't know I was this close, even though I wanted her to.

I forced myself to focus. I found the metal post where the fence met the ground, reached out, and pressed the device against it. The magnet snapped into place with a soft click. Once Jason's cousin worked his magic, I would have access to the entire house. I was just about to leave when the porch light clicked on, and I froze.

The front door opened, and Banks stepped out. He didn't look my way as he walked over to one of the SUVs parked in the driveway. I watched as he opened the trunk and pulled out a Saks Fifth bag before walking back inside. I waited until he went back inside before I slipped out and walked off. By the time I made it back to my car, my hands were shaking. It was not from fear but from the adrenaline, from the thought of what I could do with this feed once it was live.

Once I was home, I called Jason's cousin and let him know the device had been planted. I knew he would do what he had to do, and soon, I would be watching Braylen from inside the house. For the first night in weeks, I didn't watch the feed. Instead, I went to sleep, happy about the moves I'd made.

That next morning, I woke up feeling refreshed. I turned on the feed and watched it as I ate my bowl of cereal. My phone rang, and I looked down to see Victor calling. He let me know that we would be hitting casinos over the weekend and that I should be ready to bring my A-game. I agreed before getting off the phone.

I spent the rest of the day watching the feed, while I was doing minimal housework. I washed a load of clothes and the few dishes that were in the sink. Around eight that night, I got a call from Jason's cousin, whose name I still didn't know. He told me that he was able to put a rush on it and that the feed was live. He told me the link had been sent to my email.

I darted for my laptop on the table, opening it and going straight to my email. I saw the link in blue. I pressed it and saw several different camera images, all of the inside of Banks' house. I clicked on one of the images when I saw her come into view. She looked so beautiful. She was standing there, back turned to me, but I could still see her beauty from behind. I smiled, but it faded the moment I saw Banks walk up and lift her into his arms from behind before kissing her on her lips. Rage shot through my body as he carried her out the room. I searched the screen for them frantically. A few moments later, I saw them walking into a bedroom. I watched in anger as Banks removed Braylen's clothes and buried his head between her thighs.

She moaned, arching her back, as she opened her legs wider, allowing him access. I recoiled, shaking my head. I couldn't believe my wife was allowing that man to please her, to lick and kiss the very spot that was supposed to be mine. The way she moaned was unlike anything I'd ever heard. Braylen had never moaned for me in that way. I watched in agony as Banks savored her, tasting what was supposed to only be for me.

I watched as Banks stood up and removed his clothes. He laid sideways on the bed and pulled Braylen on top of him. At first, I thought I was seeing things, thought my eyes were playing horrible tricks on me. I closed my eyes, rubbing them, before opening them again. My eyes locked on that little curve of her stomach again. It was subtle but undeniable. *Oh, my God, is Braylen pregnant?* The realization slammed into me like a fist to the gut. My throat tightened, and I swallowed hard, anger twisting into something darker, colder.

I leaned in closer to the screen. I wanted to zoom in but was afraid that I would fuck up the feed altogether. *She's let that man get her pregnant? I was her husband, yet she is pregnant by another man? How could she let this happen?* I wanted to lash out, to fuck her and him up, but I couldn't. I knew she would never be with me if I did that. If I lost my head, I'd lose the only thing that mattered, and that was her.

I stormed into the kitchen, yanking open cabinets, slamming dishes together, the clatter loud enough to drown out the chaotic noise in my mind. Every break was a crack in the walls I was building around my pain. I ripped a glass from the shelf and crushed it under my heel, watching the blood from a small cut drip down slowly. My chest heaved as anger shot through me.

A guttural scream tore from deep in my soul. I punched a hole into the dining room wall before sliding to the floor. There, on the floor, curled up like a baby, I cried. I cried hard for everything. For what I'd done to Braylen. For the fact that I had lost her forever. She was pregnant by another man, and I now knew that I was the cause of it all. She was mine. She could have still been mine if I didn't fuck it up. But I did.

Just then, as if a light bulb went off in my head, I sat up. Jumping up from the floor, wiping my tears, I ran back to my laptop. I watched closely, zeroing in on Braylen's stomach. That was not a stomach of a woman who just got pregnant. She had to be at least four or five months pregnant.

"That's my baby!" The realization hit me as a smile spread across my face.

Chapter Sixteen

BRAYLEN

The water was warm enough to hug my skin, a soft contrast to the October chill pressing against the glass walls of the pool room. Outside, Michigan had traded summer's glow for shades of copper and gold. Trees stood half-naked, and branches swayed in the cool breeze. Every few seconds, a gust rattled the tall windows, and stray maple leaves danced across the patio before getting caught in little whirlwinds.

I floated on my back, staring up at the ceiling's beams, letting my body drift wherever the water wanted to take me. The surface was calm except for the ripples my arms made, my fingers cutting through like they were painting lines. My hair floated around me, heavy with warmth and chlorine. It was easy to lose track of time in here, especially when the rest of the house felt so still. I loved being home, our home. Mine and A'zir's. It had become this strange, luxurious cage that I never wanted to leave.

I heard the door open, the slow creak cutting into the hush, and when I tilted my head, there A'zir was. He was wearing a black fitted tee and a pair of gray sweatpants. His eyes found me immediately, and he smiled.

"How long you been down here? Why you let me sleep so long? I'm usually the first one up."

"You looked like you needed your sleep."

He stepped in, letting the heavy door fall shut behind him, then started pulling off his shirt. My eyes followed automatically. No matter how much time I spent with him, that man's body still did something to me, the smooth planes of muscle, the faint ridges of his stomach, the tattoos on his chest, arms, and neck. He toed off his shoes, peeled away his sweats, and the next thing I knew, he was stepping down into the pool. The water lapped at his chest when he stopped a few feet away, his eyes staying on me like there was nothing else in the room worth looking at.

"Why you so quiet?" he asked.

"I'm not. I'm just relaxed."

"Mm." He moved closer, closing the space between us, until I could feel the water shifting around my body from his. "Or maybe you're thinking too much."

"About what?"

He dipped his head just enough so that his breath brushed my cheek. "About tonight."

I swallowed, the words curling in my stomach. "Meeting your parents?"

"Yeah. You nervous?"

The way he said it made it sound like I should be, like it was something to be nervous about.

"I don't know if nervous is the word."

His brow lifted slightly. "Then what's the word?"

I sighed and let my hands drift under the surface, fingertips brushing his arm before sliding away. "Excited."

"Aww, you're so cute." A'zir laughed.

"Boy, shut up." I laughed with him. "I just know meeting your parents is a big deal, and I hope I make a good impression."

"They will love you because I do."

"Did you tell them about the baby?" I asked, hanging my head low as if I was afraid to make eye contact.

He placed his hand under my chin, lifting my head so my eyes could meet his. "I told them that you're pregnant. That's all they know. That's all they need to know. That's all anyone needs to know."

I smiled, wrapping my arms around him, as I kissed him passionately. "I love you, A'zir."

"And I love you more, Braylen."

We stayed there for a moment, just drifting in the water. His hand slid from my hip to the small of my back, anchoring me against him, and I leaned in. Outside, the clouds shifted, letting a patch of pale sunlight wash across the yard before disappearing again behind the heavy gray clouds. It was such a Michigan fall day – moody, unpredictable, and beautiful. We swam together for about another hour.

After we got out of the pool, I wrapped myself in a thick towel and padded barefoot through the hall toward the kitchen. My skin was still warm from the water, and every step felt slow and lazy, like I didn't really want to start the day just yet. Banks trailed behind me, his towel slung low on his hips, droplets rolling down his chest. The sun had moved higher since we'd first come downstairs, but now, it had drifted behind the clouds, making the day look gloomy. The big windows along the back wall of the kitchen framed the bare branches swaying in the wind, leaves swirling across the yard like little gold coins.

I moved toward the fridge, but Banks stepped in front of me, pulling the door open himself. "Sit," he said, nodding toward one of the bar stools at the island. His voice had that tone that made it sound less like a suggestion and more like an order. I sat, still clutching my towel around me, watching as he started pulling out ingredients – eggs, butter, green peppers, onions, cheese. Then, he grabbed two oranges from the fruit basket and tossed one up in the air before setting it down on the counter.

"You cooking for me? Where the hell is Marcus?" I teased, leaning on my elbows.

He gave me a quick side-eye as he reached for the cutting board. "I'm cooking for us. I gave him the day off since we having dinner with my parents tonight."

I frowned. "I hope you know what you doing. Don't have me sick and not able to go to dinner tonight."

"I am Chef Boyar Banks. Now sit yo' nervous ass down and wait on this food."

I burst out laughing. "Boy, I'm not nervous."

A'zir shook his head and turned to the stove. While he worked the skillet, I peeled one of the oranges, letting the sweet citrus smell fill the air. The sound of the peppers and onions sizzling mixed with the wind outside, making the house feel cozy. When the omelets were done, he slid them onto two plates then poured orange juice into glasses. We ate at the island, knees brushing under the counter. Every now and then, his hand would rest on my thigh. After breakfast, I started to get up to rinse the plates, but he caught my wrist and shook his head.

"Leave it and come on. I'll get it in a minute."

I raised a brow. "Where are we going?"

"Downstairs."

"What?" I asked, confused.

"I want you to paint me."

"You serious?" I asked, still looking up at him.

"Dead ass. Let's go. We got about five hours before it's time for us to start getting dressed. Do you think that's enough time?"

I took his hand, smiling from ear to ear, as I led him downstairs to my art room. A'zir took the towel from around his waist, exposing his naked body. He sat down on the sage green chair he'd purchased for the room. I turned, grabbing all the paints I would need for the portrait.

"Why do I feel like you're trying to distract me from tonight?" I asked.

"Because I am." He swung one leg over the arm of the chair. "If I can keep you relaxed now, maybe you won't overthink later."

I tilted my head back to look at him. "So, you think I'm gonna embarrass you or something?"

"Nah." His lips curved. "I think you're gonna own that whole fuckin' room. I just don't want you stressing yourself out before we even get there."

I nodded my head, letting him know that I understood. For the next four hours, I stood there, painting him, as he talked and laughed. When I was done, A'zir looked at the painting, smiling. He let me know that he was going to hang it up in our bedroom. I laughed and nodded.

I stood in front of the floor-to-ceiling mirror in our bedroom, towel wrapped around my body, my braids falling down my back. Steam still clung to my skin from the shower I'd just taken. Outside, the sky was dimming into that moody gray as the day turned to night. A'zir was in the closet, sliding hangers back-and-forth with that quiet decisiveness he had when he was choosing something to wear. He took dressing seriously, like every outfit was an announcement. I heard the faint click of shoe boxes opening, the smooth scrape of leather soles as he tested a pair in his hand.

"What are you wearing?" he called, voice deep and casual.

"I don't know yet," I said, stepping into the closet. "But I know I gotta wear something classy to meet your parents."

His mouth curved into that slow, knowing grin as he looked up from the blazer he'd just pulled from the hanger. "You damn sure don't have to be classy for my parents. They both dress to the nines, but I don't know about classy." A'zir laughed.

I rolled my eyes, though heat crept up my neck. He laid the blazer over the valet stand and kept building his outfit – tailored black trousers with a subtle sheen, a white dress shirt with a spread collar, and a deep midnight-blue velvet blazer that caught the light every time it moved. It wasn't loud, but it had that quiet richness that he always had.

"You like?" he asked, sliding into the trousers.

"Mhmm," I said, leaning against the door frame. "It's giving... 'my son's successful, and yes, we like her.'"

He smirked, fastening his belt. "And what about you? What's the statement?"

I slipped past him to my side of the closet. My fingers skimmed over hangers until they landed on the black silk slip dress I'd been saving for something special. It was cut on the bias, the kind of thing that clung in the right places and draped everywhere else. I paired it with a floor-length, camel-colored coat. It was warm enough for the weather but soft enough to feel indulgent. When I turned, A'zir's eyes were on me like I'd just answered a question he hadn't asked out loud.

"That's the one," he said, no hesitation.

I laid the dress across the ottoman and went to work on my hair, pinning my braids back into a low bun. Makeup came next, bronzed cheeks, a warm nude lip, and enough highlight to catch the light when I smiled. A'zir moved behind me, buttoning his shirt, the faint scent of his cologne already curling into the air.

"What is that you wear? It smells good," I asked, glancing over my shoulder.

He grinned like he'd been waiting for me to notice. "Parfums de Marly's Herod."

It was rich, a little spicy, with a warmth that made me want to lean into him.

"You're making it hard to concentrate," I murmured, slipping into my dress.

His gaze followed me like a slow caress, trailing from my shoulders to the slit at my thigh. "Good," he said simply, stepping into his loafers.

I reached for my own fragrance, a bottle of Tom Ford's Santal Blush. It was creamy sandalwood with a little floral bite, soft but memorable. I dabbed it at my pulse points, knowing it would mix with the warmth of my skin by the time we got to dinner.

He came to stand behind me at the mirror, his hands resting lightly at my waist. "You ready?" he asked, though his tone said he already knew the answer.

I looked at us in the reflection – him in velvet and tailored perfection, me in silk and subtle confidence. We looked good together, like we'd been doing this for years instead of months.

"Almost," I replied, smoothing the front of my dress.

A'zir adjusted his cuffs, slid on his watch, and tucked a pocket square into his blazer. Everything about him was meticulous but never stiff. I stepped into my heels and grabbed my clutch.

"You good?" he asked, watching me slip on my coat.

"Yeah, I'm good. Just ready to meet your parents."

His expression softened, and for a moment, the air between us shifted from playful to intimate. "They nosy asses ready to meet you too."

We stood there for a second longer, just looking at each other. Then, he offered his arm, the faintest smile playing at his lips. "Let's go make an entrance."

As we headed toward the door, the combined scents of Herod and Santal Blush lingered in the air, like a promise that whatever the night held, we'd face it together and look damn good doing it.

———

The restaurant looked like money but not the kind of money that screamed in bright neon or glittered like some club bottle service table. This was quiet money, the self-assured kind that spoke in silk, marble, and candlelight. The moment we stepped through the tall glass doors, I felt like I was walking into another world. The lobby smelled faintly of fresh flowers, and the polished black marble floor was so spotless it mirrored the lights from the crystal chandeliers above. Soft jazz floated through the air, played live by a trio tucked into the corner of the dining room.

I glanced at A'zir, who had his hand on the small of my back. He hadn't told me the name of the restaurant until we pulled up, and even then, it sounded like a place you couldn't just call and book. The hostess, a tall woman with sleek hair and a flawless black dress, greeted him with a warm, familiar smile.

"Mr. Banks," she greeted, her voice as smooth as champagne. "Your table is ready. Your guests are already here."

He leaned down, his lips brushing my temple in a way that felt casual to anyone watching, but to me, it was like he was telling me without words to relax. "You ready?" he murmured.

"As I'll ever be," I replied, forcing a light laugh.

We followed the hostess through the dining room. I tried to keep my eyes from darting everywhere, but the place was worth looking at. Every table was draped in crisp white linen, each one set with gold-rimmed plates and tall wine glasses that caught the light. Couples sat close, leaning into private conversations over candlelight, waiters gliding between tables like they'd been choreographed. The hostess walked us to the table where I saw Banks' parents already sitting.

His father wore a perfectly tailored charcoal suit. His salt-and-pepper hair was cut short, his jaw clean-shaven. His eyes were sharp, scanning me in a way that was polite but assessing, like he was filing away details for later. His mother was a light skinned woman with a short cut. She wore an emerald green strapless dress that showed off her sleeve of tattoos. She wore gold hoops and a diamond ring that caught the candlelight every time she moved her hand. Her smile was warm when she looked at me, but there was a weight behind it I couldn't place.

"Ma, Pops," A'zir spoke easily, pulling out my chair for me before taking his own. "This is Braylen. Bray, this is my mother, Monique, and my father, Victor."

Monique leaned in first, her voice smooth. "So nice to finally meet you, Braylen. We've heard quite a bit."

I smiled back, trying to ignore how the words "quite a bit" made my stomach dip.

"All good things, I hope."

Victor chuckled, deep and low. "We'll see."

I let out a breathy laugh, though inside, I was already reading between the lines. They were sizing me up, and no matter how polite they were, I knew they had questions. Maybe more than I was ready for. Menus were passed, but A'zir barely glanced at his. He knew what he wanted. I took longer, pretending to read the descriptions of truffle risotto and seared sea bass, but really just trying to slow my heartbeat.

The waiter brought wine, a bottle so expensive they didn't list the price. He poured for all of us. Monique talked about the vintage like she'd been in the vineyard herself, and Victor nodded along, sipping and agreeing.

"How long have you and A'zir been together?" Monique asked, her gaze fixed on me.

I swallowed, keeping my voice steady. "A little while now."

"A little while," Victor repeated, his tone curious. "And what is it you do, Braylen?"

"Braylen's an artist," A'zir spoke, answering for me.

Monique's expression didn't change, but Victor's eyes flickered, just for a second. The food arrived, plated like art. I'd ordered the pan-seared sea bass, while A'zir got the tomahawk steak, and his parents had matching plates of duck breast drizzled in something that shimmered under the lights. For the first few minutes, conversation stayed light, weather, travel, the restaurant's history. But there was an undercurrent, a tension I could feel in the space between words. Every so often, Victor's gaze would flicker to A'zir, then back to me, then down at his watch.

"You got somewhere to be, Pops?" A'zir finally asked.

"You know the money always calling. But I'm starting late tonight because I needed to be at this dinner. I had to meet the mother of my grandchild."

"I'm glad we could meet too. I told A'zir we should have met a long time ago."

A'zir reached under the table and hit my leg playfully, causing me to giggle. His hand found mine, and I held on to him. Dinner went on for another hour, and by the time it was over, Monique and I had exchanged numbers.

The second the front door clicked shut behind us, I came out of my shoes. A'zir didn't say a word. He hung his keys on the hook, his gaze cutting toward me so sharp I felt it in my skin. He moved slow, deliberate in a way that made my heart pound harder. I could hear the low hum of the fridge, the distant tick of the clock, and beneath it all... the sound of my own pulse in my ears.

He shrugged out of his coat, draping it over the chair like he had all night to deal with me. And maybe he did. His eyes told a different story, one that promised there would be no mercy tonight. I tried to walk past him toward the stairs, but his hand shot out, catching my wrist. The heat of his skin burned through me.

"Upstairs," he ordered, his voice low, dangerous, like the command wasn't up for discussion. I swallowed hard and moved. My heels clicked against the steps, and I could feel his presence behind me, close enough that my back tingled. When we reached the bedroom, I turned, but before I could speak, he shut the door with a quiet thud. He didn't touch me right away. He just stood there, watching.

"Take it off," he said.

The words were soft, but they cracked through the air like a whip. I hesitated only a second before sliding my dress down my shoulders. The fabric pooled at my feet, leaving me in lace and bare skin. His gaze dropped, slow, traveling over every inch of me like he was memorizing the view. He stepped forward, closing the space between us, until I could feel the heat radiating from his body. His hand came up, tracing the side of my neck, thumb pressing just enough to make my breath catch.

"You think I didn't see the way you were looking at me the entire time we were at dinner? You were looking at me like you wanted to put me on a plate."

I didn't answer, not because I didn't want to but because I couldn't. He tilted my chin up, forcing my eyes to meet his. He leaned forward, pressing his lips against mine. I moaned into the kiss, tasting the mint from the gum he had after dinner. My knees weakened, but his hand gripped my hip, holding me in place like he wasn't going to let me fall unless he wanted me to. When he finally pulled back, his eyes were darker, hungrier. He pushed me back until the back of my knees hit the bed. I fell onto it, looking up at him, and the faintest smirk tugged at his mouth before he followed me down.

The rest of the world faded. All I could see was him. All I could feel was him. And deep down, I knew I'd give him whatever he wanted, just as he'd given me.

Chapter Seventeen

VITA

I stood in the middle of the party supply aisle, squinting at several different shades of blue ribbon like my life depended on it. This was my girl's first baby, her first time being celebrated for something soft instead of just surviving something hard. I wanted it to be perfect because Braylen deserved perfection. I had the entire theme mapped out in my head the moment I told her I would throw the shower. It would be a Boho Blue Garden. I'd been scrolling Pinterest like a woman on a mission, screenshotting every balloon garland, flower wall, and grazing table I could find. We were talking powder blues, royal blues, soft creams, a few gold accents, and enough greenery to make it feel like we'd rented a secret garden. The vibe was going to be dreamy, delicate, and just a little bougie, exactly what Braylen deserved.

The cart I'd been pushing for the past hour was already ridiculously full. Inside, I had a stack of white ceramic cake stands in varying heights, three oversized vases for the faux eucalyptus I'd found, two rolls of rose gold table runners, and a literal mountain of disposable dinnerware that looked expensive but were just plastic. There were plates with scalloped edges, champagne flutes with gold rims, and powder and royal blue napkins, the whole nine.

As I moved toward the next aisle, my phone buzzed in my back pocket. I ignored it, too focused on finding the perfect welcome sign. I wanted something big, with the baby's name written in gold calligraphy, framed with cascading florals. I found a plain, white foam board sign just begging to be transformed and added it to the pile. Now, all I needed was a few more candles and something for the favor table.

By the time I made it to the checkout lane, I was half out of breath from pushing what felt like a small mountain in a cart. The cashier, a young girl with pink hair and silver eyeliner, gave me the kind of look that said, *Wow, somebody's really going all out.* I just smiled and started unloading.

"This is for a baby shower," I told her, mostly because I couldn't keep the excitement in. "My best friend's. She's having a baby boy."

"That's so cute," she said, scanning the cake stands. "Is it gonna be like one of those TikTok showers where everything matches?"

I laughed, more so because she was right. After twenty minutes of bagging, paying, and making a mental note to never check my bank account until after this was over, I wheeled everything out into the parking lot. The sun was high and warm, making the bags crinkle loudly as I loaded them into the trunk of my SUV. My shoulders ached, my wallet felt lighter, and my vision for the shower felt even clearer. I had just closed the trunk when my phone rang again. This time, I pulled it out, ready to ignore a spam call, but the name on the screen made me smile. It was Braylen.

"Hey, mama," I said as I slid into the driver's seat.

Her voice came through warm. "Hey, Vita. What you doing?"

"Spending too much money on you," I teased. "I just left the store. Girl, wait until you see this shower. It's about to look like it belongs in a magazine."

She let out a small laugh, but it didn't sound like her usual one. It was softer, almost cautious. "I can't wait, but that's not why I called."

The tone in her voice had my smile fading. "Aw, shit, what's going on?"

There was a pause. I could hear her take a breath on the other end, like she was steadying herself. "It's done."

I blinked, gripping the phone tighter. "Done? What's done?"

"Bitch, the divorce," she informed, relief evident in her voice. "Me and Kyrie, it's finalized. He tried to stall the divorce, but the courts finally pushed it through. I'm so fucking happy. I'm finally fuck boy free."

I sat there for a moment, staring out at the sunlit parking lot. I knew this day was coming, but it felt like it was taking so long. When Braylen and Kyrie first married, I thought that she would be dumb for him forever. But Braylen had finally smartened up, and I knew that Banks had everything to do with that.

"Wow," I breathed, finally finding my words. "I'm so glad. I know this makes you happy, and I'm happy for you."

"Yeah, I am happy. I can finally move on with my life with the man that I really love. I'm pretty sure I'm going to like this new chapter of my life better. I already am."

I leaned back in my seat, twisting one of my locs around my finger. "You walked through fire in that marriage and did it with a smile on your face. You took things that most women would have never, and it was all because you loved that nigga. I'm just happy that you finally love yourself more."

She was quiet for a beat then spoke again. "Yeah, me too. It's like I'm an entirely different person now. I'm even painting again, Vita. I have an entire art studio downstairs that A'zir put together for me. And I met his parents the other night."

"That's dope. I knew Banks was where it was at the first time I met him. He's good for you, Bray, and you deserve that."

"Yeah, I do deserve this, and so does my baby."

"What is the baby's name going to be? I want to make a sign, but I need his name."

Braylen paused. "We don't know yet. I'm still thinking. Just have the sign say Baby McFarland because I know for sure he will have A'zir's last name."

"Okay, Baby McFarland it is. I can't wait until you have him, so I can spoil Teetee's baby."

"Girl, I already know. But I can't wait to meet him either. I can't believe I'm really about to be somebody's mama."

"Well, believe it, bitch, because he gon' be here in about three and a half months. And while we on the subject, can we have the shower in your big ass house?"

"Of course we can. We can use the basement and decorate it however you want."

"Okay, cool. I'm going to finish my shopping, and I'll call you back when I get home and settled."

When we hung up, I put the car in gear and pulled out of the lot, my mind already shifting back into planner mode. The next stop was the bakery. I needed to lock in that three-tier cake with the blue ombré frosting and gold leaf accents before someone else snatched my date.

<hr>

I left the bakery with my debit card damn near crying for mercy after the purchase of a five-hundred-dollar cake. There would be no more stops for me today. I was tired and ready to go home. By the time I carried the last bag inside, my phone was buzzing across the kitchen counter. Victor's name lit up the screen. My stomach fluttered, and a smile spread across my face.

"Hey, baby," I answered, tossing my keys in the dish by the door.

His voice came smooth through the line. "I want to see you. Tonight."

I leaned against the counter. "I just got home from shopping. I'm about to shower."

"Perfect. Shower, get dressed, and come to my place. I'll send the driver."

A flicker of hesitation tickled the back of my mind. I was tired, and all I wanted to do was relax. But it didn't last long. If my man wanted to see me, then he was going to see me.

"Alright," I spoke into the phone.

"I'll be waiting," he replied then hung up.

I stood there for a beat, feeling the quiet settle around me, before walking to the bathroom. The shower was quick, just enough to wash my body twice. I dressed in a pair of dark washed jeans and a black cropped top. I paired it with a black pair of shark boots and a black puffer jacket. Once I added my gold jewelry and sprayed on my scent of the night, I was ready. When the driver pulled up, I stepped into the backseat, ready to go see Victor.

The penthouse was lit with soft lighting, warm and golden. He was already standing near the bar when I walked in, hands in his pockets, tailored shirt open at the collar.

"You look..." His eyes moved over me slowly, his voice wrapping around the word like velvet. "Like you're worth every second I've waited."

He poured two glasses of dark liquor and handed me one. The first sip burned then softened, sliding down with a heat that matched the way his gaze was burning into me.

"You trust me, Vita?" he asked suddenly, leaning a hip against the bar.

The question caught me off guard, but I nodded. "I wouldn't be here if I didn't."

He didn't smile, holding his gaze on me a beat longer before setting his glass down. "Good. Because I'm about to do things to your body that you've never had done before."

I felt that statement all over my body. His hand came to mine, warm and firm, and he led me down a hallway I hadn't been through on my last visit. The door we stopped at was heavy, dark wood with a steel handle. When he opened it, the air inside felt different, thicker some-how, carrying a faint hint of leather and cinnamon. The room was nothing like the sleek, glass-and-marble main living space. This was much deeper with rich mahogany floors and low lighting that came from recessed sconces instead of overhead. The walls were lined with racks, hooks, and shelves of neatly arranged items I didn't have the nerve to catalog right away.

And then, there was the centerpiece, the thing that pulled my eyes no matter how I tried to take in everything else – a black, leather sex swing, suspended from the ceiling by thick, silver chains. It swayed slightly, just enough to make me wonder if it had been used recently. The rest of the furniture was minimal but intentional – an armless chaise, a long, padded bench, and mirrored wall. In one corner, a tall cabinet stood closed, but I didn't need to open it to know there were more things inside.

Victor stepped behind me, his breath warm against my ear. "Wel-come to my favorite room in my home. This is where I stop guessing what you can handle and start finding out."

I looked at him with wide, but not scared, eyes. As I stood there in his playroom, the only thing I felt was curiosity. I wanted to know what came next, what he was planning to do to my body. My body shivered when his hands touched the bare skin at my stomach. He pressed his mouth to my ear before ordering me to take my clothes off, and I did. Victor watched me as I removed each piece. The moment my panties came off, Victor picked me up into his arms, my breath hitched as I wrapped my arms around his strong shoulders.

For Victor to be his age, he was in great shape. He kissed my neck gently before placing me into the swing. The leather straps were cool against my thighs as I stepped into the swing, Victor's hands guiding me like he'd done it a hundred times before. The seat cradled me, my legs spreading easily under the pull of the suspension, making me feel exposed in a way that sent heat spiraling low in my belly.

I could hear him moving behind me, the subtle rustle of fabric, the faint clink of metal. Then, darkness. The blindfold slipped over my eyes, stealing the light and heightening everything else. My breathing quickened, chest rising and falling.

"Relax." His voice rumbled close to my ear, low and commanding.

The first hum of the vibrator was soft, almost teasing, but when it touched me, my whole body jolted. My head fell back, the leather swing holding me in place, while the vibration seeped into me, deep and relentless. I couldn't see him, couldn't predict where he'd move next. My world narrowed to the steady thrum between my legs and the way his fingers gripped my hips, holding me still when my body tried to writhe.

Every nerve felt alive, like the blindfold had stripped me of every defense and left me nothing but sensation. The leather straps pressed into my skin, the chain above creaked softly, and the air felt cooler against my bare body. My lips parted, a quiet sound slipping out before I could swallow it back.

He caught it immediately. "Don't hold back, Vita," he murmured, the words vibrating through me almost as much as the toy.

The hum deepened, shifting from a playful tease to a slow thrust. Pressure shot through me so hard that every muscle in my body tightened. My fingers curled into the straps of the swing, gripping leather so hard my knuckles ached. I couldn't see him, but I could feel him. His presence felt like heat in the dark, circling me, studying the way my body reacted to every flicker of sensation. The vibrator drifted away for a moment, leaving me trembling and breathless, before he brought it back with just enough pressure to make my hips jerk.

"Uh-uh," he warned, one big hand flattening over my lower stomach, holding me still. "I decide when you move."

The command was quiet but sharp, sending a shiver down my spine. The blindfold seemed tighter, the swing more confining, like every inch of me belonged to him right then. I wanted to beg for more, for faster, for harder, but my throat felt thick with need. He kept me there, hovering in that unbearable place between too much and not enough. I could feel the heat pooling, the tension coiling inside me, but just as it began to crest, he'd pull back, letting the vibrations skim over me instead of sink in,

The toy slowed to a maddening pace, a rhythm meant to keep me teetering at the edge but never falling over it. My chest rose and fell in uneven pulls, the air feeling thick and heavy. Every second felt like forever, every withdrawal a cruel reminder that he wasn't done with me. And I didn't want him to be.

The hum faded and was replaced by silence so sharp I could hear my own heartbeat. Then came heat. Soft, wet, unrelenting heat against the most sensitive part of me. The first slow drag of his tongue stole my breath. My thighs quivered, tightening against the straps of the swing, but there was nowhere to run, nowhere to escape the way he explored me. The blindfold made it worse. I couldn't see the way he moved, couldn't predict when the next flick or curl of his tongue would come. All I could do was feel, each stroke sending little electric jolts up my spine.

Then, his fingers found my nipples. Firm, warm, confident fingers that pinched and rolled until I gasped. My back arched helplessly as soft moans escaped my lips. Every nerve in my body seemed connected now, my nipples tightening in tune with the rhythm of his mouth. His tongue pressed deeper then retreated, tracing circles that left me trembling. It wasn't just pleasure; it was *possession*. Every lick of his tongue or suck from his lips was calculated.

I was already right there, teetering on the brink. My muscles tightened, and my breath came in short, helpless gasps. Victor's hands never left my body, grounding me, while his hot, insistent tongue worked me like it was the only mission that mattered. It hit me in waves, sharp and uncontrollable, my hips jerking against the swing. A cry ripped out of me, raw and unfiltered. The orgasm rolled through me like fire, burning me from the inside out.

The blindfold was sliding away. My lashes fluttered, adjusting to the dim light, my vision clearing. My breath froze in my chest when I saw it wasn't Victor between my legs but Monique. Her full lips glistened, and her eyes locked on mine, a sly, knowing smile on her face. She licked her lips slowly as if tasting me was the most natural thing in the world. Shock came first, a sharp jolt that made my heart slam against my ribs. My mind scrambled to put the pieces together, but my body... my body was already ahead of me. The truth was that seeing her there, kneeling between my legs, looking up at me like I was dessert, made me even wetter.

It turned me on, so much so that another pulse of heat shot through me, almost as strong as my orgasm. Victor was still there, behind me, his hands on my waist like a silent permission slip. When Monique's fingers trailed up my thighs, I didn't flinch. I leaned into it. She stood, slow and smooth, until she was eye-level with me. She cupped my face, thumb stroking along my jaw, and kissed me. I tasted my own juices as our tongues danced. The kiss was soft at first then deepened, her tongue sliding against mine until my knees went weak even in the swing.

When she pulled back, her voice was low, teasing. "Your turn, Vita."

My whole body pulsed with need, every nerve screaming for more. Victor's eyes darkened as he watched us, his presence a steady force behind me, grounding me even as the heat threatened to consume me.

"You ready?" Monique whispered, her breath hot against my ear.

I didn't hesitate. "Yes."

Victor trailed his fingertips up my thighs before unbuckling me. Getting out of the swing, I lowered myself between her legs with a hunger I hadn't known I could feel. The soft heat of her skin met my lips, and I drank her in. Her taste was intoxicating, a mix of sweetness and spice that made me ache for more. My tongue flicked out, tracing the sensitive edges. Monique's quiet moans vibrated through me, encouraging me to go deeper, and I did. I pressed my hands on her thighs, steadying her, as I kissed and licked with purpose, losing myself in the taste of her.

Behind me, Victor's hands settled on my waist, strong and possessive, sending waves of reassurance through my body. I could feel him hard against my backside. And just knowing he was watching made me want to do it even more. Monique's hands found my hair, fingers threading through the curls at my nape, as she guided me, urging me on. Every lick and flick of my tongue sent shudders through her, and I loved that I was the one making it happen.

As I worked her, my own body burned hotter, the need between my legs intensifying, until it was almost unbearable. Victor's grip tightened on my hips and then his voice, low and commanding, whispered, "Arch that back."

Obediently, I shifted, putting an even deeper dip into my back as he positioned himself at my opening. His hands roamed my body, tracing the curve of my arch and the swell of my breasts, before settling firmly on my hips. He slid inside me with a slow thrust that stole my breath and sent a jolt straight to my core. I moaned against the inside of Monique's thigh before sucking her clit gently. Victor's rhythm was steady, matching the hunger that coursed through my veins. I pushed back against him, making him go deeper. Monique's soft moans mixed with the sound of Victor's breath created a symphony of pleasure that wrapped around us. Reaching one hand back, I gripped Victor's thigh as waves of sensation rolled over me, building higher with each thrust.

"Let go," Victor murmured into my ear, his voice low but thick

I surrendered completely, the tension in my body unraveling, as the waves of pleasure crashed over me. Victor's steady rhythm drove me higher, each movement synchronized with the beating of my heart. The warmth of his hands on my hips grounded me even as the sensations pushed me toward the edge.

Taking my hands from Victor's thighs, I cupped Monique's breasts, twirling her nipples through my fingers. Her eyes met mine as I looked up at her. The way she latched onto me made me even wetter. My breaths came faster, ragged and shallow, as Victor whispered words I barely caught. His lips brushed the shell of my ear, and I felt a shiver run down my spine.

"Damn, Vic, every time you thrust into her, you make her eat my pussy even better. Don't stop fucking her until I cum," Monique moaned.

And she was right. Every thrust dove me into her deeper. The pleasure built like a storm inside me, fierce and relentless. My release came shuddering through me, leaving me trembling and gasping for air. But I didn't stop licking, not until Monique came. When she did, her back arched and her fingers fisted my hair as she moaned loud. Victor's pace quickened, and he gripped my hips harder. I smiled when Victor pulled out, and a stream of warm cum hit my ass cheeks.

Monique was the first of us to get up. She grabbed her clothes, that were in a pile on the floor, and walked out the room. When she returned about ten minutes later, she was fully dressed.

"Victor, it's always a pleasure, but I have to get going." Monique grabbed her purse off the couch before turning to look at me. "I hope to see you again soon, Vita."

"I hope so too," I replied, surprising myself.

Victor smiled, wrapping his arms around me, as he said goodbye to Monique. The warmth of his body against mine was a soothing balm after the storm of passion. We lay there on the couch, tangled and quiet. The weight of the night settled around us like a dark, velvet cloak. I knew the night was just beginning, and I was ready for anything Victor had in mind.

Chapter Eighteen

KYRIE

The street was quiet when we pulled up to the warehouse. The adrenaline from the casino still buzzed in my veins, but now, it mixed with exhaustion. My head leaned back against the seat for a second longer than I meant to before Victor cut the engine.

"Let's go in here and count this money, so we can call it a night," Victor announced, opening the door and getting out before the rest of us followed.

Simone yawned as she stretched, her nails catching the faint glow of the streetlights. Tasha rolled her shoulders, eyes scanning the block like she was looking for something. I was just ready to count the money, get my cut, and get back to the feed I had of Braylen. Inside, the warehouse was dim with only a few lights on inside the entire place. We settled at the table in the middle of the room. Victor dropped the duffel bag on the table, the zipper's rasp cutting through the silence. Thick stacks of cash stared back at us, fresh from the casino floor.

"Let's count it," Victor spoke.

Victor began running the bills through the money counter until it was all counted. Between the four of us, we had made a hundred and forty thousand dollars that would be split evenly.

I let out a low whistle. "We did good tonight, y'all."

Victor was already dividing the stacks, neat and precise. "Thirty-five apiece," he confirmed, sliding the bundles across the table. "We back at it tomorrow, same time so don't be late."

"Y'all ever stop and think about how wild this is?" I asked, leaning forward. "We walk into a place meant to bleed people dry, and we walk out feeding ourselves. It's like flipping the whole system upside down."

Simone chuckled. "That's because most people don't have the discipline to pull it off. They go in chasing luck. We go in with strategy. That's a big difference."

Victor nodded slowly. "Luck runs out. Strategy keeps you in the game. Remember that."

I stacked my share into my backpack, zipped it up, and stood from my seat. It was late, and I was ready to go home. It was after four in the morning, and all I wanted to do was relax. The cold night air hit my face as I walked out of the warehouse. It was early November, and although there wasn't any snow on the ground, the air was still at freezing temperatures. I jogged to the car, tossing my backpack inside, before getting in and starting the engine. I allowed my car to warm up as I bobbed my head to an old Jeezy song. Five minutes later, I was pulling out of the parking lot and headed home.

My house was dark when I arrived. I went directly up to my room and put tonight's earnings inside my closet. I was now on my third shoe box, and I knew things would only get better from here. Once my money was put away, I peeled out my clothes and tossed them into the hamper before going to the bathroom.

The steam still clung to my skin when I stepped out the shower, towel hanging low around my waist. I didn't even bother putting any lotion on, didn't care that water spots dripped down my chest onto the carpet. My head was heavy, thoughts weighing me down. I dropped down on the couch, remote in hand, flipping through channels. I already knew what I wanted to see; I wanted to watch her. I flipped to the feed of Banks' house, and there she was.

Her face filled the screen like God was tryna punish me. Her soft brown skin glowed under the lights, long lashes brushing her pillow, looking so peaceful. Banks' big ass arm was wrapped tight around her, possessive as hell. His hand rested on her stomach like it belonged there, like he had the right to touch what was mine. My stomach flipped, chest clenching so tight I couldn't breathe. For a second, I thought maybe I was hallucinating. Maybe I was dreaming this, and none of this was actually happening. I hadn't lost my wife; she wasn't pregnant with a baby that I knew was mine and hadn't heard one thing about. Like she didn't look happy with another man.

Braylen even being with him was still something that I didn't want to stomach, no matter how it happened. She was supposed to be better than this, better than me. She was supposed to be the glue that held this marriage together, but instead, she'd allowed it to fall apart. She'd allowed her feelings for me to take a back door to what she now had with some other man. And that was something I couldn't let slide. I needed her like I needed air to breathe, and I wasn't going to go too many more nights without her.

The way she curled under him, like she was in perfect hands, made me want to throw up. Had she been this peaceful with me? This content? I'd never seen her like this before, and it made my chest tight. As much as I hated to see her with him, I couldn't stop watching. My entire body stiffened. The towel slid off my waist and rested on the couch, but I didn't even notice. I was too busy staring at the screen, every muscle in my body locking up like I might break if I moved.

"They got me fucked up," I whispered, voice shaking.

That was supposed to be me. I shot up off the couch, pacing hard across the living room floor. My fists curled so tight my knuckles popped. Every step felt heavier than the last, like anger was dragging me down, and it was.

"That's my wife," I growled, talking to myself because no one else was here to hear me. "That's my fuckin' wife."

The veins in my neck pulsed, and I could feel blood rushing in my ears like gunfire. I slammed the remote down on the coffee table so hard it cracked against the wood, batteries flying out. Images of them together burned into my skull. Braylen's soft little smile while she was sleep. The way her hair spilled across Banks' chest. How his hand was spread across her belly like he was protecting something inside her. Something that wasn't even his to protect.

The rage that hit me then was different. It wasn't the quick spark I felt before; it was a wildfire burning me alive from the inside, causing my entire body to shake. I punched the wall hard. Drywall cracked under my fist, floating down to the floor around me. My knuckles split open, blood welling up, but I didn't feel any of it. Pain didn't even matter to me at that moment. All I could see was her. Her choosing him over me. I slid down the wall, breathing hard, chest heaving like I just ran a marathon. My head dropped into my bloody hand.

"I gave you everything I could. I know it wasn't much, but I'm different now," I muttered, voice raw. "And instead of giving me a chance to prove that, you wanna lay up with him. The same man that bought you."

Tears burned at the back of my eyes, but I swallowed them down, refusing to let them fall. There were no tears left in me, only rage. Zooming in closer on her sleeping face, I swore it felt like a knife twisting in my chest. My wife was happy with a man that wasn't me. I stood again, pacing faster, words spilling out my mouth like venom.

"You think he gon' love you better than I can, Bray? I know you. We have years of history, and you wanna throw it all away for a new nigga!"

I snatched my phone off the table, thumb hovering over her Instagram. It was the only thing I wasn't blocked on. I wanted to send her a DM so bad. I wanted answers, needed them. I knew the baby she was carrying was mine; there was no way it wasn't. I wanted to ask her why she hadn't said anything about the baby. Why wasn't I notified of any doctors' appointments, but would she really tell me? There was no way I would allow her to keep me away from a child I created. And my child wasn't going to live in a broken home the way I had. So, Braylen and I getting back together was a must. She was just going to have to understand that.

Chapter Nineteen

BRAYLEN

I slept in a little longer this morning, not getting out of bed until well after ten. Banks wasn't in the room, and I knew he was downstairs helping Vita make everything perfect for me. It was the day of my baby shower, and I couldn't have been happier. Walking into the en-suite bathroom, I used it before brushing my teeth and washing my face. I slipped on my robe before walking downstairs into the kitchen. Marcus had already cooked breakfast and placed my plate on the warmer. Now, he was hard at work cooking all the food for today.

"Hey, Marcus, how are you this morning?" I greeted, placing my plate on the table before taking my seat.

"I'm good. How are you this morning? Are you excited about today?"

"Yeah, I am. I can't wait to see how everything gets decorated. My friend, Vita, has expensive taste, so I already know it's going to be over the top. I just can't wait to celebrate my little boy."

I looked down, smiling at the plate of French toast, dusted lightly with cinnamon and sugar, the edges crispy just the way I liked. A small bowl of fresh fruit sat right beside it. On a smaller plate were cheese eggs and turkey sausage. It was my favorite breakfast, and I knew Banks had told Marcus to make it for me. I couldn't help but smile. It was only morning, and the day was already perfect, so I could only imagine how the rest of the day would be. The thought made my chest swell so much I had to pause mid-chew and press a hand against my heart.

I couldn't stop smiling. Today was the day all my friends, family, and people who really cared about me would gather, not just to celebrate my baby but to celebrate me too and the new life I was stepping into. I was glowing, and it wasn't just the pregnancy glow everybody kept teasing me about. It was joy.

I thought about how far I'd come, about everything I'd endured, and tears blurred my vision for a moment. For years, I wasn't sure I'd get to feel this happy again. But God had worked everything out, and here I was, standing barefoot in the kitchen, full of life, full of hope, and full of love for the little one growing inside me.

I rubbed my belly absently as I chewed another bite. "We're about to be celebrated, baby boy," I whispered. "Everybody's coming just for us."

My heart fluttered. I imagined the way the room would look when everything was done. The balloons, tables draped in soft pastels, little games that would have everybody laughing, a table piled with gifts wrapped in shiny paper. The idea of opening onesies, bottles, blankets, and strollers while my closest friends and family cheered me on made me giddy. I wiped my hands, finished the last of my food, and padded toward the stairs. I wanted to peek at how things were coming along downstairs.

The sound of movement reached me before I even hit the bottom step. Voices, shuffling, and laughter. It was clear the decorators were still setting up. When I reached the basement, I peeked in and felt my smile falter just a little. The tables weren't covered yet, balloons were still tied in bunches on the floor, and half-open boxes of decorations were scattered everywhere. I hugged my arms around myself, bouncing a little on my toes. I knew it would all come together. Vita promised me I wouldn't have to lift a finger, but my excitement made me impatient. I wanted to see the vision complete, to step into the magic.

"Okay," I whispered to myself with a grin. "Let me go mind my business."

I turned and headed back upstairs, deciding not to hover and stress them out. When I reached the top of the stairs, sunlight spilled through the front windows, brighter than usual, almost pulling me outside. I slipped on my house shoes and opened the front door. The breeze kissed my face the moment I stepped outside. But it wasn't the air that stole my breath. It was the sight laid out before me. I gasped as I covered my mouth.

The driveway was lined with framed photographs of me. But not just any photos. They were the ones from my maternity shoot. I walked slowly down the porch steps, eyes wide, heart hammering in my chest as I took it all in. The first photo was me in that soft cream silk gown that clung to my bump so perfectly it looked like it was painted on. I was standing barefoot in a meadow, the sunlight catching on my hair, while my hands cradled my stomach. The next one was of me in black and white, turned to the side. My bare belly was exposed with one hand resting protectively on top and the other underneath. My eyes were closed in that one, lips parted just slightly, like I was listening to the heartbeat inside me. That picture had felt vulnerable when I took it, but seeing it framed so beautifully made me feel powerful.

Farther down, I stopped at another – me in a deep emerald gown that split at the thigh, flowing in the wind, as I stood on the edge of a rooftop. My hair was in wild curls tumbling down my back, and I looked fierce. That one made me tear up just a bit. Each picture told a different story. Some were soft and sweet. Me in a floral crown holding sunflowers against my belly. Some were bold and daring. Me draped in nothing but a white sheet, eyes sharp with confidence. Others were playful. Me sitting cross-legged on a picnic blanket with ice cream in hand, laughing so hard you could almost hear it through the picture.

The frames themselves were stunning, each one of them unique – gold, silver, and wood, all with carved edges. Some were even mirrored and reflected the sky above. Whoever put this together had thought of every detail, arranging them in a perfect path leading from the edge of the driveway all the way up to the house. Every picture had a stand. Some were perched on an easel, and others hung on decorative poles wrapped in ivy and flowers. It looked like an outdoor gallery dedicated solely to me and the life I carried inside me. I pressed a hand to my belly again, overwhelmed by everything.

"Oh, my God." My voice cracked. "This is beautiful."

The wind picked up slightly, ruffling the silk ribbon tied to one of the frames, making it dance like it was alive. I stepped closer to another portrait, me in a long lace robe, belly bare beneath, standing in front of a mirror. The photo had captured both my profile and my reflection, and I remembered how unsure I'd felt that day. However, as I stood there, looking at the picture, I saw just how beautiful it had turned out. I blinked quickly, trying not to cry but failing anyway. Tears slipped down my cheeks, warm and grateful.

This wasn't just about pictures. This was about honoring the life I was carrying, honoring motherhood and the journey I'd been through to get here. Every frame was a reminder that I was strong, that I was beautiful, and that I was truly loved.

I laughed through my tears, shaking my head. "They didn't have to do all this."

But they did, and it was because this baby wasn't just a blessing to me and A'zir. I walked slowly along the line of pictures, pausing at each one, my fingers brushing the edges. By the time I reached the last frame, the sun had risen higher, bathing everything in a golden glow that made the pictures sparkle.

I closed my eyes and whispered, "Thank you, God. Thank you for this moment."

I didn't even realize how much I needed it until now. This was more than a baby shower. This was my rebirth. This was me taking my life back. All the things I'd been through in my life had all led me to this moment. And this moment made it all worth it. I walked back up to the driveway slowly, still taking everything in. I couldn't believe that this was really my life. For once in my life, I could smile, and it was actually genuine. Walking into the kitchen, I grabbed a bottle of water and headed back to my bedroom.

I was halfway through my bottled water when I heard a knock on my bedroom door. I wiped my mouth with a napkin and padded over, still in my robe. When I opened it, Sabrina was standing there, grinning like she had just hit the jackpot.

"Girl, you ready for your big moment?" she asked, one hand hidden behind her back.

I laughed. "What you got up your sleeve?"

She stepped inside, pulling a long garment bag forward like it was the Holy Grail. The bag was pearl white, zipped up tight, but the way she held it made my heart flutter.

"Your shower dress," she sang, drawing out the words. "You know I couldn't let you wear just anything today. This is your baby shower, your celebration. You're about to glow so bright they gon' have to dim the lights."

I shook my head, but I was already smiling. "Sabrina, what did you do?"

She laid the bag across the bed and unzipped it with dramatic flair. The fabric spilled out in a ripple of rich sapphire blue, catching the sunlight that streamed through the window. My breath hitched.

"Oh, my God, Sabrina. This is beautiful."

The dress was everything I didn't even know I wanted – floor-length and made of a silky chiffon that shimmered with every movement. The bodice was off-the-shoulder, and it had a sweetheart neckline that dipped just low enough to be sultry without losing elegance. Tiny, hand-sewn crystals lined the bust, sparkling like baby stars every time the light hit them. The waist was fitted, cinching just above my bump, with a flowing skirt that cascaded down gracefully, giving me room to move while still looking like a queen.

The back dipped into a deep V, and a sheer chiffon cape was attached at the shoulders, trailing behind like angel wings. It wasn't just a dress; it was a statement.

I touched the fabric, almost afraid to wrinkle it. "Sabrina, this is beautiful. I don't know if I could wear this."

"Yes, you can," she interrupted, putting her hands on her hips. "You deserve to feel like royalty. You're carrying a king, girl. You think I'm about to let you walk into your shower in something basic? Nah. I now you know me better than that."

Tears pricked my eyes. "It's perfect. Blue for my baby boy," I whispered, my voice breaking a little.

"And when you step into your baby shower, everybody's gonna see you and know you're glowing from the inside out." She grinned, her excitement contagious.

"Are you coming back for the shower?" I asked, looking over at her.

"You already know I am. I just wanted to come early to give you that dress."

I hugged Sabrina, thanking her for the dress. She left after telling me that she would see me later. I stood there, just looking at the dress in amazement. It was so beautiful, and I knew it would look even better on. I zipped the garment bag up carefully before taking it into my closet and hanging it up. I didn't want anything to happen to the dress before I got a chance to put it on, so I handled it with care. I had a pair of Dior heels that would go perfect with the dress.

"I see Sabrina came to give you the gift she had for you," A'zir spoke as he walked into the room.

"Yes, and it's so beautiful. I can't wait to put it on."

"I can't wait to see you in it. Vita really outdid herself. They're not even done setting up yet, and I can already tell it's gon' be beautiful. Shit, you done got so much for the baby already, I don't think the guests even have to bring any gifts."

I smiled as I walked over to A'zir. "You mean you bought it. That money you put in the mailbox for me every week is what I been using to buy everything."

"What money?" A'zir asked, confused.

"The money that you put in the envelopes that have 'Mrs. Banks' on them."

A'zir frowned before shaking his head. "Baby, I never did that. Why would I put money in the mailbox when I could just hand it to you? How much was it?"

"It's like five stacks every week. I thought you were trying to be romantic and leave it for me."

"Fuck no! You know damn well that if I would have left money, it would have been way more than five thousand dollars. I ain't leave that shit, but I'm damn sure about to figure out who is."

A'zir started to walk off, but I stopped him. This was supposed to be one of the happiest days of our lives, and I wasn't going to let anything get in the way of that.

"All that can wait until tomorrow. Today we celebrate our son."

A'zir nodded in understanding before promising that he wouldn't be doing any work today. He kissed the top of my forehead before wrapping his arms around me. My phone buzzed just as A'zir let go. I looked down at it to see that it was Ayanna letting me know that she and her team would be here shortly for hair and makeup. About twenty minutes later, Ayanna and another woman were knocking on my bedroom door.

"Good morning, mama-to-be!" Ayanna sang out, giving me that

big, radiant smile of hers, before she wrapped me in a hug. Her arms were always warm, always full of love. "You ready to get spoiled?"

"I'm more than ready."

"Good, now relax and let us take care of you," she said, slipping off her shades. "By the time we're done, you're gon' feel like Beyoncé at the Grammys."

They wasted no time setting up. Ayanna unpacked bundles, combs, sprays, and hot tools, while the makeup artist organized palettes, brushes, and little glass jars of glowing powders. Ayanna pulled her phone out, connected to the Bluetooth speaker, and within seconds, the room filled with the smooth, timeless voice of Sade singing *By Your Side*.

"Now this is a vibe," the makeup artist murmured, snapping her fingers along with the beat.

The entire room seemed to soften under that music. Sade's voice wrapped around me like silk, and I let out a deep breath I didn't know I was holding.

"Sit your pretty self down," Ayanna said, gesturing toward the chair in front of the Ring light. "Let's get started."

I lowered myself carefully into the chair, and as soon as I did, Ayanna turned the music, up allowing it to flow through the room. After Sade, the playlist switched effortlessly into Maxwell's *Ascension Don't Ever Wonder*. My head started nodding along without me even thinking about it.

"I'm thinkin' soft waves, something timeless and elegant but still give a little drama," Ayana spoke. For the next hour, she worked her magic, braiding me down before gluing down a black lace frontal. She sectioned my hair, pressing it smooth then curling it into cascading waves that flowed down my shoulders. Every time a curl dropped and framed my face, I smiled, knowing that I would look amazing when it was all done.

Meanwhile, the makeup artist prepped my skin, dabbing foundation along my cheeks, blending until it melted perfectly into my complexion. She added warmth with bronzer, sculpted my nose, and gave me a soft but radiant highlight that made my cheekbones gleam under the lights. Then, she focused on my eyes. She brushed a deep, smoky brown into my crease and topped it with a shimmering gold that made my eyes look bigger and brighter. Then, she finished with long, wispy lashes that fluttered every time I blinked, all while the playlist moved from Maxwell to H.E.R.'s *Focus*, to Daniel Caesar's *Get You*, and then slid right into Jazmine Sullivan's *In Love With Another Man*. The music carried me. Each song felt like it was narrating some part of my story, some part of me.

When they were finally finished, I barely recognized myself. My reflection glowed. My lips were painted in a glossy nude that looked soft and kissable. My eyes sparkled under the weight of the lashes. My skin looked airbrushed and flawless, like I belonged on the cover of a magazine.

Ayanna clapped her hands together, her face lighting up. "Yessss! That's it! You look gorgeous, girl."

I blushed, my hand automatically going to my stomach. "I don't even look like myself."

"Shut up," Ayanna said with a playful eye roll. "You look like the best version of you. Now, it's time for the dress."

She pulled the garment bag Sabrina had dropped off earlier from the closet and unzipped it. The moment the fabric spilled out, my breath caught. The dress was a masterpiece – sapphire blue satin, rich and gleaming under the light. And I couldn't believe Sabrina had given it to me to wear.

Ayanna held it up to me with a wide smile. "Sabrina outdid herself. You ready to put it on?"

I nodded, though my throat felt tight with emotion. She helped me step into it, adjusting the fabric carefully, so it laid perfectly over my bump. When she zipped me up and I turned to face the mirror, tears immediately welled in my eyes. I looked stunning, regal even. The blue satin hugged my body in all the right places, and the way it shimmered made my skin glow even more. My hair fell in soft waves over my shoulders, and my makeup tied everything together like I belonged at the most glamorous event of the year.

"You're crying," Ayanna whispered, her hand landing softly on my shoulder.

"I just…" I shook my head, pressing a hand to my chest. "I never thought I'd feel this beautiful while pregnant. I'm big as a damn house, but I've never felt more beautiful."

"Baby girl, you're not just beautiful," she said, her voice thick with emotion. "You're radiant. You're glowing. You're the definition of divine right now. Don't you ever forget that. You are about to bring a life into the world, and that is a wonderful gift."

I nodded, wiping at my tears carefully, so I wouldn't ruin my makeup.

Ayanna wasn't done though. "Now for the finishing touches."

She opened a small velvet box and revealed a necklace with delicate diamonds set into a thin chain, elegant and understated. Matching studs sparkled in her palm.

"These are for you," she said softly.

"Ayanna, I can't. This is too much."

"You can, and you will," she cut me off, fastening the necklace around my neck herself. "Because every queen deserves her crown."

I stared at my reflection again, the necklace catching the light and drawing even more attention to my neckline. It was perfect.

Finally, Ayanna handed me a bottle of perfume. "One last thing."

I recognized the bottle immediately; it was Bianco Latte. I sprayed it lightly at the base of my neck then at my wrists, closing my eyes as the scent wrapped around me. When I opened my eyes again, the room had fallen quiet. Ayanna and the makeup artist were just staring at me, smiling.

"Braylen," Ayanna said softly, her voice cracking for the first time. "You're everything."

I couldn't even speak. I just stood there, breathing in, trying not to cry again because if I started, I might not stop. I took one last look at myself in the mirror before thanking them and telling Ayana that she was welcome to come to the baby shower. She agreed, telling me she would go change and be back by the time it started. I walked Ayanna and the makeup artist to the door, and the doorbell chimed the moment I got to it. Opening the door, I smiled.

Standing on the other side in an emerald, two-piece pants suit was my mother. The six-inch heels she wore added to her already tall stance. Her skin was deep brown and smooth like butter. She wore her hair in long, pressed waves that brushed her shoulders, streaked with a little silver that only made her look more regal. Her huge, almond shaped eyes looked at me with excitement.

"My baby," she whispered, her voice breaking.

"Ayanna, this is my mother, Lorraine, but most people just call her Rain."

Ayanna extended her hand. "It's every nice to meet you.'

Mama shook her hand and stepped inside the house as Ayanna stepped out.

"You look beautiful, baby girl. I can't believe I'm gonna be a glam ma." My mama smiled.

"Thank you, Mama. I'm so happy." I smoothed my hands over the curve of my belly, the hem of my flowing blue dress swishing against my legs.

"I'm so glad you're happy. Is everything set up yet?"

"It should be by now. Let's go see."

I took my mama's hand and led her to the basement steps. We walked down together, slowly. The moment we reached the bottom step, I froze, my hand instinctively flying to my chest as tears prickled my eyes. The basement had been completely transformed. This was no longer a basement. It was a garden dream. A pale blue canopy of fabric was draped overhead, cascading like the sky itself. Fairy lights were woven through it, glowing softly like stars, while hanging greenery, ivy, eucalyptus, and delicate baby's breath, gave the illusion of stepping into an enchanted garden.

Every table was clothed in linen the color of misty blue, topped with wildflower centerpieces tucked into mason jars wrapped in twine. White lanterns with flickering candles were scattered throughout, casting a golden warmth. Against one wall stood a balloon arch in shades of powder blue, cream, and hints of sage green, framing a wicker chair draped with plush pillows. It was clearly my throne for the day, the "mama-to-be" seat where I'd open all my gifts. A sign above it read in swirling script: *"Baby Boy McFarland."*

The dessert table nearly made me gasp again. There were tiers of cupcakes, frosted with pale blue swirls, macarons in shades of ivory and sky, and chocolate-dipped strawberries sprinkled with edible glitter. At the center sat a three-tier cake, frosted in watercolor shades of blue, adorned with sugar flowers, and topped with a gold baby carriage. To the side was a refreshment station offering glass dispensers filled with sparkling lemonade, blueberry-infused water, and iced tea, each labeled with handwritten calligraphy tags.

The final touch was the floor itself. Faux grass rolled out beneath my feet, sprinkled with petals and scattered with small white garden stools. It didn't feel like a basement anymore. It felt like a secret oasis carved out just for me.

My throat tightened. I pressed my hand against my belly, my voice barely a whisper. "This is perfect."

"This is beautiful.." Mama smiled, looking around the room.

When I felt the baby kick, I knew that he agreed. My heart was swelling with gratitude, and I was so glad that I let Vita plan this. This was finally my moment to celebrate my little blessing, and I couldn't wait. Everything was going great, and today, I finally realized just how perfect my life really was.

Chapter Twenty

VITA

Everything had been set up for Braylen's shower, and I was now on my way back to my house to get dressed. My heart was filled with joy, and I couldn't wait to see her smiling face when she saw all the love she would receive today. It was all well-deserved, and I was happy my girl was able to get some light at the end of that dark ass tunnel. Banks was good for her. He had completely changed her life, and as long as he kept a smile on my girl's face, he was alright in my book.

I rushed into my house and went straight to the bathroom to take a shower. It was already one in the afternoon, and the shower started at three. With me being the host, I would need to get there before the other guests started to arrive. Once I was out the shower, I wrapped myself in a towel, brushed my teeth, then walked back to my bedroom.

I'd laid my clothes out the night before – a blue and white Balenciaga sweater dress and a pair of blue thigh high boots. I sat at my vanity and applied my makeup. It was nothing fancy, foundation, contour, eyeliner, and lip gloss. When I was done, I laid my baby hairs and allowed my long locs to hang down my back. I oiled my body and put on my clothes. I slid the pair of gold Louis Vuitton hoops that Victor had gifted me into my ears. I sprayed myself with Burberry Goddess and looked at myself once more in the mirror. I smiled, already knowing I looked good. I grabbed my blue Balenciaga bag that was also a gift from Victor and was on my way out the door by two fifteen.

It was ten minutes to three by the time I made it back to Banks' and Braylen's house. Thankfully for me, the guests were on CP time because I didn't see any cars in the driveway. I walked up the stairs, and the door opened before I even rang the doorbell.

"Hey, Vita," Banks greeted. "Come on in. I'm not sure where Braylen is, but she's somewhere in the house, probably downstairs looking at the beautiful decorations. Man, you outdid yourself. It looks beautiful down there."

"I'm glad you like it. This is her first child, so I had to go all out."

"Come on. I'll come down with you. I'm sure that's where she is."

I nodded, following Banks through the house and down to the basement. Just as he thought, Braylen was downstairs. My eyes widened when I saw Braylen's mother, Rain. I screamed, rushing over to her and hugging her tightly.

"Girl, look at you, over here thicka than a Snicka," I joked.

"Vita, this is so beautiful. Can you believe Braylen ass bout to be somebody's mama? Girl, I never thought I would see the day. I'm just glad that it's not by that ol' knuckle head ass Kyrie." Rain turned to Braylen. "Speaking of, when am I gon' get to meet this new man of yours? Mr. Big Money Grip with this big ass house," Rain joked.

Braylen smiled before wrapping her arm into Banks'. "Mama, this is A'zir. A'zir, this is my mama, Lorraine."

"You can just call me Rain. A'zir, huh? Why does that name sound familiar?" Rain asked, stepping up closer to Banks. "What's your last name, A'zir?"

"It's McFarland."

"That last name don't ring a bell, but you look familiar. It's gonna come to me, just give me a second."

Banks chuckled and nodded his head. "Okay, let me know when it does."

A few moments later, guests started to arrive. Braylen's cousins and aunts walked in, all complimenting the house and the decorations. And they were right about everything they said. The decorations were beautiful, and my vision had come to life in the most perfect way. The Boho Blue Garden was the perfect theme for this baby shower. Sky-colored drapery spilled from the ceiling, pooling against the walls like soft clouds. Woven wicker chairs and rattan baskets were everywhere, layered with pampas grass, eucalyptus, and pale blue roses. String lights glowed above like a canopy of fireflies. The gift table was already overflowing with glossy bags and carefully wrapped boxes tied with ivory ribbons.

I sat down at one of the circular tables draped in cream linen, smoothing my dress over my thighs. Guests trickled in – old friends, family, women from Braylen's job, even a couple of Banks' boys and their girlfriends. Music played low, soft R&B that kept the atmosphere calm and elegant. Everyone was smiling, hugging, and congratulating Braylen and Banks on their new bundle of joy.

"Vita," Braylen called, brushing past me with her glow in full effect. Pregnancy agreed with her in the most wonderful way. She was radiant. Her dress flowed and made her look like she was floating. "Help me make sure the desserts are lined up right before Banks' people eat half of them."

"Girl, you know damn well we got staff to do that but come on." I stood to my feet anyway and walked with Braylen.

At the dessert table, I adjusted tiers of cupcakes topped with edible pearls and tiny fondant baby booties. A tower of macaroons glistened in shades of blue, cream, and gold. Banks walked over to us, smiling, before speaking.

"Baby, my mom and dad are about to pull up. I want to introduce them to your mom," Banks announced.

"Aww, shoot. I'm finally about to meet Mr. and Mrs. Banks," I joked.

"You silly. Please don't call them that. They not married at all, and they names is Victor and Monique."

Victor and Monique? Please tell me that them are just common names, I thought. I froze, my fingers digging into the edge of the table. My chest caved as the air left my lungs. *He can't be talking about them, right? Nah, that would be too crazy.*

I didn't have to wait long to find out. They came walking in, and my entire world crashed. I'd been fucking the grandparents of my god child. They walked in like royalty, heads held high. Victor was in a tailored, navy suit, broad shoulders filling the jacket like it was made for him. That sharp jawline I'd kissed and licked. That mouth that had whispered filth and praise in equal measure. My chest burned as I thought about just the other night.

Monique was stunning like always, a vision in a fitted cream dress that hugged every curve she had. Her hair fell in perfect waves, catching the soft glow of the string lights. She smiled with that same mouth that was just kissing between my thighs. It was enough that I was fucking the daddy, but I had to be fucking the mama too? What the hell was I supposed to do? It wasn't like I could run away. *Just keep it together, Vita. Don't make a scene and embarrass yourself.* Before I could say anything, Victor walked up to me and hugged me, wrapping his arms around me tightly.

"Baby, why didn't I know you would be here?" Victor asked before placing a gentle kiss on my forehead.

My heart skipped a beat when his soft lips touched my skin. The way his body pressed against mine. The way I could feel his heat even through our clothes. The way he called me baby in front of everyone like he didn't care who knew I was his. Before I could say anything, Banks spoke.

"Baby? Hold up, Pops. You two know each other?"

"Yeah, Vita's my girl. But I didn't know the two of you knew each other."

"Vita is Braylen's best friend," Banks announced.

"It's very nice to see you again, Vita," Monique chimed in, stepping up with an extended hand.

The moment I looked into her eyes, I instantly got wet. Looking at her in that dress, with her sleeves of tattoos on full display even in winter, made my thighs tingle. Her hair was different from the last time I saw her, but the style still worked. There was no way she had a child my age. She didn't look any more than thirty-five her damn self. I was stuck, and as much as I tried to hide it, I knew my face showed it all. I shook her hand, feeling her soft skin on mine.

"Ma, you know her too?" Banks asked in surprise.

"Yeah, Vic has brought her to the shop."

It wasn't a total lie because Victor had indeed brought me to the shop. And I knew she could just come out and say *and I ate her pussy until she came.* Heat flushed my cheeks as I switched my gaze to Victor.

"I didn't know this was your son. If I would have known, then I would have told you I was going to be here."

"Wait, so this is Victor?" Braylen spoke, louder than she needed to. "What the hell are the odds this shit would happen?" Braylen laughed as if this was the funniest thing she'd ever heard.

Before I could even speak, Rain came over to introduce herself, saving me from the embarrassment. Victor kept his arm around me, like he wasn't ashamed. And neither was I, not of him. Just of the fact that I'd unknowing fucked two of my god child's grandparents.

"Ma, this is A'zir's parents, Victor and Monique."

"Oh, okay," Rain said, smirking at me. "It's very nice to meet you both."

"So, wait, Pops. How long have you been with Vita?" Banks asked, still looking confused.

"For a few months. This my baby though. So, y'all gon' be seeing us together a lot now," Victor answered.

We stood there, talking for a few moments. I was glad that Monique hadn't said everything we did, and I hoped she never would. Rain continued to look at A'zir, never taking her eyes off of him.

"You good?" I mouthed to her, and she shook her head yes, but her eyes were still locked on A'zir. As Braylen made her way over to her seat so that she could eat the plate that was prepared for her, I took my seat next to Rain.

"Rain, I know something is up, so what is it?" I asked, leaning in so that only she could hear me.

"I know that A'zir from somewhere, and I'm going to figure it out."

Chapter Twenty-one

BANKS

The room was dressed in pastel blues and creams, balloons gathered in archways, tables laid out with gifts, all for our baby. But the best part of this entire day was her smile. Braylen's happiness was a light that filled every corner, brighter than anything else ever could. I leaned back in my chair, drink in hand, and let myself watch her. The way she leaned her head back when she laughed, or the way she touched her stomach in every picture she took, I could tell she was happy, and that made me happy.

It didn't matter to me that the baby didn't have my blood. I didn't care that he wasn't biologically mine. Braylen was mine, and anything that came from her was mine as well. I would never treat this little boy like anything other than my son because that was what he was. I hadn't given Kyrie a second thought – not until today when Braylen let it be known that she was getting envelopes of money that wasn't coming from me. That meant he had been coming to my house and dropping them off. That shit didn't sit well with me.

I'd promised Braylen that I would let today be the joyful celebration it was supposed to be. And I meant that. However, I knew if I didn't deal with Kyrie quickly, then he was going to try to be a problem. Every time I looked over at Braylen's smiling face, it was enough to make me hold off on Kyrie just one more day.

From across the room, I caught sight of Vita. She was dressed sharp, laughing with a few of the women, her glass of champagne catching the light. I'd known Vita through Braylen. She was pretty cool from what I'd seen, and I knew she genuinely loved Braylen. She was a grown woman that could handle herself; however, Victor McFarland wasn't an easy man to love. My father was charming and powerful in his own right, but that charm was laced with steel. He had expectations that could suffocate most people. And women? They never lasted long around him. He demanded too much – too much energy, too much loyalty, too much everything.

I wasn't judging Vita for wanting him because most women did. However, this was Braylen's best friend, and I didn't want anything that my father did to affect me and Braylen's relationship. I didn't say a word out loud though. Not today. Today was about Braylen and our baby. But a part of me kept my eyes on Vita and my pops, watching.

I watched as Vita walked to the front of the room, announcing that it was time to play the games. Once we started playing, I surprised myself by how much I actually enjoyed them. Normally, I was not the type to do silly shit in front of a crowd, but with Braylen right there, I couldn't say no. The first game was baby bingo. Cards were passed out, markers handed over, and number were called. I caught myself laughing when one of the old aunties smacked her card down and hollered, "Bingo!" like she'd just won the lottery. The whole room erupted, and Braylen leaned against me, laughing so hard she had tears in her eyes.

Next came the bottle race. They handed us baby bottles filled with juice, and the task was to see who could finish theirs the fastest. I could admit I underestimated it. Drinking out of a bottle? Easy, right? Wrong. That shit was work. The little nipple made it damn near impossible to get more than a trickle at a time. Watching grown men in designer fits red-faced, sucking on bottles, had the whole room doubled over in laughter.

Braylen was cackling so hard she nearly fell out of her chair. "You look ridiculous, A'zir!" she teased, her smile wide and open.

I couldn't do anything but laugh because I knew it was true. Malik's competitive ass was right there with me, trying to win. I continued sucking down the juice, determined not to quit. I wasn't about to let these people think I couldn't win a simple game. When I slammed the empty bottle down, victorious, the cheers went up. Braylen clapped as she congratulated me.

The diaper changing relay came next – tiny baby dolls, diapers, and blindfolds. I got roped in, of course, and though I'd never changed a diaper in my life, I wasn't about to back down from a challenge. Fumbling blindfolded, I managed to get it on, crooked as hell but on. The crowd roared, and Braylen laughed so hard she had to wipe her eyes. For hours, the games went on, and I found myself losing track of everything and had a good time.

After the last game wrapped up, everyone gathered around for the gifts. The table was stacked high, bags stuffed with tissue paper, boxes tied with bows, tiny clothes folded neatly. Braylen settled into the chair in the middle, her belly rounding under her dress, her smile stretching wide as she prepared to start unwrapping. I stood at her side, one hand resting on the back of her chair, ready to see what people had bought for our baby. She looked up at me, smiling, before she pulled the first bag over. Just as the first gift bag was being torn open, I felt a presence at my side. I turned, and there was DeShawn. His expression was tight, his jaw set, eyes darting around like he didn't want anyone else to hear.

"We need to talk," he muttered, low and firm. "It's important."

And just like that, the laughter, the lightness, the bubble of joy around me cracked just a little. The way DeShawn's voice cut through the noise of the shower had me instantly on edge. I didn't like the look in his eyes either. He wasn't just being cautious; I could tell this was something serious. I glanced at Braylen, who was busy laughing at a onesie she'd just pulled from a bag, a tiny little thing with "Mommy's Boss" stitched across the front in gold. Her whole face was lit up. I hated to step away from that, but I knew I had to.

I leaned down, kissed the side of her temple, and murmured, "Be right back, baby." She looked up at me with a curious smile then went right back to unwrapping the next gift.

I motioned to DeShawn. "Office," I said quietly. "We'll talk there."

He nodded once then jerked his chin toward Tariq and Malik across the room. They caught the signal immediately, falling into step behind us. The four of us slipped away from the party, weaving through the noise of chatter and laughter, until we were upstairs, the door to my office shut tight behind us.

"Alright," I said, lowering myself into the chair behind my desk. "What's up?"

DeShawn didn't waste time. He reached into the inner pocket of his jacket and pulled out his phone. The screen was lit up with a mess of red pings, maps, and scrolling code I couldn't begin to decipher.

"Soon as I got here, my tracker lit up," he spoke, voice low. "At first, I thought it was a glitch, but it kept pinging. Strong as hell too. That's when I realized someone was bouncing into the systems. Not just watching my signals. They're tracking movements. The movements from inside this house."

My jaw clenched. "Tracking me how?"

"Through your own shit." He gave me a pointed look. "Cameras. Smart devices. Anything connected to the Wi-Fi in this house. They're watching through it."

I leaned back in my chair, hands gripping the arms. My mind went immediately to Braylen downstairs, laughing and glowing and unguarded. *Somebody is watching us through our own damn devices?* I felt heat rise under my skin as a mix of fury and unease came over me.

"You telling me I got rats in my walls?" I muttered.

DeShawn was already moving. He pulled a small black case from his bag and flipped it open on the desk. Inside was a neat arrangement of gadgets – handheld scanners, cables, and little blinking boxes that looked like they belonged in a spy movie. He picked up a small rectangular device with an antenna and flicked it on. It started humming softly, the screen lighting up with waveforms.

"This right here will sniff out signals bouncing where they shouldn't," he explained, his hands moving quick and sure, like he'd done this a thousand times. "I'll sweep your office first then work through the house and around the property outside. If there's a leak, I'll find it."

Tariq leaned against the wall, arms folded, watching. Malik perched on the edge of the window ledge, his face tight but calm.

I kept my eyes on DeShawn. "So, what, you think this is cops? Feds?"

"Could be," he said, voice flat. "But the way they're running it feels like something different. This ain't no sloppy government crawl. Whoever's doing this knows what they're looking for. They're patient and precise. This ain't no small spike, Banks. This shit loud as hell, meaning the shit is all through the house."

The humming in the room deepened as DeShawn moved the scanner slowly across the shelves, the desk, the corners of the ceiling. He paused, tapped the screen, adjusted the antenna. "See this?" He held it out, so I could see jagged red lines spiking across the display. "That's interference. Someone's piggybacking on your connection."

I narrowed my eyes, blood thudding in my ears. "So, they're in my house? Right now?"

"Yeah, they for sure watching you. They could even be recording. I don't know yet. But I'm damn sure gonna find out."

The words sat heavy in my chest. I thought about every late-night conversation Braylen and I had in this house, every touch, every moment we thought was private. The idea of some faceless bastard watching us like it was entertainment made me sick. DeShawn set down the scanner and pulled another device from the case. This one looked like a miniature laptop with cords hanging off it. He plugged it into the router on the shelf by the window, and the screen lit up with scrolling text, code racing down faster than my eyes could catch.

"I'm tunneling in," he said, his fingers flying over the small keys. "If I can trace the breach, maybe we can figure out who's behind it."

I leaned forward, elbows on my desk, staring hard at the back of his head. "And if you can't?"

His shoulders stiffened. "Then we burn it all. Wipe every system, every feed, every smart device in this house and start fresh."

For a moment, the only sound in the room was the rapid-fire clack of his fingers and the faint hum of his gadgets. Tariq shifted against the wall, while Malik drummed his fingers against his thigh. The tension was thick, pressing down like a storm about to break.

Finally, DeShawn cursed under his breath. "Son of a bitch."

"What?" I snapped.

"They're good, real good. They're masking their IP, bouncing signals all over the damn world. But..." he pointed at the screen, at one tiny line of code that glowed brighter than the rest. "They slipped. Just once. And when they did, I saw a fingerprint."

"Meaning?"

"Meaning whoever this is, they're not untouchable. I can find 'em. But it's gon' take some time."

I exhaled slowly, fighting to keep my composure. Downstairs, Braylen was still smiling, still laughing, oblivious to the storm brewing above her. And I knew, sooner or later, that storm was going to come crashing down on us.

"Do whatever you gotta do," I told DeShawn. My voice came out low, edged with steel. "I want names and locations. And when you find out whoever is doing this, I want to be the first to know."

DeShawn nodded once, eyes back on the screen, determination carved deep into his face. Although I wasn't sure who was watching me, I knew that DeShawn was going to find out. Until then, I would have to make sure that I kept Braylen safe.

"If the cops or Feds are watching, then maybe we should check all of our houses," Malik suggested.

"My house good. I never got any pings. But I can check your and Tariq's houses when I'm done here," DeShawn spoke.

DeShawn continued sweeping the house as I returned to the shower. Although I didn't want to alarm Braylen, I knew we would not be sleeping here tonight, or any other night, until I found out exactly what was going on. I stood next to Braylen as she finished opening all the gifts she'd received. Once everyone left and Braylen and I went upstairs, I simply told her to pack a bag.

"Pack? Baby, I'm tired. I just want to shower. Where are we even going?" Braylen asked, voice low.

"No! Don't shower here!" My voice came out harder than I meant it to. "Baby, just come on. Please. I'll pack your bag, and I'll tell you everything once we get there."

Braylen looked at me for a short moment before nodding her head. She walked into the closet, grabbing a bag. before putting clothes into it. I followed suit, putting clothes into another bag. Once we were done, we got into the car. DeShawn was already at the house in Palmer Wood, making sure there was no breach there. If there wasn't, then that was where me and Braylen would be staying. I hated that we had to leave our home, but there was no way we would be staying there with muthafuckas watching us.

When we pulled up to the house, I left Braylen in the car with Zeek, while I went to talk to DeShawn. I was hoping that we would get the all clear for this house because if not, a hotel was our next step. Walking inside, I saw DeShawn in the living room, placing all his gadgets back inside his bag.

"What up doe, D? We good here or…"

"Yeah, Banks, you good here. I triple checked, and there's nothing here. Just give me a few days to find out what's going on. But from what I've come across this far, I don't think it's the Feds. There's no trackers in this house or none of ours. My guess is this is something personal, and I'm going to figure it out."

I nodded before walking outside to get Braylen and the bags. When DeShawn left, I sat Braylen down and told her what was going on.

"This is Kyrie, A'zir. He's doing this. I think he's who's been leaving the money in the envelopes."

"Kyrie might be leaving the money, but you think he got enough reach to hijack our Wi-Fi?"

Braylen stepped closer to me, eyes wide. "He's a different person now. He's working with your dad and getting money now. I didn't know til today when I found out that your dad was the same Victor Vita was fucking with."

"He's been working with my pops? That nigga been this close the whole time? Say less."

This day was getting crazier by the minute, but I knew I was going to get to the bottom of this. There was no way I was going to allow anyone to come in and fuck with my family. And if this was Kyrie that was doing this shit, I was going to kill him with my bare hands.

Chapter Twenty-two

KYRIE

I sat on my couch, watching the baby shower as if I were really there. Braylen looked so happy. Her family and friends were around her as the room filled with laughter. They were celebrating our baby, and I wasn't even invited. The decorations were beautiful, and Braylen looked amazing. But all I wanted to do was rush in and pull her out. She needed to know that she was not going to raise my baby with anyone else. I didn't give a fuck about what I did to her in the past. She belonged to me, and it was high time that I went to collect. Braylen was coming back to me one way or another – even if I had to tie her up and put her in my trunk to get her here.

I saw the man when he whispered something to Banks. I also saw Banks and three other men walk away from the baby shower, but I was so focused on Braylen that I really didn't give a damn what they were going to do. I wanted to see Braylen open each and every gift she received for our baby. So, that was what I did, not taking my eyes off the screen until the very last gift was opened.

Once she was done, I rushed upstairs to the bathroom. If I was going to do this, I couldn't keep thinking about it. I had to do it now. I didn't know how nor did I have a plan. But I knew the more I thought about it, the less likely I was to actually do it. Going up to my bathroom, I took a shower, trying to wash off the fear of what I was about to do.

When I got out the shower, I dried off and placed a black durag over my braids. I then walked into my bedroom and put on a fitted black tee and a pair of black joggers. I grabbed a pair of back Forces and put them on my feet before putting on a black hoodie. I put the hood over my head and tied it low before looking at myself in the mirror.

"It's now or never," I said to myself before walking out my room and heading back downstairs.

I looked at the screen one last time. The guests were leaving, and I knew that Braylen and Banks would be winding down for the night. I watched as they walked to the master bedroom. Grabbing my Glock 19 from the lockbox in my living room, I grabbed my keys and walked out the house. I didn't give a fuck what I had to do next. Braylen was coming back with me.

I had been driving for about ten minutes, but my mind was spinning faster than the wheels beneath me. The longer the road stretched out in front of me, the tighter my chest felt. Every light I passed through, every sign on the side of the freeway, felt like it was mocking me, telling me I was too late and had already lost her. I gripped the steering wheel tighter, knuckles turning white, but it wasn't enough to stop the storm raging in my chest. The thought of her being with that man was like pouring gasoline over a fire I couldn't put out.

I hated the way he carried himself, like he owned everything he touched, like he had earned her. He hadn't earned her. He bought her, and she actually stayed with him. That was the part that really got me. Now she thought she was going to raise my baby with Banks. Fuck no. That would only happen over my dead ass body.

The road hummed beneath my tires, but my thoughts were louder. I replayed every memory I had of her. The way she used to smile when she looked up at me. The way she laid on my chest when she slept. I wanted that back, needed it back. Braylen was my home, and she belonged to me. So, tonight was the night that I took her back – back to me, back home, and back inside my heart. The baby that she was carrying was mine, and he wouldn't get to take my wife and my child.

I pressed harder on the gas, weaving between cars. It was like the faster I drove, the quicker I could erase the months she'd spent under Banks' roof. The baby shower, the pictures they took like they were the perfect couple. The way she looked in that dress when I saw her over the feed. That image had nearly broken me. Seeing her glowing, smiling like she was truly happy, like she had chosen him and forgotten me, that shit made my blood boil. Today was the day I made her remember. Remember just who she belonged to and why she could never really get away from me.

She was about to see just who I was now. I wasn't the dumb boy she'd married. I'd grown into a man – a man who wasn't going to allow anyone else to come in and take his family. The only thing I cared about now was getting my family back. To do that, I had to remind them both that she was mine first and would forever be mine. My chest tightened, and I let out a low growl. The steering wheel creaked beneath my grip. I had sacrificed too much, lost too much, to let another man stand in my place.

The neighborhood was coming into view now, and I knew I was just minutes away from getting my wife back. I slowed as I approached the gate. I parked right in front of their house, not giving a damn. My heart was pounding now, a steady, violent rhythm that echoed in my ears. Every second that passed brought me closer to her, closer to the moment I had been waiting for.

I imagined her face when she saw me – shocked at first, maybe even scared. But then there would be relief. She would remember who I was and what we had been together. She would feel it the same way I did, no matter how much time had passed.

I killed the engine and sat in the car for a minute, staring at the house like it was taunting me, that huge, beautiful home that looked more like a fortress. Every window was blacked out, the porch lights on, like Banks had set the stage for me to lose my mind. My hands were locked around the steering wheel, and I had to remind myself to breathe. Braylen was inside, and I was finally about to go get her.

All the nights I stayed awake, thinking about her laying in his bed, maybe laughing at something he said, maybe touching him the way she used to touch me, it was enough to make any man's blood run hot. I could taste the jealousy on my tongue like copper. But this was the night I was taking her back. I popped the trunk and pulled out the crowbar I'd stashed under the lining. My palms were sweaty, but I tightened my grip. I wasn't stupid enough to walk up and knock. I knew Banks had cameras, alarms, and maybe even people watching. I had to move smart, like every step was life or death, because it was.

Creeping up the side of the house, I studied the windows until I found one cracked open in the back, a kitchen window. Banks thought he was slick with all his muscle and his toys, but even slick men got sloppy. I wedged the crowbar under the frame, gave it a hard snap, and the lock popped like it was nothing. I froze, waiting for an alarm to scream out into the night. But nothing happened.

"Too easy," I muttered under my breath, sliding the window up and hauling myself inside.

The kitchen smelled like lemon cleaner and fresh coffee grounds. I shut the window behind me, crouching low, every nerve on edge. My shoes were silent on the tile. The silence in the house was suffocating, like the walls were holding their breath, waiting to see what I'd do. I gripped the crowbar like a weapon and crept into the hall. The first door I opened was a pantry with rows of expensive liquor, wine, snacks, even imported shit I couldn't pronounce. I slammed it shut. The next door was a bathroom, spotless and smelling like lavender, but still not what I needed. *Where the hell is she?*

I crept up the stairs, each step slow, steady, and careful not to make them creak. My hand rested on the gun at my waist. I'd brought it just in case, but all I wanted was to find her, pull her out of this place, and remind her who she belonged to. The master bedroom was the first door I tried. The bed was massive, neatly made, pillows lined up perfectly, like some damn hotel. My chest tightened. I imagined her laying there, wrapped in silk sheets, whispering Banks' name instead of mine. My hand clenched around the doorknob so hard I thought it might snap. But the room was empty. I yanked open the closet doors. Rows of designer suits and shoes lined up in order on one side, while Braylen's clothes, shoes, and purses were lined up on the other.

"Where are you, Bray?" I whispered.

Room after room, I searched. Guest rooms, an office, even an indoor pool and sauna. However, there was no sign of Braylen anywhere – or Banks for that matter. Panic clawed at me. I tore through drawers, checked under beds, even yanked back shower curtains like maybe she was hiding. My chest burned with each breath, the rage rising up like fire in my throat. I was too late.

They weren't here. I was halfway down the stairs when I heard the sound of a door unlocking. My whole body froze as I heard the footsteps. I ducked into the shadow of the hallway, pressing my back to the wall, gun in my hand before I thought about it. The front door opened, and a man in a chef's uniform stepped inside. I knew his face instantly from the feed. He looked into my eyes, shocked to see me standing there.

"Who are you, and what the hell are you doing here?" he yelled.

I didn't think or plan in that moment. My finger squeezed the trigger before I even realized what I was doing. The shot cracked through the house, loud as thunder. He stumbled, clutching his chest, his mouth falling open like he wanted to curse me but couldn't find the words. Blood spread across his shirt, blooming dark and fast. He hit the floor with a heavy thud, eyes wide open, staring at the ceiling. My ears rang, and my hands shook. For half a second, I stood frozen, staring at what I'd done. I hadn't meant for it to go this far, not yet. But once you pulled the trigger, there was no taking it back.

I heard the silence that was now heavier than before. The house was no longer just empty; it was dangerous. I had seconds before somebody else came, before this turned into a war. So, I bolted. My feet pounded against the floor as I tore back through the kitchen, slamming open the window I'd come in through. I half-fell half-jumped into the yard, hitting the grass hard and rolling. I scrambled up, sprinting for the car, the gun still hot in my hand.

I threw myself behind the wheel, shoved the key in the ignition, and the engine roared to life. My chest was heaving, hands trembling on the steering wheel. I didn't look back. I slammed the car into drive and peeled off into the night, tires screeching, smoke curling behind me. My pulse was wild, my thoughts scattered. I'd come for Braylen, and I'd left with blood on my hands instead. But it wasn't over, not until Braylen was back in my arms and we were a family. Just me, her, and our baby.

Chapter Twenty-three

VITA

I didn't get home until about ten that night. It had been a long day, but it had been so beautiful, and Braylen kept a smile on her face the entire day. I still couldn't believe that Victor and Monique were Banks' parents. I could never tell them about Monique and would never. However, they seemed to be cool about me and Victor being together. Pulling off my dress and boots, I went to take a shower.

The moment I stepped out, my phone chimed. I looked down to see a text from Victor letting me know he was on his way over. I texted back a quick okay and oiled my body. I put on a red lace panty and bra set before spraying myself with Prada Paradoxe. The knock at the door wasn't loud, but it carried through the quiet of my place like thunder. I knew it was Victor. I smoothed my hands down the red lace that clung to my hips, felt the delicate straps of the bra press against my shoulders. My skin was warm, flushed, before I even touched the knob. When I opened it, I didn't say a word. I didn't have to. His eyes swept over me in that slow, claiming way they always did, and my breath hitched in my chest.

"Damn," Victor murmured, voice deep, almost rough.

Before I could think, he had me off my feet, my chest pressed against his as his arms locked under me. I gasped, clutching his shoulders, as I wrapped my legs around his waist. He carried me like I was weightless,

173

like I belonged there, and the quiet click of the door shutting behind us seemed to seal something between us.

"Victor," I whispered, my throat tight.

He didn't answer. His mouth found mine before I could say more, stealing the air right out of me. His kiss was hungry but controlled, the kind that made my toes curl and my body melt against him all at once. Every step he took down the hall toward my bedroom made my heartbeat race harder, anticipation coiling deep in my stomach. The moment we crossed the threshold, he laid me gently on the bed. My sheets felt cool against my skin, but the way he looked at me made fire crawl up my spine. He stood there for a second, towering over me, pulling his shirt over his head with that unhurried confidence that only he had.

I took in the sight of him, every muscle, every scar that spoke of stories he didn't share but that I longed to know. My fingers itched to touch him, but I stayed still, waiting, because part of me craved the way he led, the way he made me feel like the world narrowed down to just his hands on me, his voice in my ear.

"Vita," he said, low, like my name was meant for only him to say. "You don't even know what you do to me."

His words sent shivers racing down my body. When he lowered himself onto the bed, covering me with his warmth, I arched up into him instinctively. His mouth traced the line of my jaw, down my throat, until I was trembling under the drag of his lips. I wrapped my arms around him, nails digging lightly into his back, as I whispered, "Then show me."

Victor kissed me until I couldn't think straight, until every nerve in my body was awake and begging for more. His hands explored with a reverence that made me ache, slipping over the lace, teasing me with slow strokes that left me breathless. When he finally pulled the straps of my bra down and freed me from the delicate fabric, I gasped his name, my body arching up to meet the heat of his mouth. The rest of the night blurred into nothing but sensation. The weight of him pressing me into the mattress, the rhythm of his movements, the way he said my name like a promise every time I cried out for him. It wasn't rushed; it wasn't careless. It was deliberate, every touch designed to make me feel claimed, cherished, undone.

When it was over, I was trembling in his arms with his heartbeat pounding against mine, and I realized something I hadn't wanted to admit before. This wasn't just about heat or lust. Not anymore. With him, it felt like something deeper, something I wasn't sure either of us was ready for. But as I lay there, tangled with him, his hand tracing lazy circles on my skin, I knew one thing for certain. I didn't want to let him go. We fell asleep just like that.

By the time we woke up, it was after eleven the next morning. I walked into the bathroom to handle my business before heading to the kitchen to cook breakfast for Victor and I. I made two western omelets and some hash browns. I was just buttering the toast when Victor walked into the kitchen.

"Good morning, gorgeous. I see you in here cooking. You got it smelling good in here, lil mama."

"I just wanted to put something together for you. After last night, you deserve at least a meal."

He chuckled, and we sat down to eat. In that moment, we talked about our future and the things we wanted to do together. Victor told me that he saw himself with me and never wanted to let me go. I hadn't realized it before, but I felt the exact same way about him. After breakfast, Victor and I took a shower together before going into my living room and putting on a movie. We cuddled up on the couch.

We were only about five minutes into the movie when my phone chimed. Looking down to see it was Braylen calling me, I answered.

"What up doe, baby mama? You put away all them gifts yet?"

"Girl, no. I didn't get to put away shit because I couldn't even stay at my house last night. Some shit is going on, and me and A'zir had to leave right after the shower."

I heard Victor's phone ring, but I was so into my conversation with Braylen that I wasn't worried about what he was saying. That was until I heard Victor getting angry.

"Oh, I know that nigga don't think he means more to me than my own son. Fuck you finding that nigga, I can bring you right to him, and we can handle that shit together."

I watched as Victor stood to his feet and walked to my room. I was still talking to Braylen, but now, I was worried about him too.

"What shit went down, Bray?"

"Girl, somebody's been watching us inside the house. I think it's

Kyrie's ass. A'zir just went back to the house to see what he could find out."

Before I could answer, Victor walked back into the living room, fully dressed.

"Hold on right quick, Bray." I placed the phone on mute before looking up at Victor. "Where you going? I thought we were about to watch some movies."

"I'll be back, but my son needs me right now." Victor kissed my lips before walking out the door.

"Okay, Bray, I'm back." I spoke as I placed the phone back to my ear. "Where are you now? Do you want me to come over?"

Braylen told me she did, and she texted me the address. The moment we got off the phone, I put on a pair of black leather pants and a cream sweater before walking out the door. About fifteen minutes later, I was pulling inside the Palmer Woods community and parking in the driveway of the address Braylen gave me. Without a second thought, I rushed to the door. Braylen opened it, and I walked inside.

"Bitch, what's going on, and whose house is this?"

"Girl, someone hacked into our system at home and has been watching us through all of our smart devices. Then, on top of that, someone been putting money in our mailbox every week. I think it's Kyrie."

My eyes widened in shock. "Girl, what? Kyrie has been watching you at home? That sick fuck."

Braylen motioned for me to follow her to the living room. "A'zir don't think it's him, but I know it is. I don't know how he did it, but this got his name written all over it. I don't put nothing past his ass. That nigga is the same crazy muthafucka that sold me to A'zir in the first place. Who knows what else he would do?"

"Girl, I can't even believe this is the shit that's happening right now."

Braylen sat there, just shaking her head. We sat there, talking about how her life had gone from perfect to crazy in less than twenty-four hours. Her phone chimed, and she looked down, noticing it was her mother, and she answered it on speaker phone.

"Hey, Ma. You on speaker, and Vita's here with me," Braylen answered.

"Hey, Rain. How you over there doing?"

"I'm good, Vita... Braylen, you remember yesterday when I kept saying that I knew A'zir from somewhere?" Rain spoke into the phone. "I just figured out where I know him from."

Before Braylen could answer Rain, she screamed before doubling over in pain. She held her stomach as she looked up at me.

"Vita, something is wrong. I gotta get to the hospital. It's too early for me to be in labor. I'm only eight months."

Without another word, I helped Braylen to her feet and rushed her to my car, ready to take her to the hospital.

Chapter Twenty-four

BANKS

I woke up wishing it was a dream. But the second I opened my eyes and saw the unfamiliar ceiling above me, that little fantasy fell apart. Although the house was mine, it was used for meeting with the crew, not for sleeping. This wasn't my bed, and the fact that I couldn't even get up and go down to the indoor pool was really pissing me off. And that meant what happened last night, what DeShawn told me, what I saw with my own eyes, wasn't just some nightmare. Somebody had hacked into my system, my home, the one place in the world where I thought I was untouchable.

I sat up slow, elbows braced against my knees, head hanging low. The sheets slid off me, cool against my skin, but my blood was running too hot to feel the chill. I rubbed both hands over my face, like I could scrub away the memory of DeShawn pulling out all that equipment, his voice calm but tight, as he explained what the hell was happening. Someone had been inside my world, watching me and Braylen, while we thought we were alone.

The thought twisted my stomach into knots. I'd built my whole life on control, on staying five steps ahead. If somebody had cracked into my system, they had eyes on me when I was supposed to be invisible. That wasn't just a crack in the foundation; it was a damn earthquake.

I pushed up off the bed and moved through the quiet house. It didn't matter how comfortable the place was; it wasn't where I lived. I wanted to be at my house. Braylen was still laying in bed, sleeping, her hand resting on her stomach. I didn't wake her, didn't want to worry her any more than she already was. So, instead, I walked into the bathroom.

The bathroom mirror didn't do me any favors when I looked at it. My eyes were heavy and jaw clenched. I turned on the shower, steam curling up from the spray, and stepped inside, letting the heat pound against me. For a moment, I let my head fall back and closed my eyes. The water cascaded down my shoulders, running over the tension, but it couldn't rinse it away. I kept replaying everything DeShawn said. Someone was watching us through our smart devices.

Somebody was close enough to set it up and smart enough to cover their tracks. My phone buzzed against the sink counter. I let out a sharp breath, grabbed a towel, and stepped out of the shower, water still dripping down my skin as I swiped the screen. It was DeShawn.

I answered. "What up doe?"

"They're not inside your house." His voice came through steady, calm like always, but I could hear the edge underneath it. "I checked again this morning. Whoever did it, they didn't break into your network. They used a router to piggyback off your Wi-Fi."

I gripped the phone tighter. "So, where the hell is it?"

"Outside somewhere, I'm guessin'," DeShawn said. "Close enough to pull from your system, far enough you wouldn't notice. Could be in a car. Could be in a neighbor's yard. Could be anywhere within range."

I wiped my face with the towel, jaw tightening. "We gotta find this shit."

"Yeah, I'm going to do the sweep of the outside area. I'm gon' be heading to your place soon."

I looked at my reflection in the mirror again. This wasn't how I planned to start my day. I wanted to wake up next to Braylen's smiling face, but instead, I was searching for the ghost that had been watching us. Braylen told me it was Kyrie, but I wanted to be sure before I went off the deep end.

"I'll meet you at my house," I informed.

"You sure?" DeShawn asked. "You don't have to."

"I'm sure." My tone left no room for debate. "If they're outside my house, I'm not hiding from them. I'll be there in a half hour."

DeShawn was quiet for a moment before he said, "Bet. I'll bring the equipment."

The call ended, and I stood there for a second, towel wrapped around my waist, heart beating hard against my ribs. This wasn't just about a router. This was about someone testing me. Pushing me. Seeing if I'd fold under pressure. They picked the wrong man if that was what they thought.

I called Zeek and told him to pick me up in fifteen minutes. I got dressed fast, black jeans, black tee, and a black hoodie, sliding my Glock into its holster like it was an extension of my body. I didn't know what I was walking into, but I wasn't going unprepared. The ride back to my house felt longer than it was. The city was awake, morning traffic starting to clog the streets, but my focus tunneled in. Every car we passed, every pedestrian on the sidewalk, every corner where somebody lingered too long, it all felt suspect.

When we pulled onto my street, the tension in my chest doubled. My house sat at the end of the block, quiet, untouched on the outside. But I knew better. Just because the front door looked the same didn't mean the inside was safe. Zeek slowed the car, scanning, but we didn't see anything that looked out of the ordinary. We pulled into my driveway and parked at the front door. I looked at my house, eyes narrowing. If somebody thought they were going to watch me, they were about to learn the hard way that I didn't get watched. I did the watching. I stepped out the car, hoodie pulled up, as I felt the cold air hit my face.

"You can leave, Zeek."

Zeek nodded his head before pulling off. DeShawn was already outside, walking around the property in search of the router. He had a small black device in his hand that he was running over everything he saw. I could tell that he was thinking hard. I knew DeShawn wanted to find out who was doing this just as much as I did.

"Appreciate you pulling up, bro," I spoke, clapping his hand and pulling him in for a half hug.

"Of course," he replied, voice low, calm, but carrying weight. "But we need to get straight to it. I don't like how this looks."

Before I could answer, Malik's black SUV eased up slow, followed by Tariq in his blue Charger that he loved so much. The two of them hopped out, both posted like soldiers ready for war.

"What up doe? What's the word?" Malik asked, adjusting his fitted cap, while his eyes scanned the street.

"We gotta sweep this property," DeShawn said, no hesitation in his tone. "Somebody's been in Banks' system, but I know it ain't the Feds. If they're running a router out here, they ain't just watching. They're damn near living in his pockets. We gotta find it before anything else moves."

That lit a fire in me. It wasn't just the thought of somebody tapping into my world; it was the violation. The disrespect. Somebody thought they could sit back and play Big Brother over me, over my woman, over everything I was building. Nah, they weren't gon' play with me like that. We split off, pacing slow around the yard like hounds on a trail. I moved methodically, scanning the edges of the house, checking under the deck, sliding a light along the siding, just to find nothing.

"Shit clean over here," Malik called from the far side.

"Nothin' back here either," Tariq added, though his voice carried that edge of impatience he always had when he couldn't see the immediate picture.

We kept at it though. Minutes bled into an hour; an hour bled into two. Sweat started to bead on my forehead even though the air was cool. I wasn't tired, but my patience was thin, each second stoking the fire in my chest. Whoever set this up had been bold enough to plant something on my turf, and that alone meant they either knew me too well or didn't know me at all. Either way, the ending was the same.

"Hold up," DeShawn's voice cracked through the quiet. I turned quick to see him crouched low at the back fence. His hands were already moving, pushing back vines and dirt, until a small, black box came into view.

"Here you go, muthafucka," he muttered.

I stepped closer, crouching beside him, staring at the thing. It was small, no bigger than a deck of cards.

"That it?" I asked. I couldn't believe that something so small caused so much trouble.

"Yeah, this is it. Somebody set up a secondary router, been bouncing your whole system through it. Smart move. It lets me know that whoever it is ain't no rookie."

I clenched my jaw so hard it felt like my teeth might crack. "Take that shit down."

DeShawn nodded once, pulling out tools from his bag. Tariq and Malik flanked us, watching the perimeter, while he unscrewed panels, disconnected wires. Every movement of his hands felt like a countdown. By the time he had it free, I was already on edge.

"Inside," he said, standing with the device. "I'll crack it and see where it's feeding from. Maybe even who set it."

We didn't waste time. The four of us moved inside, boots heavy against the hardwood, silence hanging thick. DeShawn laid the device out on the dining table, his bag spilling wires, laptops, and different gadgets. He got to work, fingers dancing across keys, while the rest of us stood guard, waiting.

That was when it hit me, a smell that was both sharp and metallic yet familiar. It was a smell I'd smelled hundreds of times. It was blood. I froze mid-step, nostrils flaring, as the scent wrapped around me. My gut dropped, low and heavy. I walked out the dining room and looked down the hall. The moment I turned the corner, I saw him.

"Yo," I whispered, voice low, thick.

I moved closer, every step heavy. My chest tightened, breath caught halfway in my throat, as I saw Marcus slumped against the wall. His eyes were wide open, mouth twisted in the stillness of death. A pool of dark crimson spread beneath him, already drying into the floorboards. For a second, everything around me blurred out. All I saw was Marcus. All I felt was the storm boiling in my chest, rage and grief fighting for control.

"Fuck!" I yelled loudly.

Malik's voice broke in behind me, sharp with shock. "Yo, is that... Damn!"

Tariq cursed low, pacing back a step. "Man, what the hell? Is that your chef?"

But I wasn't hearing them. I was locked on Marcus, the way his body was laid out like trash in my space, like a message left just for me. Whoever had done this hadn't just killed him. They left him here for me to find. And I knew, right then, this shit was bigger than a router, bigger than surveillance. This was war.

"We gotta check the cameras, so I can see who the fuck came in here last night. I can bet you that whoever did this was the one that put that router out there and the same one that's been watching me and my woman."

"The cameras didn't work last night. I cut off the Wi-Fi, so whoever was watching couldn't look in anymore. But give me a minute to track the router. We can find them that way."

My jaws clenched as I nodded my head. I leaned against the wall, arms crossed, watching DeShawn hunch over his laptop like some mad scientist. I'd seen him work before, but this time, it was different. It was personal.

"Talk to me, DeShawn," I spoke, my voice low but sharp. "You said you had a way to trace it."

He didn't look up. "I do. Whoever planted that router thought they were slick. Masked the IP, bounced it off a couple satellites, layered proxies like a damn onion. But they got sloppy. When it first booted up, it pinged back to a local network for just a few seconds before it hid. That gave me a thread. I've been pulling on it ever since."

I stepped closer, my patience running thin. "And?"

"And," he said, finally glancing up, "that thread leads me to a specific ISP in Detroit. Narrowed down to a house in Chandler Park. Belongs to some fool named Terrance. That's who registered the line. That's where the signal keeps bouncing."

I smirked, a cold curl at the edge of my mouth. "Terrance? I don't know no damn Terrance."

DeShawn shrugged. "We'll find out. But I can tell you this. If he was paid to do this, it was done in cash. Ain't no digital trail. Somebody wanted eyes on you, and if it wasn't him, he knows who it was."

Malik cracked his knuckles from the couch. "Sounds like we got ourselves a little visit to make."

Tariq stood, sliding his gun into his waistband. "What we waitin' on?"

I pushed off the wall, the decision already made. "Get the truck. We're going to Chandler Park. If Terrance knows something, we'll make him talk. If he don't..." I let the silence finish the sentence. I climbed into the SUV, Malik at the wheel, Tariq in the back with me, and DeShawn up front with his laptop open.

DeShawn tracked the signal in real time, his screen pulsing like a heartbeat. "It's still active," he muttered. "Still bouncing from that house. He's probably got the router plugged in right now."

"Good," I said, pulling on my gloves. "That means he can't lie."

When we pulled up on the block, the house looked like nothing – a small, two-story place with peeling paint and an old Buick in the driveway. Malik pulled up and parked a few houses down. We moved quickly until we were at the front door. Tariq pulled a slim crowbar from under his hoodie, slid it between the frame, and popped the lock without a sound. The house smelled like fried food and stale smoke the moment we stepped inside. A TV was playing low in the living room. A man, who I assumed was Terrance, was sitting on the couch.

"What the..." he started, but Malik's fist caught him in the jaw before he could finish. His beer bottle shattered on the carpet, foam soaking in. Terrance went down hard, groaning, holding his face.

I crouched next to him, calm as ever, pulling my pistol from its holster and pressing the cold steel to his forehead. "Mornin', Terrance. We're here for a little talk. You gonna make this easy, or you gonna make it hard?"

He stammered, blood dripping from his split lip. "I-I don't know what you talkin' about, man. I don't even know who the hell you are."

I sighed, shaking my head. "That's the wrong answer."

Malik grabbed him by the collar and dragged him into the kitchen, slamming him into a chair. Tariq tied his wrists to the arms with a roll of duct tape we'd brought, wrapping it tight enough to bite into his skin. DeShawn set his laptop on the counter, turning the screen toward Terrance.

"See this? That's your house, your network. This router's signal bouncing from right here. You let somebody pay you to set this up, or you the nigga that's been watching him?"

Terrance's eyes flickered from the screen to me, wide and scared. "I don't know what y'all talkin' about. Ain't nobody pay me for nothin'. That's just my Wi-Fi, bro."

I leaned in close, so he could feel the weight of my voice. "You lying to me? You know what happens to liars, Terrance?"

He swallowed hard but stayed quiet. I nodded to Malik. Without hesitation, Malik ripped a knife from his belt and drove the tip straight through Terrance's hand, pinning it to the wooden table. Terrance screamed, body jerking against the duct tape. Blood spread fast across the surface.

"You feel that? That's mercy. Because Malik could've gone for your throat."

Tears welled in his eyes. "Man, please, I swear I don't…"

Tariq cut him off, stepping forward and slamming the butt of his gun into Terrance's ribs. The crack of impact echoed in the room, followed by another scream.

"Talk!" Tariq barked. "Who paid you? Who told you to put that router in?"

Terrance coughed, gasping for air. "Okay, okay, okay! Damn, y'all crazy! I'll tell you, just stop!"

"Now you're ready to speak. So, speak."

He closed his eyes, jaw trembling. "My cousin's friend, Kyrie. Said he wanted to keep eyes on his wife. At first, it started off with a drone outside the house. Then, he came to me and told me it wasn't enough. He said he needed to be inside. I suggested the router, and he paid."

Kyrie, I fucking knew it. His name lit a fire in my chest. I'd suspected him, but hearing it confirmed made my blood boil. That little bastard had been playing too much, and I was about to show him I was not to be played with.

I stood, holstering my gun, my voice a low growl. "That's all I needed to know."

Terrance looked up at me desperately. "You ain't gonna kill me, right? I told you what you wanted. I ain't got nothin' to do with this. It was just a job!"

I stared at him for a long moment, weighing his fate. Then, I turned to Malik. "Clean this up. We're done here."

Malik yanked the knife from his hand, and Terrance howled again, clutching the wound. Tariq ripped the tape loose and shoved him back in the chair. Blood soaked through his shirt, dripping on the floor.

As we walked out, I heard him sobbing behind us. In the SUV, DeShawn closed his laptop with a snap. "So, it's Kyrie. He's the one who planted it."

I lit a blunt, taking a slow drag as the anger simmered in me. "Yeah. And now that I know, I'm gonna deal with him myself."

The smoke curled out of my mouth as we pulled away, leaving Chandler Park behind. But in my mind, I was already planning my next move. Kyrie thought he could watch me, but now, he would never see me coming.

<hr>

We pulled up to my house with my adrenaline through the roof. I couldn't believe Kyrie had been watching me and Braylen in my house. That little broke ass, half fingered, cornrowed bastard really thought he could get one up on me. Tracking my woman like she was some toy. I didn't even sit down. My phone was already in my hand before I even realized it, scrolling to my pops' contact. I hit call. The line clicked once, twice, then his deep voice came through.

"What up doe, Zir?"

"Pops, I got problems. That nigga that works with you, Kyrie. He's a problem for me. I need to find his ass. It's important."

Pops didn't ask any questions. He knew when I said it was important that some shit was going down. He agreed and hung up. I posted at the front window, watching the long driveway, until I saw the sleek black Benz roll up. Pops stepped out, smooth, tailored pants, dark turtleneck, like he was just leaving some exclusive lounge in the middle of the day.

I opened the door before he could knock. "Come in."

He smirked. "Somebody sound tense."

I motioned him to my living room, closed the door, then leaned against the wall with my arms folded. "Sit down, Pops."

Pops looked at me for a second before he lowered himself into the leather chair, legs crossed like he owned the place. "Tell me what all this is about?"

"You got a nigga counting cards with you by the name of Kyrie? A skinny nigga with cornrows that's missin' a finger?"

"Yeah. Why, you know him?"

"He Braylen's ex-husband. That nigga put a router on my property and hijacked my Wi-Fi, so he could watch Braylen from inside my house."

"What?"

"No lie. DeShawn tracked the router, and we just came from the dude's house. He confirmed that it was Kyrie."

"So, what you wanna do, son? Because I'm down with whatever you down with."

"That nigga gotta go. Tonight," I spoke, raising one eyebrow.

"Say less, Zir. I can have that nigga to you tonight. I'll text you in a few hours with a time and place."

I nodded, dapping my pops up, before he walked back out the door. He hadn't been gone five minutes when my phone rang. Looking down to see it was Braylen, I answered.

"Hey, baby, it looks like I'm gonna be out for a few hours, but I'll be back to you as soon as I can."

"Banks!" Vita screamed into the phone. "You need to come to the hospital. Braylen is in labor."

Chapter Twenty-five

KYRIE

I couldn't breathe. My chest felt like somebody had their whole hand wrapped around it, squeezing with every step I took toward my front door. The gunshot was still ringing in my ears like a bell I couldn't silence. Every little sound – the car door slamming a few blocks away, a dog barking, even my own footsteps – made me twitch. *I killed him.* The thought kept pounding in my skull. I'd replayed the scene a dozen times already on the drive back, but every version ended the same way – him hitting the ground, his eyes wide, blood spreading across his shirt, and me standing there frozen like an amateur.

When I finally made it inside, I locked the door and leaned back against it. My hands were shaking so bad, I dropped the keys. They hit the floor with a loud clatter, and I jumped like it was a gun going off again. I crouched down quick, snatching them up, then stood still for a second, just listening. The silence was worse than noise. It gave my mind too much room to run wild. What if somebody saw me? What if a camera caught me running across the grass? What if Marcus wasn't dead, and he started talking?

I stumbled toward the bathroom, every nerve screaming. My shirt and hoodie clung to my skin, damp with sweat and Marcus' blood. I ripped my clothes off before I even hit the hallway, tossing them to the floor like they were trying to burn me. The shower was already running before I could think twice. I jumped in, water pounding down on me, hotter than I normally kept it. Steam filled the air until it felt like I couldn't get enough oxygen. I scrubbed at my arms, my chest, and hands, but the soap and water wasn't enough. I swore I could still smell the iron, still see the red dripping off me. I grabbed the soap again, scrubbing harder this time, until my skin was raw. I closed my eyes and let the water rush over my face, but behind my eyelids, I kept seeing his face and the look he gave me when he saw me standing somewhere I shouldn't have been in the first place.

"Fuck," I muttered, smacking the wall with my palm. The sound echoed. I leaned against the tile, letting the heat sting my skin, hoping it would wash everything away. When I finally turned the water off, my legs felt weak. I dried off fast, wrapping the towel around my waist, then picked up the clothes off the floor. I didn't even want them in the house. I shoved the bundle of clothes into a trash bag and tied it tight. I put on a pair of joggers and a coat and carried the bag outside. The night air hit me, cool and sharp, but it didn't calm me. Outside was quiet. Every time a branch creaked or the wind blew, I thought somebody was watching me.

I popped open the lid of the BBQ grill, dumped in a handful of charcoal, then pulled out a lighter. My hands shook so bad it took three flicks before the flame caught. I touched it to the edge of the bag, and it went up fast, plastic melting, fabric curling, smoke twisting into the night sky. The smell was awful, a mix of burning cotton, rubber, and blood-soaked cloth. I gagged and stepped back, but I didn't take my eyes off of it. I had to make sure it was all gone.

The fire hissed and crackled. The flames flickered high, and for a second, I felt almost hypnotized, like if I stared long enough, I could burn the memory too. I paced around the yard, chewing the inside of my cheek. When the fire finally died down to glowing embers, I poked through it with a metal rod, making sure nothing was left but ash. Thankfully for me, everything was gone. I closed the grill, my heart still racing, then went back inside.

I sat on the couch, elbows on my knees, running my hands over my face. *What the fuck did I just do?* I thought I was ready for this life. Thought I could handle what came with it. But nobody told you about the way it ate at you, how the sound of the shot never left your ears, how the smell stuck to you even after you scrubbed your skin raw. I picked up my phone, scrolling through TikTok for a moment, before sitting my phone back down. I leaned back on the couch, staring up at the ceiling. I could hear the clock ticking in the kitchen, every second louder than the last. I wanted to sleep, but I knew I couldn't. Not with my mind like this.

I got up and poured a drink instead, Hennessy straight. The burn down my throat was sharp, but it grounded me for a second. I poured another then another until the edge of my nerves dulled just enough that I could sit still without my leg bouncing. But even drunk, I couldn't shake the paranoia. I kept getting up, checking the windows, making sure the door was locked, looking out at the street. Every pair of headlights that passed made me duck down. Every voice in the distance made me tense up. By the time the sky started to lighten, my nerves were shot. I hadn't slept a minute. My stomach twisted, my hands wouldn't stay steady, and my head pounded from the liquor.

I walked to my room and got into my bed, but I couldn't get comfortable. No matter how many times I flipped the pillow or turned on my side, my body refused to rest. Sleep wasn't coming. Every time I closed my eyes, his face was there – the way his eyes widened when I pulled my trigger. My heart was still racing hours later. My hands wouldn't stop shaking, even though I'd scrubbed them raw in the shower. I kept looking down at them like there'd still be blood there, like the water didn't do enough. I knew it was gone, but my mind kept playing tricks on me.

I kept telling myself it had to be done. He had left me no choice. When he walked in and saw me, I knew it was either kill or be killed. I could very well be the one laid out dead if I hadn't shot him first. I stretched out on the bed, but all I could do was stare at the ceiling. My mind replayed it over and over. The weight of the gun in my hand. The sound of the shot. The chef stumbling back. The way his body hit the ground. I pressed the palm of my hands against my eyes and groaned.

By the time the sun started creeping through the blinds, I still hadn't slept. My body was heavy, but my head wouldn't shut down. My stomach growled, but food didn't even sound right. What I needed was peace, and that was the one thing I couldn't buy. I tried closing my eyes, but every time I drifted, that chef came back. His voice, his face, that last breath. I sat up, sweating. My shirt stuck to my back. My hands trembled as I reached for my phone, just to distract myself.

It buzzed before I even picked it up. Looking down, I saw it was Vic. I almost didn't answer. My nerves were shot, and my voice felt like it would give me away. But I swiped anyway, forced my tone steady.

"What up doe?"

"Kyrie." Vic's voice was smooth, calm, like always. "You good?"

I swallowed hard. "Yeah. I'm straight."

There was a pause, then he began speaking again. "Aight. Listen, we hittin' the casino tonight. Just me and you. Tasha and Simone took the night off."

"Okay, I'm down with that. What time you talking about?"

"I'ma pick you up around nine tonight so be ready. It's just gon' be me and you, so once we get to the casino, keep yo' eyes open."

"Bet, I'll be ready," I assured.

I laid in that bed, staring at the ceiling, chest rising and falling heavy like I had weights pressing down on it. I knew I would need to get some sleep if I was going to be on my A game tonight. I couldn't let shit get in the way of me getting my money. Getting out of the bed, I went into the bathroom and took two melatonin before making my way back to my room. I turned on the TV and went to YouTube, putting on one of them ASMR videos Braylen used to watch to fall asleep.

I was finally able to go to sleep, and when I woke up, the day had turned to night. My phone ringing shook me up. The screen lit up with Vic's name. My stomach tightened before I even answered.

"What up doe?" I answered, voice scratchy.

"Kyrie, get up. I told you we was hittin' the casino tonight. I'ma be there in twenty."

I sat up in bed, looking around the room for a second, before I took a quick shower. I dressed in a pair of black slacks and a black turtleneck before finishing it off with a black peacoat. By the time I made it outside, Vic's black Escalade was pulling up, shiny under the streetlights. He rolled down the window, grinning like the night was already his.

"Hop in, young blood."

I slid into the passenger seat, the smell of his cologne mixing with leather and smoke. He had his usual confidence, one hand on the wheel, the other tapping against it with the beat of the music low in the background. We pulled off, heading toward the freeway. The city lights flickered in the rearview as we left the neighborhood behind. I leaned back, arms crossed, just trying to breathe normal.

At first, I thought nothing of the route. We hit the highway, driving smooth. Vic was quiet except for the occasional humming with the music. But after a while, I noticed we passed the exit for Greektown, MGM, and MotorCity.

I frowned before I sat up straighter. "Yo, Vic. Where you going? You passed all the casinos."

He didn't look at me, just smirked, eyes on the road. "We ain't staying local tonight. We headed to Ohio."

"Oh, okay, got it." I sat back in my seat and continued to enjoy the ride.

I stared out the window, the streetlights stretching long across the freeway. The farther we drove, the darker it got – less city, more empty road. I felt uneasy, like I was walking blind into something. Before I could say another word, I heard the click behind my ear. Then, cold metal pressed against the back of my head. I froze, my breath catching.

"Don't move," a voice growled low, a voice I knew too well.

It was Banks. My entire body went stiff. My eyes darted to Vic, but he kept driving, calm as ever, and I knew this was part of his plan all along.

"Banks," I whispered, not daring to turn.

"Don't say my name," he snapped, the gun digging harder into my skull. "Just sit still."

My heart hammered so loud I could barely hear the road beneath the tires. Sweat beaded at my hairline. I knew why Banks was here, and I knew what he was about to do. I thought Vic could be trusted; now I was on my way to my demise. The betrayal cut deeper than the gun pressed to my head. This was the man who'd been teaching me, guiding me, making me believe I had a shot in this world. And now, he was driving me straight into death. The car ride stretched into forever. Silence filled the space except for my uneven breathing. Banks never moved, never eased up. Just sat back there, steady, like he'd been waiting for this moment. And I knew he had.

After what felt like an eternity, we turned off onto a dark road. No lights, no houses. Just fields stretching wide and empty under the moonlight. Vic pulled over onto the dirt, the crunch of gravel under the tires sounding final, like a door closing.

"Out," Banks ordered.

My legs felt weak as I opened the door and stepped onto the cold ground. The night air hit me. Banks got out too, keeping the gun on me. Vic shut the driver's door and came around, standing with his arms crossed like he was just there to watch. The field was quiet except for the wind moving through the tall grass. No one was around for miles. It hit me then that this was really it. Banks stepped closer, the moonlight catching his face.

"You know what's crazy, Kyrie?" Banks said, voice steady, almost calm. "The baby Braylen carrying? That's yours. Not mine. But I'll be the one raising him. You did all that watching of my house and us, but you couldn't see that? You couldn't see when a woman was really done with you. You did this to yourself. You should have just walked away."

His words ripped through me worse than the gun could. My knees buckled, but I forced myself to stay standing. "No, no, man. Don't do this. Please."

He tilted his head, studying me like I was an insect under a glass. "You ain't fit to be no father. You couldn't protect her; you the one she needs protecting from. Couldn't even protect yourself from this shit happening. You weak. And I don't let weak men live."

Tears burned at the corners of my eyes, but I clenched my jaw, refusing to let them fall. "Banks, I swear I'll stay out your way. I'll disappear. Just don't..."

"Too late for that," he cut me off, raising the gun.

The barrel gleamed in the moonlight, steady and aimed straight at me.

I turned to Vic, desperate. "Vic! Please, man. Don't let him do this. You been teaching me, helping me."

Vic shook his head, his face cold and unreadable. "I taught you the game. But the game don't save everybody. You was cool, young blood, but this is my son, and you crossed him."

My chest tightened, my breaths shallow and quick. The world seemed to slow around me, every sound sharper. The wind in the grass. My own heartbeat pounding. *His son?* Banks stepped closer, so close I could see my reflection in the gun metal. "Say goodbye, Kyrie."

Before I could speak, before I could beg again, the gun went off. The shot exploded through the night, tearing into me, fire spreading through my chest. I gasped, stumbling back, the ground rushing up. The stars above blurred as I hit the dirt, my body convulsing. Pain seared through me, stealing my breath. Banks loomed over me, his shadow the last thing I saw before everything faded to black.

Chapter Twenty-six

BRAYLEN

I lay in the hospital bed, trying to breathe through the pain. The cramps had been coming and going all day, sharper than usual, but I told myself it was just false labor. I wasn't due for another couple of weeks. At first, I thought they were Braxton Hicks until they got too painful. Vita had rushed me to the hospital and called A'zir as she drove.

The contractions were coming harder now, and every time one hit, I felt like I was breaking apart. I bit down on the sheet, squeezed Vita's hand, and cried out.

"You're okay, Bray," Vita whispered. "You're stronger than you think. You got this."

I heard what she was saying, and I was glad that my best friend was here, but in this moment, the only person I wanted was A'zir. Between contractions, I kept glancing at the door, praying he'd walk through it. Every second felt like forever, every scream leaving my throat raw. The fear of doing this without him settled heavy in my chest. My mama had arrived five minutes after we did, and she was sitting right next to me, trying to help me with breathing exercises.

The door opened and in walked A'zir. The second my eyes landed on him, a sob ripped out of me that had nothing to do with the pain. Relief washed over me so hard I almost collapsed into the bed.

"A'zir," I whispered, my voice cracking.

He moved straight to my side, his presence swallowing the whole room, grounding me. He took my hand from Vita and held it firm, his other hand stroking my cheek with a tenderness that made tears spill down my face.

"I'm here," he spoke softly. "I got you, baby."

The sound of his voice, the feel of his hand, it was everything to me. For a moment, the pain faded into the background, and all I felt was his love. I didn't care that I was sweating, crying, and screaming just seconds ago. I didn't care that I was early or that I was scared. All that mattered was that he was here, and I wasn't doing this without him. I didn't think I'd be here this soon. The doctor said my due date was still weeks away, but my body had its own plans.

"Don't cry, Bray. You're strong. You got this," he whispered, his voice low and steady.

I clung to him like he was my anchor. "I'm scared," I admitted, letting the words break free.

He bent down until his forehead pressed against mine. "Don't be. I'm right here. We're about to meet our son."

Those words gave me strength I didn't know I had left. The nurses came in, moving fast, checking monitors and calling out numbers I barely heard. All I could focus on was breathing. Vita rubbed my arm in circles, and my mom whispered little prayers under her breath.

"Alright, Braylen," the doctor said, sliding on gloves. "You're fully dilated. It's time to push."

A'zir kissed the side of my head. "You hear that? Let's get him out, baby."

The contractions came like waves, and every time one hit, A'zir coached me through it. "Deep breath in, hold it, now push. Push, Bray, push."

I screamed, gripping his hand so tight I thought I might break his bones. He didn't even flinch. He let me pour all my pain and fear into him, and he just absorbed it.

"That's it, baby girl," Vita encouraged, leaning close. "You're doing so good."

"You almost there," my mom added, her voice trembling with excitement.

The room blurred, but their words anchored me. And when the

doctor said, "One more big push," I gathered everything I had left. A'zir was right there, his lips brushing my ear, his voice fierce and full of pride.

"Do it for him, Bray. Bring our son into the world."

I bore down, screamed, and then, just like that, it happened. The cry that filled the room was the most beautiful sound I'd ever heard. Thin but strong enough to make my heart break wide open. Tears spilled down my face as the doctor lifted him up.

"It's a boy!"

They placed him on my chest, warm and slippery, his tiny fists waving in the air. My breath caught as I looked down at him. He was perfect. A'zir's hands hovered like he was afraid to touch him, then finally, he laid one big palm over our son's back, his voice breaking. "Damn... Bray, look at him."

The nurse called out his stats. "Six pounds, four ounces. Nineteen inches long."

I laughed through my tears. "He's so small."

"He's strong," A'zir corrected, brushing his thumb over our son's cheek. "Strong like his mama."

I kissed the top of his damp head and whispered, "Welcome to the world, Nyair."

The name felt right the moment it left my lips, like it had always belonged to him.

A'zir repeated it, his voice soft but firm. "Nyair." He bent and kissed my forehead then kissed our son. "My little man."

Vita was crying. My mom had her hands pressed over her mouth, whispering thank yous to God. But all I saw was A'zir and the tiny life we were going to raise together. In that moment, nothing else mattered. Not the pain, not the fear, not the chaos of the world outside that hospital room. Just us. Me, A'zir, and Nyair, our family.

For the next few hours, we talked and cooed over Nyair before Vita finally left. A'zir left for a couple hours to handle some business, leaving my mama to stay with me until he got back. We ordered dinner and watched TV, while I waited on A'zir to return.

"I can't believe my baby is really a mama."

"Me either, but I'm going to be the best mom I can be to this little guy."

"I already know you are, Bray. You deserve this."

"Ma, you called me before I went into labor and told me you realized where you knew A'zir from. But you never got a chance to tell me where."

Before she could answer, A'zir walked into the room. It was late, and he looked tired. But when he looked at me, he smiled.

"Gone head, A'zir. I'll see y'all at the house when you get out the hospital." My mama kissed my forehead before saying goodbye to A'zir and Nyair. She walked out the room, closing the door behind her.

"What is she talking about? Where does she know you from?"

A'zir took a seat in the chair before grabbing my hand. "When I was eight, I saw my older brother murdered right in front of me. That was the worst day of my life. I screamed so loud, and nobody came to help us. After that, I just stopped talking. I felt like nobody heard me; nobody saw me. Because if they did, they would have helped me that day.

"For years, I didn't say a word. My parents took me to all types of specialists, but none of them could make me talk. Then, one day, you were coming out the store by your aunt's house, and you looked at me. We were twelve. The smile you gave me that day did something to me. When you said hi to me, my entire body lit up, and I did something I hadn't done in years. I spoke.

"Everyone on the block teased me because I was a mute, told me I was a weirdo for being like that, when they had no clue the trauma I was holding inside. But you were different. You made me want to talk. I have loved you since the first day I saw you all those years ago. And when Kyrie offered you up to pay his debt, I thought that this was the universe finally giving you to me. It was never about the money for me. It was always about you."

A single tear fell down my cheek as I listened to the most beautiful love story I'd ever heard.

"I remember you now. I never knew your name though."

"And now look at you, about to have my last name."

Before I could say another word, A'zir pulled a velvet box from his pocket and opened it, revealing the most beautiful diamond ring I'd ever seen.

"Braylen Nicole Parker, would you do me the honor of being my wife?"

Tears streamed down my face as A'zir placed the ring on my finger.

"Yes, baby. I'll marry you."

A'zir kissed my lips passionately. "You have made me the happiest man alive. I love you so much, baby."

Epilogue

VITA

One Year Later

I leaned back against the arm of the sofa, watching the makeup artist dab at Braylen's face with the soft precision of somebody who'd done this a thousand times before. The bridal suite was filled with the sound of strings and soft piano drifting through the speakers, wedding music that already had half the room sniffling before the ceremony even started.

"Girl, if you don't stop crying, she gon' have to start your whole face over again," I said, shaking my head. "And I'm not about to let you be late to my wedding because you can't control your tears."

Braylen laughed through her sobs, the sound shaky, watery, but real. She dabbed at her eyes carefully with a tissue the makeup artist handed her, trying not to smudge anything. "I can't help it, Vita. Look at you."

I frowned, confused for a second. "Look at me?"

"Yes, you." She turned her head toward me, her eyes glossy and soft. "You look so beautiful in that gown. I swear seeing you dressed up like this just made the water works start. I keep thinking about everything we've been through, everything you've been for me. And now here I am, standing by your side on the biggest day of your life. I can't stop crying."

"Girl, yo' pregnant ass just emotional. My little niece or nephew got you that way. I can't believe you're pregnant again, and Nyair just turned one."

"Bitch, you already know. I'm gon' give A'zir as many kids as he wants."

I couldn't do anything but chuckle because I already knew Braylen was telling the truth. As much as I begged my best friend not to get pregnant before my wedding, she still came up to me a couple months again, telling me that was exactly what happened. I couldn't get too mad because I understood how it felt to be in love now. Victor had come in and completely changed my life. So, if he told me he wanted ten kids, then I would be on my back spread open every night.

"I'm serious, V. You look so beautiful." Braylen smiled at me, her tears starting to form again.

Her words hit me like a weight pressed straight against my chest. My throat tightened, and I had to look away for a second before I joined her in her tears. The last thing we both needed was two ruined faces. I looked at myself in the mirror. My mermaid gown hugged every one of my curves just right. It was strapless and had a sweetheart neckline with intricate lace applique. The back was cut low with a delicate line of satin buttons running down the spine. My train was long and swept the floor when I walked, and my elegant sheer veil was lined with black lace. My jewelry was minimal with a diamond choker gracing my neck and a pair of diamond studs in my ears.

"Bray, don't do that," I whispered, fighting my own tears. "Don't make me cry too. You know how long it took me to get into this damn dress without messing my hair up?"

She giggled through her tears, and the sound eased the heaviness between us. The makeup artist smiled faintly, still working, her brushes sweeping like magic wands across Braylen's glowing skin. The bridal suite around us buzzed, bridesmaids fixing curls, laughter bubbling from the corner, the faint smell of hair spray and perfume lingering in the air. But in that moment, it felt like it was just me and her.

I stood up and walked closer, reaching out to squeeze her hand gently as she sat in the chair at the vanity. "You're the most beautiful bridesmaid I've ever seen. Don't ruin it with puffy eyes, okay? Hold it together until you make it down that aisle at least. Then you can cry all you want."

She sniffled, smiling at me, her lips trembling. "Deal."

The moment had finally arrived. I had dreamed about this day since I was a little girl twirling around in my mother's too-big heels, pretending I was walking down the aisle to marry the love of my life. But no fantasy, no childish daydream, could have prepared me for what it actually felt like. The reality of it settled into my chest like a weight, heavy but sweet. The venue was nothing short of a dream, a masterpiece painted in black and white, every detail, every corner, gleaming with sophistication. The ceremony space stretched before me like a scene from a movie with rows of chairs dressed in white covers tied with black satin sashes creating a checkerboard rhythm that seemed to pulse with life under the soft lighting.

White roses and black calla lilies sat in tall crystal vases at the end of each aisle, their stems submerged in glass cylinders filled with clear stones. They glowed faintly as the light hit them, catching the delicate gleam of the floating candles around them. The aisle itself was draped with a white carpet runner trimmed in black lace that shimmered as though tiny stars had been sewn into its edges. Above, a grand chandelier spilled light like liquid diamonds. Tiny crystal beads refracted the glow into a soft halo that seemed to bless every guest sitting in anticipation. And behind it all was an elegant arch made of intertwined black branches and white flowers, curling into one another like lovers locked in an eternal embrace.

The music swelled, violins and a soft piano playing a melody so sweet it made my throat tighten. I pressed a hand lightly to my stomach, willing myself not to cry before I even took the first step. My father was standing tall and proud beside me, squeezing my hand. His eyes glistened, but he was determined not to let a tear fall.

"You ready, baby girl?" he whispered, his voice rough with emotion.

I nodded, swallowing the lump in my throat. "More than ready." I breathed, though my knees felt like water.

The doors opened. A collective sigh seemed to ripple through the room as every guest turned in unison, eyes settling on me. For one dizzying moment, I felt the weight of every gaze, the rush of admiration, curiosity, and love. But then, I saw Victor. He stood at the end of the aisle, sharp and regal in his black tuxedo. The white pocket square gleamed against his chest, a single black rose pinned to his lapel. His posture was strong, his expression unreadable at first, until our eyes locked. And then, the mask slipped, and all I saw was love, a love so raw and consuming it was almost frightening. He didn't just look at me; he looked into me, through me, as if this moment was the only thing anchoring him to the earth. At that moment, every fear I had melted away.

The aisle stretched out before me like a path carved just for us, and with my father guiding me, I began to walk. Step by step, the hem of my gown whispered against the runner. I could hear faint gasps, soft murmurs of admiration. Someone whispered, "She looks like an angel." But none of it mattered. All I could hear, all I could feel, was the thundering rhythm of my own heart as I walked toward the man who held it.

Victor's eyes never left me. When I reached the altar, my father kissed my cheek and whispered, "Be happy, baby girl," before placing my hand into Victor's. Victor's fingers wrapped around mine, strong and steady. The warmth of his touch anchored me, chasing away the last remnants of nervousness. My father stepped aside, and for the first time, it was just us. The officiant began to speak, his voice smooth and solemn, but I barely heard the words. All my focus was on Victor and the way his thumb brushed against my knuckles, the way he tilted his head slightly, as though even now he was memorizing me.

Our vows came next. Victor went first. His voice was deep, steady, but threaded with emotion that cracked at the edges. "Vita," he began, and my breath caught just hearing my name on his lips, "from the moment I met you, I knew you were different. You didn't just walk into my life. You transformed it. You gave me peace when I didn't know what peace felt like. You gave me laughter when I thought I'd forgotten how to smile. You gave me love when I thought I wasn't capable of being loved the way I deserved." His eyes softened, shimmering faintly. "Today, in front of God, our family, and our friends, I promise you that I will love you without condition. I will protect you without hesitation. I will honor you without fail. No matter what life throws at us, I will stand by your side. You are my heart, my strength, my everything. And I am yours."

Tears blurred my vision. I couldn't stop them this time, not when his words pierced through me like sunlight breaking the darkest clouds. It was my turn. My hands trembled, but my voice was clear.

"Victor," I spoke softly, feeling the weight of every eye on me but only caring about his, "I never believed in fate until I met you. I never thought love could be this powerful, this healing, this consuming. You are my safe place, my anchor, my home. With you, I've learned that love is not about perfection; it's about choosing each other every single day, no matter what." I took a breath, steadying the storm of emotions swirling inside me. "So today, I choose you. I promise to love you when it's easy and when it's hard. I promise to lift you when you are weak and stand with you when you are strong. I promise to laugh with you, cry with you, dream with you, and fight for you, for us, always. Today, I give you my heart, my soul, and my forever."

The officiant smiled. "By the power vested in me, I now pronounce you husband and wife. You may kiss your bride."

Victor didn't hesitate. He pulled me into his arms and kissed me with a passion that made the room disappear. The guests erupted into applause, cheers echoing like thunder, but all I felt was the warmth of his lips, the strength of his arms, the overwhelming certainty that this was exactly where I was meant to be. We were married, and forever had just begun.

THE END

Did You Enjoy?

Did you enjoy the read?
Let us know how much by leaving us a
review on Amazon and Goodreads.

Other Books By

URBAN AINT DEAD

Tales 4rm Da Dale

The Hottest Summer Ever

Hittin' Licks For The Holidays: Atlanta

Wet Dreams On Lockdown: The Nurse

How To Publish A Book From Prison

How To Invest In The Stock Market From Prison

First Summer Out With My Prison Bae

By **Elijah R. Freeman**

Despite The Odds

Despite The Odds 2

By **Juhnell Morgan**

Hittaz

Hittaz 2

Hittaz 3

Hittaz 4

Hittaz 5

Hittaz 6

Coldhearted

Coldhearted 2

Coldhearted 3

By **Lou Garden Price, Sr.**

A YN'S Muse For The Summer

Wizdom: Forever Your Gangsta

Charge It To The Game

Charge It To The Game 2

Charge It To The Game 3

A Summer To Remember With My Hitta

Snatched Up By A Hitta

Santa Sent Me A Real One For Christmas

Wet Dreams On Lockdown: The Unit Manager

Thug Me The Right Way 2

Thug Me The Right Way 3

Seizing A Gangsta's Heart For The Summer

Yours For The Taking

Wrapped Up In A Hitta's Love For Christmas

By **Nai**

A Set Up For Revenge

A Set Up For Revenge 2

Wet Dreams On Lockdown: The Librarian

By **Ashley Williams**

Trickin' On A Heaux For Christmas

Homie Hoppin' For The Holidays

Wet Dreams On Lockdown: The Female C.O

Letters Of His Love

By **Telia Teanna**

The State's Witness

The State's Witness 2

The State's Witness 3

This Time Won't You Save Me

This Time Won't You Save Me 2

His Summer Side Piece

A Holiday Heist

Healing The Heart Of A Detroit Gangsta

Summer Vows With A Detroit Gangsta

The Promissory

By **Kyiris Ashley**

Stuck In The Trenches

Stuck In The Trenches 2

By **Huff Tha Great**

Melted The Heart Of A Menace

Wet Dreams On Lockdown: Lieutenant Grace

By **P. Wise**

Merry Trapmas

By **Mia Sky**

Thug Me The Right Way

By **DiamondATL & Nai**

Wet Dreams On Lockdown: The Counselor

By **Paris Iman**

Wet Dreams On Lockdown: The Male C.O

By **Tamyra Griffin**

Wet Dreams On Lockdown: The Captain

By **TN Jones**

Wet Dreams On Lockdown: The Warden

By **Shawnice**

Atlantastan

Atlantastan 2

By **Chris Green**

IN The Streetz

IN The Streetz 2

IN The Streetz 3

IN The Streetz 4

IN The Streetz 5

By **Tron Hill**

Hittin' Licks For The Holidays: New York

Bandemic

By **Freshh Moneyy**

Coming Soon From
URBAN AINT DEAD

Drill
The Hottest Summer Ever 2
THE G-CODE
Tales 4rm Da Dale 2
How To Build Your Credit From Prison
By **Elijah R. Freeman**

Despite The Odds 3
By **Juhnell Morgan**

A Felon's Promise
By **Nai**

Atlantastan 3
By **Chris Green**

IN The Streetz 6
By **Tron Hill**

Bandemic 2
By Freshh Moneyy

* 9 7 9 8 2 1 8 7 7 7 0 5 0 *